Magic Touch

A Brooklyn Girls Story

Magic Touch

A Brooklyn Girls Story

Treasure Hernandez

www.urbanbooks.net

Urban Books, LLC
300 Farmingdale Road, NY-Route 109
Farmingdale, NY 11735

Magic Touch A Brooklyn Girls Story

ISBN 13: 978-1-62286-588-8
ISBN 10: 1-62286-588-X

First Trade Paperback Printing November 2017
Printed in the United States of America

10 9 8 7 6 5 4 3 2 1

Distributed by Kensington Publishing Corp.
Submit orders to:
Customer Service
400 Hahn Road
Westminster, MD 21157-4627
Phone: 1-800-733-3000
Fax: 1-800-659-2436

Chapter 1

New Beginnings

Loud reggae music blared through the house and competed with the clang of pots and pans. The smell of curry and fried plantains wafted through the air so strong the aromas had dragged Simmy out of her sleep with hunger pangs. As she stretched her arms over her head and wiggled her toes, Simmy could also hear the bustling noise of the block party preparations going on outside of her window: loud Calypso music, steel pan bands practicing and, of course, the screaming of, "Ayo!" and, "Yo, son!" up and down her block, and extra noise associated with the extra people who came out to Brooklyn for their annual block party, bustling up and down the street. It was definitely a typical noisy, hot summer weekend in August.

If Simmy had her way, it would be a good weekend of partying and celebrating to mark the end of summer. She was looking forward to her last year of high school and finally graduating. Now, if she could get her hands on some money so she could buy herself a decent outfit, that would make her day.

She threw her legs over the side of her bed and sat up. Although it was the last weekend in August, the sun still blazed as if fall weren't around the corner. Simmy fanned her face with her hands trying to make what little breeze she could.

"Who took my fan?" she mumbled, looking around the small, cramped front room where she slept.

The room was so hot, long, loose strands of Simmy's hair stuck to the side of her face and snaked down her neck like ivy growing on an old building. Her T-shirt clung to the wet parts of her chest and back.

"They always touching my stuff," Simmy groaned, scanning the small space to see what else her cousins might've touched. She sighed loudly when her eyes landed on the big gray plastic bins with purple covers that served as her dresser. A few pieces of her clothing hung over the sides and, Simmy noticed, just below the stack of plastic bins her neat row of shoes had been touched, too. Two pair were missing. A flash of heat exploded in Simmy's chest.

"I'm telling," she grumbled, stomping out of her room. As soon as she got into the hallway, she paused. There was a commotion so raucous she could hear it even over the music.

"I don't care what you say, Mummy. All of these shift-less-ass adults in this house should be contributing. I am tired of doing everything around here. You let Marcus do whatever he wants and bring his lazy woman here to live with kids. She hasn't worked in six or seven months. Then she got the nerve to say she's a profressional hairdresser." Sheryl stopped talking and put her hand up over her eyes. "Hairdresser? Where?" She looked around as if she were looking for something.

"She don't bring a dime to you. The bills are piling up, the taxes on the house are not paid, and what about the crazy high light and gas? Who is supposed to do all of this? Me?" Sheryl yelled, her second-generation Jamaican accent occasionally creeping into her words.

Simmy crinkled her brow and rolled her eyes at the sound of her aunt's loud voice. She could just picture Sheryl standing in the middle of the floor, bent slightly at the waist with her head rolling, her finger pointed and going in and out and the veins in her neck visible at the surface of her fair skin.

Sheryl was always complaining, and there always seemed to be an argument going on in the house. If it wasn't Sheryl and Simmy's uncle Marcus, then it was Simmy and Marcus's kids or Marcus's kids and Sheryl's kids. The arguments were usually about money: the high light bills, the cable turn-off notices, or the past due water bills. Or that someone ate someone else's food out of the refrigerator even though it was labeled DO NOT TOUCH. Or that someone wore someone else's shoes or clothes, which Simmy remembered was the whole reason she had been drawn out of her room.

Simmy shook her head and bit down on her bottom lip as she listened. With each point Sheryl made, Simmy felt more and more like a burden. She hated living in her grandmother's crowded house. It was times like this, listening to her aunt, that Simmy missed her parents the most.

She peeked from the corner of the kitchen door as her grandmother, Patricia, lovingly known to her children and grandchildren as Mummy Pat, sucked her teeth and continued moving her long-handled spoon in circular motions inside of the huge silver Dutch pot, mixing her curry goat gravy for the right thickness. Mummy Pat was short and wide now, but Simmy could still see some semblance of an hourglass shape, or what Jamaicans called a Coke-bottle shape, left over from Mummy Pat's younger days.

"Oh, so you just going to act I'm not talking about the truth right now, Mummy? I am the only one in here working and bringing in money. Things falling apart around here and nobody cares. You've been taking a shower with no showerhead for months. Just water pouring out of the wall and that's fine with you? And why? Because you're waiting for me to go to Home Depot and replace it, that's why. But, you got Marcus and Donovan coming and going like they're Jamaican kings and bringing all their random women and kids here to eat and sleep. I can't do this anymore, Mummy. I'm soon going to be gone from here, and the whole damn house gonna fall in around you," Sheryl went on, getting closer to Mummy Pat's ear.

Mummy Pat waved her hand near her ear as if she were shooing away an annoying fly buzzing around her head. But, she still didn't say a word to Sheryl.

"Don't act like I'm not right. Even this." Sheryl opened her arms wide and moved them slowly over the table where Mummy Pat had at least fifteen foil pans filled with delicious West Indian dishes all sealed tight with aluminum foil covers. "It's Labor Day weekend, and here you are spending what little money you have to buy stuff and cooking up all of this food. For what? For your hungry, no-life-having relatives to come throw their legs under the table and freeload off of you? Everybody in here is old enough to work. You running a halfway house for no-goods and for the kids of no-goods too." Sheryl folded her arms over her chest and pouted. "Just stupid."

Finally, Mummy Pat slammed down the cover on her pot with a resounding clang. She rounded on her daughter, with fire flashing in her eyes.

"Let me tell you one thing here now, Sheryl," Mummy Pat said, her thick Jamaican accent coming on strong now. She extended her metal spoon toward Sheryl for emphasis, and it moved with her words. "Don't tell me how to run my house, hear? When you lost everyt'ing running behind a man and almost lost your mind with depression, this same house full of shiftless people was here for you. Your same brothers you complaining on went to find that man after he boxed your head and left you bruised from here to hell, and they beat his ass within an inch of life. They could've lost everything but, for you, they did that. You came here without a dime, and nobody said a word. Marcus was the one who would hustle up and give you a few dollars and get the kids things that they needed. Oh, yes, we banded together and put you back on your feet. Now you working for the city driving a bus and want to big up your chest? You want to be like you're better than all of we? Nah, man, it doesn't work that way. This is my house, and I run it the way I want. If you don't like it, you know what to do."

Sheryl's head jerked like Mummy Pat's words were an openhanded slap to her face. "Okay, so now you going to throw stuff up in my face. It's all right, Mummy. You're right. I know what to do."

Simmy pressed her back against the hallway wall and closed her eyes. She let out a long breath. The constant bickering in the house did something to her mood every day. She had been reading up on depression, and she was convinced that she was depressed.

"And you."

Simmy's eyes popped open to find her aunt Sheryl standing in her face wearing a mean scowl.

"You can start pulling your weight around here too. Seventeen means you can work. I bet you're still not used to living like this, Miss Princess. Your mother and father gave you everything, but where are they now? Locked up like animals. All that money and look at you now, left here for everybody else to take care of you and all your shit. You need to start contributing around here. Better use all that tits and ass you grew overnight to get a man to take care of you like your mother Carla did with my brother. She snagged Chris with her fast ass, and now he's not around to help out his own mother, and they left you here to be a burden on top of everything else,"

Sheryl whispered harshly, before pushing past Simmy and storming away.

Simmy hung her head; suddenly, she wasn't hungry anymore. She turned on her heels and headed back to her tiny room. Sheryl had been right about one thing: her parents had given her everything when they'd had it to give.

Simmy sulked back into her room and picked up the framed picture she kept on the seat of a small, white plastic chair that doubled as her nightstand. She stared at picture and smiled. It was an oldie but goodie of her parents. Her mother was so young back then, with a fresh, innocent, dimple-cheeked smile, rocking her hair in the classic nineties high-low cut that female rappers Salt-N-Pepa had made popular, wearing two pair of gold doorknocker earrings, a neck full of rope chains, and a fly MCM navy blue and tan monogram sweat suit with a pair of brown Travel Fox boots.

Simmy's father was eight years older than her mother and, although his facial expression in the picture was serious, the way he held her mother from behind and rested his chin on her shoulder showed that he loved her. Simmy always laughed looking at that picture of him in his tall black leather hat that sat high on his head, with his long, thick dreadlocks hiding underneath it. Simmy always thought he looked like a Dr. Seuss character in that hat. But, she loved to stare at the big gold rings her father wore on each of his fingers. One was the shape of a thick gold nugget, one was the shape of his birth country, Jamaica, and one spanned three of his fingers with the word JAH spelled out across it.

Simmy realized that, although her parents looked funny to her now, back then their outfits showed that they had money. She'd heard her family refer to them as hood rich, but she never cared about their name-calling.

They'd had it all: a big house on Long Island, a different luxury car for every day of the week, and the finest clothes money could buy. Simmy was the only child, and there was nothing too expensive for her. She remembered when her father had first moved them out of their small, cramped apartment in Brooklyn.

The ride seemed so long, and Simmy asked, "Are we there yet?" about twelve times before her father finally pulled his big-body Benz up to a set of tall black wrought-iron gates with a big gold J in the center of each.

"What's this, Daddy? Where is this?" Simmy asked, bouncing on her knees in the back seat.

"Simone. Simone, baby. You have to have patience," her father sang, laughing at her insistence.

He pulled up to a small box and rubbed a white card against it. Simmy watched as the gates parted slowly and seemingly invited them inside. She felt like fireworks were going off inside of her and she could barely keep still. Her father drove slowly up the circular driveway and stopped the car right in front a huge set of white marble steps.

"This looks like a castle, Daddy," Simmy gasped, craning her neck to see out of the car window.

"It's our castle because you're my princess. Now, c'mon, baby girl. Let's go see," her father said, smiling wide as he scrambled out of the car and rushed around to her side to open the door for her.

Simmy never entered or exited a car without waiting for her father to open her door. He'd told her that real men open doors for their ladies, and that had stuck with her.

When her door swung open, Simmy practically jumped out of the car. Once both of her feet were planted firmly on the ground in front of her new house, she paused with her mouth wide open and raised her head as far as it would go to look up at the house.

The gray sandstone mansion boasted eight regal white Roman columns on each side of the grand porch. The smooth, shiny white and tan speckled marble steps seemed like the stairway to heaven. Simmy was too young to even count far enough to account for all of the windows on the front of the house. In her mind, there had to be over one hundred of them. As they stood there taking it all in, Simmy's mother walked through the huge solid cherry wood doors.

"Hey, baby girl. You like your new house?" her mother chimed, opening her arms wide.

Simmy bounded up the steps so fast the air whipped over her face and dried her lips. She jumped into her mother's arms and squeezed her tight. "I love it, Mommy!" Simmy squealed.

"All of this for my baby," her father said. "All of this for you, princess."

"I miss you, Mommy and Daddy," Simmy whispered to the picture. She pressed the glass to her lips and closed her eyes. Her shoulders slumped, and suddenly her stomach ached. Not a day went by that she didn't think about her parents and how fast her life had changed when they'd gotten locked up. It was too much to think about, too much to relive.

She wished she could see her parents or at least be able to talk to them. Unfortunately for her, she hadn't seen or spoken to them since they'd been arrested. She remembered asking her aunt and grandmother when her mom and dad were coming home but they refused to tell her. Instead, she was told to stay out of grown folks' business. Now, almost four years later, she still didn't have a clue. She had tried asking Mummy Pat again, but her grandmother was still tightlipped about it. This time around, though, Mummy Pat did explain to Simmy why she hadn't been taken to see them since they'd been imprisoned. She admitted to Simmy that her parents made her promise to never bring her to see them. As much as it hurt them to know that they weren't going to see their little girl for a long time, they both didn't want her to be exposed to that environment. They wanted to keep her innocent and protected from that world.

Simmy put the picture down and grabbed her favorite book, *The Color Purple,* from the side of her bed. Reading was her favorite distraction from the madness and the memories. Simmy loved to escape into books and pretend she lived in another place and time. She walked over to the long wooden platform in front of her window and sat down.

Just as she opened her book, she heard, "Simone! Simone, come down here!"

Simmy closed her eyes, clapped her book shut, and sighed at the sound of Mummy Pat calling her name like there was an emergency. Peace and quiet was surely hard to come by in that house.

"Coming, Mummy Pat," Simmy called back. She rushed down to the kitchen.

Her grandmother greeted her with her usual warm smile. Simmy was starting to see the age show up on Mummy Pat's face. The fine lines branching from the corners of her eyes and the deep parentheses around her mouth seemed to have appeared overnight. Mummy Pat had fair skin, hazel eyes, and sandy brown hair. Most people mistook her for Hispanic, until she opened her mouth and that thick Jamaican Patois came out.

"Simone, baby, I need some things from the store. The rice and peas needs a little zing, and I run out of coconut milk, and Scotch bonnet peppers. Please run down to the store for me, baby."

Simmy smiled. "Okay, Mummy Pat. Anything for you."

That was true. There was nothing Simmy wouldn't do for her grandmother. Mummy Pat was the only person in the house who didn't make her feel like an outsider. When her parents got arrested, Mummy Pat was the one who stepped up and took guardianship of her when everyone else said no. If it hadn't been for her grandmother, she'd have probably been in a foster home right now. Simmy was grateful for Mummy Pat, and she had the utmost respect and a great deal of love for her.

She ran back to her room, put some sneakers on, and ran out, not bothering to change or fix her hair. She figured she could shower when she got back since she was just doing a quick run to the store.

Halfway to the store, Simmy wished she had grabbed a bottle of water before heading out. It was a hot, dry summer day and the heat was blazing. She could feel the sunrays burning her caramel skin. The sun was shining so bright it was almost blinding. The more she walked, the thirstier she felt. She could feel beads of sweat forming over her upper lip. Her long, curly hair was already in a ponytail, but she could feel the hairs sticking to the back of her neck. She couldn't wait to get back home and take a nice, cold shower to freshen up.

She put her hands over her eyes to shield herself from the blazing sun, and that's when she saw him. As soon as Simmy realized he was walking toward her, she wanted to turn and run back to the house.

Shit. Not now. I look a hot mess. Literally!

Her stomach immediately cramped up, and more sweat beads lined up at her hairline like ready soldiers. She definitely wasn't dressed or prepared to run into her all-time biggest crush, Kyan Barkley.

Simmy dug into the pocket of her shorts in hopes that she had something she could use to wipe her sweaty face.

Of course I run into him when I look tore up from the floor up! Simmy thought, biting down on her bottom lip, which was the thing she did whenever she was nervous. Simmy's heart jammed against her breastbone when she locked eyes with him.

Dang! Now he would know for sure that she saw him. Still, Simmy quickly averted her eyes, put her head down, and crossed the street, acting as if she hadn't see him.

Kyan was a young dope boy who Simmy had had a crush on since fifth grade. They attended the same high school, but all Simmy could do was watch him from a distance. He was out of her league. Way out of her league.

Simmy had watched Kyan go from the neighborhood bum kid with run-down outlet sneakers, dirty, bar-gain-center T-shirts, and ripped no-name jeans to one of the best dressed young dudes in her school and neighbor-hood. All of the girls on her block were pining for Kyan. Simmy had recently heard that he was dating a gorgeous girl from across town named Ava. Even Simmy knew she couldn't hold a candle to Ava's beauty. Everyone in school said Ava looked like a young Nia Long and Simmy had to agree.

What Simmy failed to realize was that her perfectly clear, smooth caramel skin, thick, curly hair, and deep-set almond eyes made her beautiful in her own right as well. Not only did Simmy have a beautiful face, but she had a body that many women would pay for. Simmy had a Coke-bottle shape like her grandmother. Her thick thighs led up to her round, firm bottom. She had a small waist and perky C-cup breasts. Grown men often gawked and tried to approach Simmy whenever she'd walk to the store or through the mall. At seventeen years old, Simmy had the body of a grown woman.

Simmy rushed into the grocery store relieved that she'd managed to avoid Kyan. She was glad that he had only seen her from a distance. Now she prayed that no one she knew was inside, since she had to use Mummy Pat's EBT card for her purchases. Simmy rushed around the store picking up the things off the list, all the while silently praying that nobody she knew entered.

Simmy finally finished paying for the groceries, and she was in the clear. She wiped sweat from her forehead and breathed out heavily. No one had spotted her using the card. She grabbed the four plastic bags and headed out the door.

"Oh, my God," she wheezed, stumbling backward. She had bumped hard into someone. The plastic handle on one of her bags popped and her grandmother's groceries went scattering on the ground.

"I'm . . . I'm sorry," Simmy stuttered, setting the other bags down as she bent down to pick up the items that had fallen. She was so thrown off by the body crash, she hadn't even looked up.

"No. I'm sorry. That was all my fault. I wasn't watching where I was going," a smooth voice said.

Simmy moved her head in slow motion. It was him! She had touched Kyan! Her heart leaped in her chest, and her hands started trembling.

"You're Simone, right?" Kyan asked, although he already knew her name very well. They had been in school together for years.

"Ye . . . yeah," Simmy answered, still unable to stop shaking.

"I'm sorry. I didn't mean to knock you over," he said, flashing his gorgeous smile. He bent down and helped her gather up her scattered items.

Simmy could feel her cheeks burning from embarrassment. She hurriedly tried to pick everything up so she could be on her way. She couldn't believe she had somehow managed to bump into him after she tried so hard to avoid him. This had to be the worst day ever.

Kyan extended his hand to help her stand up. Simmy took his hand into hers and felt like someone had attached her to an electric current. *God, he looks like an angel.* She could've sworn she saw a bright flash of yellow-tinged light glowing around Kyan.

"Um, thanks for helping me," she said, unable to hold eye contact for fear that he'd see into her eyes and somehow see how crazy she was about him. She felt her heart racing and palpitating against her chest.

"You're welcome." Kyan gave her a wide smile. "You live around here now?" Kyan asked. "I know you used to live on Long Island awhile back, but you still came to school out here."

"My grandmother lives around here," Simmy said, shifting her weight from one foot to the other, too ashamed to admit that she no longer resided in her home on Long Island. "I'm visiting her for a while. But, not really living here." Technically she wasn't lying about what she'd said. She loved her grandmother, but she had never felt comfortable in that house. In the years that she had been living there, she had never felt like she was home. There were just too many people living there, and none of them were nice people.

"A'ight, that's what's up. That means I'll get to see you for a while then," Kyan said smoothly, licking his full lips.

Simmy's legs felt weak, and she could barely hold on to her bags. She was having crazy thoughts. *Grab him and kiss him all over his face!*

"Well, I, um, I gotta—" Simmy struggled to find the words so she could get out of this awkward encounter.

"Hey, Kyan," a squeaky voice cut Simmy off. "You out here helping charity cases now?" Loud laughter followed.

Simmy turned to find three girls standing behind her, pointing and laughing. It was the tallest girl of the group who had made the charity comment; the other two were standing on either side of her, sniggering.

"C'mon. Get out of here with all that." Kyan waved them off. Simmy's face flushed.

"Well, we didn't think you like girls who wear last season's cutoff Levi's, Forever 21 two dollar tanks, and run-down Converses," the tall girl said, looking Simmy up and down.

All three girls busted out laughing again. "Yeah. Converse cost $49.99, so who wears them until they're filthy like that?" one of the other mean girls chimed in.

"I gotta go," Simmy said, barely opening her mouth.

The girls moved together, blocking her path. "Kyan ain't checking for no cheap-gear-wearing chick like you. And, look at that hair. Who did it? Your blind grandma?"

More laughter.

"You don't know nothing about Chanel and YSL, do you?" the tall girl said, patting the letters on her T-shirt and then hitting the front of the bright red Chanel bag that hung at her side.

Simmy's honey-colored face turned almost burgundy. She clutched the plastic handles of her grocery bags so tight the circulation in her fingers was cut off. Her eyes darted from one girl to the next and, each time, she felt lower and lower. Looking at how fly all three girls were dressed, Simmy felt like a dirty homeless person standing there. She definitely recognized the brands—Gucci, Chanel, and Louis Vuitton—that the girls rocked, but those were way out of her league these days.

"Kyan, I'm so disappointed. I thought you had better taste," the tall girl said. "You out here looking trill as hell, rocking Balenciaga, but you trying to rap to a bum bandit?"

Simmy's jaw rocked, but there was no way she would be any match for those three who had encircled her now.

"Leave her alone and get the hell on, Trisha," Kyan snapped, putting his arm around Simmy's shoulders so he could lead her out of the mean girl circle.

"Yeah, leave her alone and get the hell on, *Trisha,* before I catch a fucking case out here," a familiar voice boomed from the left.

Simmy's eyes went wide. "Jayla!" Simmy's shoulders relaxed with relief, and she almost dropped all of her bags at the sight of her older cousin busting through the mean girl circle like a superhero.

"What's up, little cousin?" Jayla smiled. "You a'ight? Anybody touch you?

Simmy shook her head no. Jayla turned to the mean girls, her face all of a sudden pinched tight into a scowl. "Y'all see her?" Jayla pointed at Simmy. "Just know that's me. Don't ever let me catch y'all trying to play her out here again or it's going to be a fucking problem. Y'all already know what I'm working with. I ain't been gone from BK that fucking long, so y'all know exactly what it is," Jayla said, pointing down to her gunmetal gray Chanel boy bag.

"And you. Pretty boy with the curly hair and fancy footwear." Jayla rounded on Kyan and pointed in his face. "Stay the hell away from my little cousin if you ain't going to protect her. How you got these basic bitches rolling up on my blood and you ain't slap the life out of one of them? Fuck outta here if you ain't about it," Jayla snarled.

With that, she grabbed Simmy by the arm and pulled her toward the corner. "C'mon, before I really lose my shit on these little nothing-ass girls. I'm too dressed up for the bullshit," Jayla said, flipping her hair out of her face. It was true. Jayla rocked a white tunic, the hottest multicolored Giuseppe Zanotti knee-high gladiator heels, and a pair of pearl-accented Chanel shades. Her hair was all out, with bouncy, blond-streaked curls bouncing around her fresh, professionally made-up face.

Simmy stumbled along but managed to look back over her shoulder at Kyan as he shoved his hands deep into his pockets and hung his head as she walked away.

"Yo, Simmy, what the fuck was that?" Jayla asked her cousin.

"Huh? What are you talking about?"

"Listen, Simmy, I don't care who it is. Don't stand out here letting nobody play you like that. Ever," Jayla scolded her.

Simmy sighed. It was hard to defend yourself when the girls teasing you had a point.

"Chicks will try you every day because of that light skin, them pretty eyes, and that beautiful long hair. It don't matter who they are; you gotta hold your own against these ugly weave-queens hiding behind some clothes they had to sell ass to get. I know you grew up on Long Island for a minute but you been out here long enough to know how to handle yourself. Simmy, you gotta act real Brooklyn at all times," Jayla lectured on. "What if Mummy Pat didn't send me over here to see what was taking you so long? You was just gonna let them shallow-ass chicks play you like that? Nah, can't happen like that, Simmy. If I don't teach you nothing else, remember I told you to never let another bitch make you feel less than. You are always your own number one fan. Always."

Simmy nodded her understanding. "I wish you still lived here, Jay. I hate it here without you," Simmy said sadly. Simmy and Jayla had only lived together for six months before Jayla moved out of Mummy Pat's house, but they had grown up together, so they had always been close cousins.

"Aw. I know, baby girl." Jayla softened. "But, for me, Harlem is where it's at right now. I couldn't do the crowded house thing no more. Everybody coming and going like it was a short-stay hotel. People touching your shit without permission. I had to get away, make my own money, you know? Spread my wings."

Simmy nodded as they crossed the street. She knew all too well what Jayla meant about Mummy Pat's brownstone being like a revolving door for anyone who fell hard and was down on their luck. Jayla's mother, Chrissy, was Simmy's father's sister. Chrissy had been killed in a drug deal gone bad when Jayla was eleven. Jayla, just like Simmy, had been left parentless. Simmy's dad, Chris, wanted Jayla to live with them but, with his illegal business, he couldn't risk filing for custody and having them look into his finances. Jayla was left to fend for herself at Mummy Pat's house.

Despite Jayla not being able to live with them, Simmy's father still made sure she was taken care of. Every month he would drop off money to Mummy Pat so she could buy whatever Jalya needed. Chris felt responsible for his sister's death since he was the one who had set up the drug deal that got her killed. He felt the least he could do was make sure that Chrissy's daughter was taken care of and didn't go without.

When Jayla and Simmy got to the front door of Mummy Pat's brownstone, Jayla held on to Simmy's arm to stop her from entering. "And, why you ain't call me and tell me you needed things?" Jayla asked, gesturing at Simmy's dirty sneakers and cutoff Levi's.

Simmy looked down at her feet, her mouth sagging at the edges. "I just don't like being a burden to anyone. I try to make the best out of what I have left in the account my father left. And I know Mummy doesn't have a lot to give me, so I just try to get by with whatever clothes I have. And you know I hate asking anybody for anything. And, besides, I really don't care about what people think of my clothes and stuff," Simmy lied. She cared very much about what people thought of her. She hated her clothes, and the comments mean girls would make when she walked past them didn't help. "I know I can't buy any of the expensive clothes everybody out here wearing so I don't even think about it. Right now I'm just trying to focus on finishing my senior year and graduating." Simmy gave her cousin a halfhearted smile.

Jayla sucked her teeth. "And you really want me to believe all that shit you just tried to feed me?" Jayla smirked. "C'mon, Simmy, I know you care about your clothes. You ain't got to lie to me, little cousin. I know what the deal is. Didn't I tell you before I got you? You ain't no damn burden. And, I don't throw shit in people's faces when I do for them. You've seen me bring Jordans for Marcus's boys, and fitted hats, sneakers, them stupid-ass thirty dollar Nike socks, and all of that for Sheryl's kids, so why wouldn't I hook you up if you asked? Remember, Simmy, I've been where you're at right now."

Simmy parted a halfhearted smile and gnawed on her bottom lip. "I know. But, I just can't get used to asking people for stuff. And I don't want you to think I'm being shallow just trying to look fly."

"Oh, my God, Simmy! You know I don't think like that," Jayla said, waving her hand like Simmy was being ridiculous. "Now take them bags inside and let's go."

Simmy crinkled her brow and tilted her head. "Where we going?"

"Just go and drop off Mummy Pat's shit so we can go do something with that bird's nest you call hair and get you some wears. Shit, you can't be out here representing me and not really representing me," Jayla said, laughing lightly afterward.

Simmy smiled wide and rushed into the house. She returned so fast Jayla had to laugh.

"Damn, little cousin. You wasn't playing, huh?"

Simmy blushed.

"To new beginnings," Jayla said, locking arms with Simmy. They bounced down the street, giggling. It was the happiest Simmy had felt in a long while.

"You still ain't say where we're going."

"If you must know, nosey, straight to the Dominicans you go. Can't have all that beautiful long hair looking crazy like this. So, first stop: hair. Second stop: Saks and Neiman for some shit that will knock those little bitches out the box. You about to level up, little cousin."

Simmy was too excited by the thought of new clothes and a new hairstyle that she never bothered to ask her cousin how she was going to pay for it all.

Chapter 2

Learning the Ropes

Simmy didn't return to Mummy Pat's house that entire weekend. After she'd gotten her hair laid for the gods by the girls at the Dominican shop, Jayla had whisked her away on a whirlwind shopping spree in Roosevelt Field Mall on Long Island.

Bloomingdale's, Neiman Marcus, BCBG Max Azria, and Nordstrom were just a few of the stores they had blazed through, grabbing things like money wasn't an issue. Simmy was amazed watching Jayla whip out her credit cards, sparing no expense.

Balmain dresses, Givenchy T-shirts and bomber jackets, Moncler coats, BCBG pants suits, Gucci sneakers, Aquazzura boots, and Sophia Webster pumps were just a few of the things Jayla bought for Simmy during their shopping spree.

"All the hood ratchets wearing red bottoms now. We off that," Jayla had chided her, snatching the shoe from Simmy when she'd picked up a pair of Christian Louboutins while they were in Neiman.

"You'll learn the difference between high fashion and fashion frontin' hanging with me, little cousin." Jayla had winked. Simmy had smiled. She was a willing student excited to learn her cousin's shopping tricks.

Simmy stayed the entire weekend with Jayla in a suite on the top floor of the Aloft Hotel on Duffield Street. Jayla had said it was far enough away from all of the crazy J'ouvert and Labor Day activities, but still in

Brooklyn so they could party and not have to travel all
the way to Jayla's place up in Harlem.

Simmy didn't care where they stayed, so long as she
was getting a break from being in Mummy Pat's hot,
crowded house. Simmy felt alive and carefree being away
from the house. Jayla never made her feel unwelcome or
as if she were a burden.

"Wake up, girl." Jayla nudged Simmy.

Simmy groaned. It felt like she'd just gone to sleep.
Jayla had picked up a fake ID for her little cousin, and
they had decided to go out one more time before Simmy
had to go home. They had just gotten back to Jayla's
hotel room at five in the morning from partying all night.
Staying up until the wee hours of the morning was not
something Simmy was used to. This was all new to her.

"It's almost noon. Sleepyheads don't get paid," Jayla
said, nudging Simmy again. "I have to take you home. I
got business to take care of."

Simmy finally sat up. Disappointment flashed across
her face.

"It's all good. I'll be back. I promise," Jayla said, flop-
ping down on the bed next to Simmy.

"Heard that before," Simmy murmured.

Jayla looked her in the eyes and raised her right hand.
"I promise on my mother's grave, I will come back more.
I'm going to make sure we have more weekends like this."

"Swear?"

"Swear," Jayla said, putting her right hand over her
heart.

The girls showered, got dressed, and grabbed a quick
breakfast before heading back to Mummy Pat's. Simmy
felt her heart racing as they got closer and closer to the
house. She felt as if she were being brought back to jail
after the little taste of freedom she'd gotten over the last
few days. The way they'd gone shopping this weekend
took her back to how it used to be before she had to
move back to Brooklyn. She missed her big house on

Long Island. She missed her bedroom, her clothes, shoes, accessories. Most of all she missed her parents.

"Simmy!" Jayla snapped her fingers in front of Simmy to get her attention.

"Huh?"

"Damn, bitch, you zoned out on me." Jayla chuckled.

"I'm sorry, Jayla. I just hate having to go back there. I love Mummy Pat, but everyone else in that house is a bunch of jerks. I usually just stay locked up in my room to avoid them." They pulled up to the house just as she said that. Simmy placed her hands in her lap and looked down at them.

"Simmy." Jayla reached over and put her hand on her cousin's shoulder. "I know what it's like in there. And I hated it just as much as you do. But, I promise you, it's gonna be all right. And I'ma be here for you, no matter what."

Simmy looked up and locked eyes with Jayla. She could see that Jayla was being genuine. She mustered up a smile. "Thanks, Jayla."

"Of course, little cousin. I gotchu." She winked. "Now let me help you get your bags out the trunk. You're gonna be the flyest bitch in school!" The two girls shared a laugh. They grabbed the bags and were headed inside when Jayla's phone rang.

"Go ahead. I'll be right there." Jayla dropped the bags and reached for her phone in the car.

"Okay," Simmy yelled back as she put the bags down to open the front door.

"My, my, my, look who decided to show up," was the first thing she heard as soon as Simmy took a step inside.

Great, now I have to deal with her crap. Here we go. "Hi, Auntie Sheryl." Simmy did her best to sound nonchalant.

"Oh, don't you 'hi' me, little girl," Sheryl snapped. "You up and left without telling anybody where you were going or when you were coming back. Where have you been?

And where the hell did all those bags come from?" Sheryl questioned as she pointed toward Simmy's full hands.

"I was out with Jay—"

"She was out with me," Jayla interrupted with an attitude as she entered the living room and stood right in front of her aunt.

"Oh, shit. It's even worse than I thought. Simmy, you have no business hanging out with no-good people like her," Sheryl said as she eyed Jayla up and down.

"Oh, please. You right about me not being no good. I'm great!" Jayla snapped. "You're just jealous because you don't have half the shit I have and don't nobody like you. You wish you were doing as good as I was."

"Little girl, you're not gonna talk to me like that in my own motherfucking house!" Sheryl took a step toward Jayla.

"First of all, this ain't your house. This is your mother's house, and you're just living in it. Second of all, you must be crazy if you think I'm gonna let you take a jab at me and I ain't gonna say nothing to you. You may be my aunt but let's not forget the only thing you ever did for me was treat me like shit the whole time I lived here. I couldn't say or do nothing back then, but I'm a grown woman now so if you wanna act all big and bad and talk shit then go ahead, but don't think I'll hesitate to put my pretty, manicured hands on you."

"What's going on in here?"

Simmy was relieved to see Mummy Pat walk into the room. One more minute and she was afraid she was going to end up caught in a fight between the two women bickering.

"Hi, Mummy Pat," Jayla said as she walked toward her grandmother and gave her a big hug and a kiss on the cheek.

"Hey, baby. How you doing, child?"

"I'm great, Mummy. I was just dropping Simmy off. I took her shopping for some clothes for school."

"Oh, that's so nice of you, Jayla. Thank you."

"No need for thanking, Mummy. We're family and family looks out for each other." As she said this, she glanced at Sheryl, who just stood there without saying a word. "Mummy, I can't stay because I need to get to work. I'll come by another day." Jayla hugged her grandmother.

"Simmy, I'll see you soon." She winked at her cousin and left without even bothering to look at her aunt, Sheryl.

"Well, I'm going to head to my room and put my new clothes away." Simmy excused herself before giving Sheryl a chance to say anything to her.

Simmy couldn't wait for the first day of school. She'd laid out several of her new items the night before, pondering which high-end outfit she would rock. She'd narrowed it down to a silver and pink Gucci bomber jacket, a pair of purposely faded black Balmain jeans, and Gucci sneakers, or a close-fitting Balmain dress and a pair of Fendi booties.

When the sun crept through her window and her annoying cell phone alarm blared, Simmy popped out of the bed like a jack-in-the-box. She picked up the picture of her parents and spoke to it. "It's going to be a good day."

As Simmy passed through the metal detector at Clara Barton High School, she could already see all eyes on her. Her hair was freshly braided in thick, feed-in braids all going back with her edges carefully slicked into tiny waves. She donned a pair of sparkly, rhinestone-accented Gucci sunglasses and carried the black classic Chanel bag that Jayla had loaned her. She definitely turned heads.

Simmy heard the hushed murmurs passing down the hallway as she walked through in her black Balmain jeans and white, red, and green Gucci sneakers. She smiled, feeling as confident as a runway model.

Simmy rounded the hallway corner heading to her homeroom when she heard the rapid tap of feet behind her.

"Simone! Hold up."

Simmy slowed down, but she didn't stop and turn around. The person caught up to her.

"What's up?" Kyan huffed. "I was trying to get your attention when you first walked in. But, you wasn't trying to hear it. What's up?"

"Ain't nothing," Simmy replied, purposely adding a slight attitude to her tone. Jayla had told her if she wanted a dude to really be interested in her, she'd have to act disinterested in him. *Men like a challenge. If you're too easy, you're boring, and they hate boring girls.* Simmy replayed Jayla's words in her mind.

"Can I walk you to class?" Kyan asked.

"Looks like you're already doing that," Simmy said, trying her best to keep up the disinterested act when really her organs were jumping inside with excitement.

Simmy noticed all of the usual popular girls watching her as she glided through the hallways riding on her new cloud of confidence.

"All eyes on you," Kyan remarked, noticing as well.

"Maybe the eyes are on you. Everybody loves you," Simmy came right back with.

"A'ight, you got that one." He laughed.

"This is my class." Simmy stopped at the door.

"Can I stay in touch with you though?" Kyan asked.

Simmy wanted to scream, "Of course you can! I've been waiting for this day for years!" She wanted to throw the Chanel bag down and do a little dance. But, she kept her cool.

"If I give you my number, your little posse from the other day won't be playing on my phone, will they?" Simmy asked facetiously, making reference to the mean girls who had surrounded her the day she had bumped into him.

"Nah. You'll never have to worry about nothing like that again. I just want to get to know you better. I've been wanting to get to know you for a minute."

Simone mentally thanked Jayla again for the phone she had just bought her. If this had been two weeks ago, she would've felt really dumb having to explain to Kyan that she didn't have a cell phone.

"A'ight, put it in your phone." Simone gave him her number, and she headed into her classroom.

Simmy found it impossible to concentrate on anything the teacher was saying. She tapped her feet impatiently, stared at her pretty pink nail polish with the rhinestone embellishments, and secretly checked her cell ten times.

All of her classes turned out the same. She couldn't help but to keep checking her phone. She was excited to get a text or a call from him. She daydreamed and replayed the scene with Kyan over and over in her mind. She had actually given Kyan Barkley her number! The most popular dude in their school and in her neighborhood had her phone number.

Simmy smiled wickedly thinking about all of the jealous girls watching, looking like they wanted to rip her head off, as she had punched her number into Kyan's iPhone. Simmy felt extra special now. It was the first time in her entire four years of high school that she felt she was getting some clout. Jayla was right; all it took was a little sprucing up: fresh hairdo, banging nail job, hot name-brand clothes, and a lot of attitude to send Simmy to the it-girl side of life.

When the last bell rang, Simmy raced for the exit doors. She couldn't wait to be able to use her cell phone to see if Kyan had called or texted her yet. She exited the school and heard her name being called and the blare of a car horn. Simmy stopped and looked around with her eyebrows furrowed.

"Over here!"

Simmy's eyes lit up. "Damn. This girl stay getting it," Simmy whispered, her mouth hanging open.

"C'mon, little cousin." Jayla waved her over. "Stop looking crazy and bring yo' ass over here," Jayla joked.

Simmy smiled so wide she was sure every one of her teeth, even the back ones, could be seen. She could feel the heat of everybody watching her. Simmy felt like sticking her tongue out and screaming, "Suckas!"

As the other lame kids made their way to the train stations or bus stops, Simmy was rushing over to a shiny black Audi A8 with low-profile tires and gleaming silver rims.

"Jay, wha . . . where'd you get this car?" Simmy gawked.

"Why you ask so many questions? I promised I would be back and what better way to come than in luxury?" Jayla replied, leaning on the car. "Now stop acting like you work for the feds with all of these damn questions, and get yo' ass in and let's ride."

Simmy felt like her body melted against the butter-soft leather seats in the Audi. "You are so fly, Jayla," Simmy said, running her hand along the door. She looked over in pure adoration at Jayla's thick gold Cartier bracelets and her diamond-encrusted Rolex. "I don't know how you can afford it all. You look like a rich lady."

Jayla laughed. "You're too cute, Simmy."

"For real. If I could only be half as fly as you, I would never worry about girls frontin' on me, ever."

"Don't worry, little cuz. Stick with me. You'll be learning the ropes and being just as fly or flier than me in no time. Matter of fact, lesson one starts today. You ready?"

"Okay," Simmy quickly agreed before she even knew what she was agreeing to. She didn't care, either. At that point, she would've followed Jayla into the fiery pits of hell if she'd asked.

"You're older now, so I think it's time. I feel like I can trust you, too. You always been real loyal," Jayla said.

Simmy shook her head vigorously. She wanted Jayla to trust her. She just wanted to be down.

"We both know growing up in Bed-Stuy, in our hood, appearance is everything. Chicks and dudes are more interested in what you wearing than what you saying, feel me? Everything you wear, down to the socks, represents you. I don't even go to the store looking half ass. That's the one thing I want you to learn. Just like the celebrities do: never leave home looking less than fabulous, Simmy."

Simmy nodded. She was hanging on her cousin's every word, but she could still read the highway signs. The last one had said CONNECTICUT. Simmy didn't dare ask any questions, though. She wanted to be anywhere Jayla was going.

"So today I'm giving you your first taste of how you get it out here," Jayla said. "The way I get it ain't always legit legal but, as you can see, it provides well."

Simmy turned and looked at the side of Jayla's face. "How do you get it?"

"Boosting, baby girl. Boosting."

Simmy laughed out loud like Jayla had said the funniest joke ever. "Please. Stop playing, Jay. I know plenty of boosters in the hood and ain't none of them living like you. You have to be doing something else. It sure ain't just boosting," Simmy said, doubt creasing her face.

"Dead ass. I'm telling you, Simmy. That's what I do. Like everything else, there are levels to this shit. I just happen to be on a level most of them hood boogers can't even begin to imagine being on," Jayla declared.

"How you get on the next level, then?" Simmy asked, her eyebrows raised into arches on her face.

"Let's just say, I had a good teacher. If you want to learn, I can teach you. But I gotta be able to trust you," Jayla said.

"You can trust me," Simmy said, raising her right hand as if she were taking an oath.

"Girl, you can stay fresh and always keep cash in your pockets. Ain't no tricks to this; you just gotta be willing to listen and learn. It's really up to you how far you go can go with it. You can choose to be like me, or you can choose to keep struggling," Jayla said, quickly turning her head to look at Simmy before turning her attention back to the road.

Simmy was staring at her older cousin, contemplating what she'd just said. The way all of those mean girls had stared at her in awe earlier and the way Kyan had practically run her down in the hallways helped to quickly make up Simmy's mind. There was no other choice and nothing much to think about. She wanted to be just like Jayla. She always had.

"I choose to be like you," Simmy said, her voice barely above a whisper. "I want to learn."

"Uh-uh. You can't be sounding all quiet and unsure and shit. You have to convince me you're ready," Jayla scolded her.

"I choose to be like you. I'm ready to stop struggling and make some money," Simmy said much louder this time. "I want you to teach me how."

"Good. So you all in?"

"I'm all in," Simmy said, her heart pounding so hard she wanted to cough.

Jayla smiled. "A'ight, then, baby cousin. Welcome to the life."

Chapter 3

Becoming a Pro

"Put these on and wrap your head with this like I'm about show you," Jayla instructed, passing Simmy a pair of dark oversized oyster-shell Chanel shades, and a silky white scarf with the gold Cs and the iconic Chanel chain strap printed on it.

Simmy slid the shades on, then turned and watched her older cousin carefully so she could learn how to wrap the scarf correctly. When Jayla was done, she looked like Jackie O with the way she had her scarf draped around her head and her round-lens Jackie O–style shades on. Jayla put on a coat of deep red lipstick and dabbed her lips to make it look like she'd been wearing the lipstick all day. Simmy was amused at her cousin's transformation.

"Is this, like, a disguise?" Simmy asked, her eyes still wide with amazement at Jayla's transformation from hood-rich chick to high-society shopper.

"Not a disguise, but a little trick so that we fit in with the other snobs out here. If we walk up in there looking like we just came out the hood, that's exactly how they're going to treat us. We can't have them following us around and playing us close, or else this would be a wasted trip. Feel me?"

Simmy nodded and opened her mouth a little. She felt like a little kid watching her idol get ready for a big performance. In her eyes, Jayla was the smartest person she knew. Simmy decided right then that she wanted to be just as successful as her cousin. She wanted to get her game plan together so she could move out of her grandmother's and live the good life like Jayla.

"First things first: here." Jayla handed Simmy a wad of cash. Simmy took the money, examined it in her hand, and looked back up at Jayla with furrowed brows.

"Put that in your purse until we make it out of there and I'll get it back once we get back to the car. This is just in case—I repeat, just in case—any of those store clerk bitches try to front on you. You can pull this out and make them feel like shit for hawking you. Once they see you really do have money, they'll leave you alone and run away, too scared they might get pulled up for harassing a legit, paying customer. I've had to set more than a few bitches straight in my time doing this," Jayla explained.

Simmy took the thick, rubber-banded roll of cash and stuffed it into her borrowed Chanel bag. She checked the mirror to make sure she'd gotten her look right, just like Jayla had showed her. Simmy smiled. She looked classy, just like her mother used to look whenever they went out to fancy places out on Long Island.

"I'll give you a bag from the trunk. It's already kitted out for what you need to do. Don't move anything inside. I'll show you once what to do, and then you've got to be smart after that. This shit is all about how smart you are and using your natural instincts to your advantage. Trust me, it is not that hard. Just follow my lead and, like I said before, you'll become a pro in no time," Jayla said, grabbing her Louis Vuitton tote from the floor behind Simmy's seat.

"Okay," Simmy said tentatively. She had no idea what Jayla meant by "the bag is kitted out," but Simmy trusted Jayla wholeheartedly.

"These are the things we need to get out of this trip." Jayla dug into her bag and then passed Simmy a folded piece of paper. Simmy unfolded it and read:

Two pairs of men's Balenciaga sneakers any size
Two pairs of any color Giuseppe Zanotti sneakers
Any color Chanel espadrilles
Any handbag worth $1,200 or more.

Simmy's eyes were stretched so wide she was sure she looked like a crazy person. She turned to Jayla with a quizzical look on her face: furrowed brows, mouth hanging open, crinkled nose, head tilted.

"What? You thought we were just coming out here to get gear for ourselves?"

"Ye . . . um, yeah," Simmy answered honestly.

Jayla laughed. "Oh, my God, Simmy. You have so much to learn. No, that's not how it works. The way you make real money is getting shit you can sell in the streets for slightly less than it costs in the stores; that's called fencing your goods. I mean, when we are inside getting the stuff, in the process, if you see something you like and you can get it, fine; but the goal here is to get enough shit to get paid cash. What we look like taking a risk just to look fly walking up and down Brooklyn? I already told you, we leveling up. Top level. The goal is always cold, hard cash in hand."

Simmy blinked a few times like a bright light bulb had gone off in her head.

"Once you sell your goods, then you take that cash and go buy whatever the fuck you want. But always remember I told you this: in this lifestyle, it's mandatory that you spend a little and save a lot, you know, for rainy days," Jayla continued, her tone motherly. "Because in this business sometimes there's going to be rainy fucking days. . . . " Jayla's voice trailed off like she had just remembered something horrible. Simmy was getting ready to ask Jayla what she meant by her last statement, but Jayla shook her head, let out a breath, put her hand up, and smiled at Simmy.

"You're ready. I can see it in your eyes, little cousin. So let's go. We wasting precious time."

What does she mean by rainy days?

Simmy snapped her lips shut and dismissed her thoughts. She didn't know how relevant the question's answer would be and how soon.

Simmy and Jayla had gone into five stores, and Simmy was feeling more confident with each store.

"You're becoming a pro," Jayla had said to her as they exited Nordstrom loaded with items. "Last thing. Shoes. You did real good, little cousin," Jayla told her.

Inside of Neiman Marcus, Jayla continued moving like a consummate professional. She smiled and waved at the sales associates as she glided through the shoe salons like she had been born shopping like this. Simmy followed along, a willing protégé.

"Can I see these both in a size eleven?" Jayla asked, turning to a tall, dark, and handsome men's shoe salon associate who was dressed in a neat, fitted suit. He seemed to be so enthralled with Jayla's round hips and perky tits that he probably would've given her the shoes to leave the store with if she'd asked. He took the men's sneaker display model from her hand, looked at a tag inside, and handed it back to Jayla.

"You're a gem," she said. He blushed.

When he was gone, Jayla placed her kitted-out bag down next to her legs. The man returned with the shoes, smiling like a silly schoolboy with a crush on his teacher.

"Let me see," Jayla squealed acting excited. When the associate put the shoeboxes down in front of her, Jayla ran her fingers over the top of his hand.

"I have never seen a man with such nice hands," she flirted. "I guess working in retail has its advantages." She giggled.

The man stepped back with a smile so wide his mouth resembled a row of piano keys.

Jayla examined the shoes and crinkled her nose. "You know what? Can you get the size twelve? I think I'll need to compare them because these, they kind of look small for my dad." Jayla was sure to put the emphasis on the word "dad."

The sales guy seemed more than overjoyed to keep helping her, especially once he figured she wasn't looking to buy the shoes for her man. The handsome guy disappeared through a doorway at the side of the register and Jayla went to work.

She put the new pair of sneakers in her bag and took an old pair out of the bag and placed the old pair in the box. She took the box that still had the other new pair inside and stacked it neatly on top of the box with the old pair inside. When the sales associate returned, Jayla smile brightly. "You're quick," she said, winking at him. She opened the box with the size twelve sneakers inside. "Hmm, okay. Still not sure." Jayla tapped her nail against her perfectly straight, gleaming white front tooth: the signal. The sales guy seemed mesmerized by her flirty antics.

"Excuse me, sir. Can I see these in a size ten?" Simmy asked from behind him.

The sales associate jumped nervously like he'd been caught peeking at a naked woman through a window. He looked over his shoulder to see if he saw any of his coworkers; then he looked at Simmy. She could see that he was slightly annoyed when he realized he was alone, and would have to leave Jayla to help her.

He let out a long breath. "Um, okay. Just a minute," he replied, talking to Simmy. Then he turned to Jayla. "I have to help this customer. If you need anything else, anything, my name is Kofi. I'll be right back," he said, smiling again.

"You're too sweet, Kofi," Jayla sang. When he was gone, she went about her work on the second pair of shoes. She repeated the same thing: out with the old, in with the new. Simmy was pacing; her nerves were getting the best of her now. She kept looking up at the ceiling. She was sure there were cameras but, for some reason, Jayla didn't seem to care.

"Let's go," Jayla huffed, springing up from the chair, snatching the handles of her kitted-out shopping bag, and speeding toward the door. Simmy was hot on her heels, running behind her like a lap dog.

As they made it to the door, it seemed to Simmy like things were moving in slow motion. Each person they passed caused more hairs to stand up on the back of her neck. Were they all watching her? Did they know what she and Jayla were doing? Was someone going to call security or, worse, the police?

Simmy felt lightheaded, and her entire body was engulfed in heat. Her heart thrummed so hard she could feel the large vein in her neck pressing hard against her skin. Her nerves were so wiry she felt like a scarecrow trying to balance on straw legs. When the thick, humid outside air finally hit her face, Simmy took a deep breath and held it in. They had made it out! She exhaled loudly.

"You a'ight, little cousin?" Jayla chuckled. "You look pasty as hell."

Simmy couldn't even speak. Her nerves were too bad. She thought she'd seen the golden gates of heaven when she spotted Jayla's car within walking distance. Simmy wanted to sprint to the car, but Jayla sauntered like nothing, so she followed her cousin's lead.

Once they got to the car, Simmy rushed inside, rested her head on the passenger side headrest, placed her hand on her heaving chest, and tried to slow her rapid breathing. She wondered if what she was feeling was how people felt when they got high for the first time. It was a rush that she couldn't explain. She could literally feel the adrenaline coursing through her veins.

Jayla slid into the driver's seat and cranked up the car. They were pulling out, seemingly as fast at they'd pulled in.

"Talk to me. How do you feel?" Jayla asked, excitement apparent in her voice.

"Oh, my God. I still can't stop shaking, Jay," Simmy confessed, holding out her trembling hand so Jayla could see what she meant.

Jayla laughed. "That's how it is the first few times, chick. After a while, you'll be a pro at this. You'll be fly as shit and have mad cash in your pockets. You'll be addicted. Just wait."

Chapter 4

Coming of Age

For the next month, Jayla picked Simmy up from school in a different luxury car almost every day. They'd travel to malls in Connecticut and Delaware. Simmy always wondered why they'd always bypass New Jersey when logically it seemed like the easiest out-of-state stop. She never asked because she didn't want to seem nosey, or for Jayla to think that Simmy was questioning her.

"I'm taking you back to my place today," Jayla announced one day, as they pulled out of a mall loaded with the stuff on the day's list and a few extra items for themselves. "You've been doing so good, Simmy. I want you to see where this all can take you. You have to set goals in life, or you'll be stuck doing the same shit forever like everybody in Mummy Pat's house. I want better for you, little cousin. You're smart, beautiful, talented. I really want better for you."

Simmy smiled. She felt proud of herself for how fast she'd learned the ropes under Jayla's tutelage. It had been a long time since anyone had shown enough interest in her to teach her and show her how to help her elevate in life. Her mom and dad used to have chats with her but those days were long gone now.

"Whose idea was the foil-lined bags and shoeboxes?" Simmy asked, seemingly out of the blue.

Jayla glared at her. "Don't get gassed because I gave you a compliment now," Jayla said with an attitude.

"Never ask about the techniques, Simmy. That only means you're overthinking things. When you start overthinking, you start slipping. When you start slipping you fuck things up for all of us. You hear me? Don't overthink shit," Jayla scolded her.

Simmy slid down in her seat and stared out of the passenger side window of Jayla's newest car, a pearly white BMW 535i. She had definitely been enjoying the new clothes, being able to get a new hairdo every week, and all of the attention she was getting at school and especially the attention from Kyan. But, Simmy was still not sure boosting was something she was cut out to do for the long haul like Jayla. She had seen firsthand what could happen to you when you get too caught up and involved in illegal things. Boosting was not something she wanted to do for too long. She wouldn't dare tell Jayla that, though.

"This is it," Jayla sang as she pushed open the door to her Harlem high-rise apartment. "My humble abode."

Simmy's mouth dropped open as she crossed the threshold of Jayla's door. She spun around in wide-eyed amazement. The colors—grays, silvers, deep purples—were so majestic.

"This is gorgeous, Jay," Simmy gasped, overwhelmed by all of the glittery accessories, glass-covered tables, and beautiful, ultra-modern furniture. She rushed over to the wall of windows in front of her, and the view of the city skyline and the Hudson River almost snatched her breath away. Simmy practically pressed her face against the glass.

"This view," she whispered, "is everything."

"Ain't it pretty?" Jayla came up next to her. "Stick with me and you'll be living like this in no time, Simmy."

Simmy could only dream of having her own place like that someday. It was definitely a far cry from her cramped little room in Brooklyn. Simmy wondered how much boosting Jayla had to do to afford an apartment like that. Her adoration for Jayla had just grown bigger.

Jayla gave Simmy the tour of her apartment. Jayla's master bedroom had to be Simmy's favorite room. Jayla's silver suede tufted wall-to-ceiling headboard was enough to make Simmy want to never leave the room.

"These glass-covered dressers are so pretty, Jay. And, these silver beaded crown-shaped pillows are perfect for you. This room looks like it's for a queen, for real."

"Yeah, I may have overdone it with the sparkles. But, I love everything sparkly. That's why you see all the sequined pillows and shiny glass everything. I think after all I've been through in life, I deserve to shine, literally," Jayla said, laughing afterward. "C'mon. Let's go count up our takes for today so we will know what we getting paid."

As Simmy followed Jayla back into her living room, Simmy's cell phone rang. She went to answer it, but Jayla grabbed her hand.

"Nah. When we are on a paper chase, social shit comes second. Right now, we conducting business. That little boy can wait," Jayla said firmly. Simmy's heart sank and her mouth sagged at the edges. She never ignored Kyan's calls. Shoot, she was happy that he was calling her every day, three and four times a day. Street dudes never did that and Simmy knew it. Kyan genuinely seemed interested in getting to know her. He'd ask her about what her likes and dislikes were, and he actually took the time to listen to what she had to say. She really liked him, and she didn't want him to think that she was blowing him off by not answering his call.

"If there's one thing I teach you in life, it's never to put no nigga before yourself, your business and, most importantly, your family," Jayla said, her tone serious. "Those niggas will never do the same for you. You hear me?"

"I hear you," Simmy acquiesced, although she really wasn't happy about not taking the call. She hit IGNORE on Kyan's second and third calls. Finally, as Jayla laid out all of the things they had boosted that day, Simmy just turned her phone off. *Family and money over everything,* she told herself.

Simmy walked into Mummy Pat's kitchen the next day and proudly dropped on the table the six bags of groceries she'd purchased. Mummy Pat was at the stove, as usual, and she turned around with a warm smile.

"What is that, Simone?" Mummy Pat asked, still smiling.

"I got you some stuff from the store. Your favorite chamomile tea, a few cans of corn beef for the days you don't want to really cook, a big bag of rice, some . . ." Simmy rattled off as she pulled items from the bags.

"Where you getting money from now, all of a sudden?" Sheryl walked into the kitchen, her voice filled with suspicion.

Simmy rolled her eyes. "I've been working," she answered dryly.

"Oh, yeah? Since when?"

"I go to Harlem every day and help Jayla out at her job," Simmy lied with ease, repeating the story Jayla had given her just in case this day ever came. *"Always have your story ready, Simmy. Never get caught slipping without that backup plan,"* Jayla had preached.

"What kind of money you making helping out at an office that you can afford five thousand dollar handbags and eight hundred dollar shoes and sneakers and clothes for all the kids in here?" Sheryl pressed, looking Simmy up and down and pointing to the bags Simmy had left by the kitchen entrance.

Simmy shifted her weight from one foot to the other and bit down on her bottom lip. She didn't answer the question.

"And, Jayla ain't fooling anyone, either. She only thinks she's smarter than the rest of us. I know she don't work in anybody's office. Whatever she's into, and whatever she's dragged you into, it definitely involves fast money. And, we all know where fast money gets you, don't we?" Sheryl continued.

Simmy could feel heat rising from her feet and climbing up to her face. The vein at her temple throbbed. She went to open her mouth to defend Jayla and herself with more lies, but Mummy Pat stepped between her and Sheryl and got in Sheryl's face.

"Would you please, Sheryl? First you say you want people to pull them weight around here. The girl is trying and helping out; now you complain. I don't understand what will make you happy," Mummy Pat said defensively.

Sheryl scoffed. "I'm just trying to make sure she doesn't end up like her mother and father, Mummy. The only jobs I know you can perform to afford these rich people things is all illegal jobs. Remember, Mummy, I was the one who first told you Chris was selling drugs back before he became some big kingpin. You turned a blind eye, and now—"

Mummy Pat threw her hand up, halting Sheryl's words. "Don't you dare mention my son in a bad light in front of his only child. Don't you dare. Leave this girl alone and let her work and finish school in peace. She's coming of age, and nicely, given the circumstances she was left to deal with. She's a good girl. She's not out there in the streets cutting school, or hanging around different boys, acting fast like some girls you see out on the road. She didn't have to bring this food here. She could've kept her money and spend it all on nonsense like you do. Leave her be." Mummy Pat gritted her teeth, her Jamaican

Patois coming on real heavy like it always did when she was mad.

Sheryl threw her hands up. Hurt passed over her facial expression like a dark cloud over a sunny field. "Suit yourself, Mummy. But, when it comes out, don't you dare say I didn't tell you so." She turned her sights to Simmy and spoke directly to her. "I'm just trying to look out for you, Simone. I'd rather you not contribute a thing around here, than for you to be caught up in something illegal to do it. Jayla is not who you think she is; you'll learn that in time. Right now, you're being manipulated, but you'll see soon," Sheryl said with feeling.

Simmy sucked her teeth and bit down on her bottom lip until it was painful. It was all she could do to keep herself from saying something disrespectful to her aunt.

"No matter what you think of me, I do have your best interest in mind. I don't want to see you waste your young life away for a little bit of fast money. Trust me, you'll regret it in the end." With that, Sheryl stormed out of the kitchen.

Simmy collapsed into one of the rickety dinette chairs, her legs suddenly weak. She stared at all of the groceries spread on the table. All she wanted to do was help out. She had no idea buying groceries would be such a big deal. She just wanted to help.

"Thank you for the food, baby," Mummy Pat said, touching Simmy's shoulder gently.

Simmy parted a halfhearted smile and placed her hand on top of her grandmother's. "No problem. No problem at all."

It was still worth it. I made Mummy Pat happy and it was worth it, she told herself. It was what she needed to get her aunt's foreboding words—*"Jayla is not who you think she is; you'll learn that in time. Right now, you're being manipulated, but you'll see soon. You'll regret it in the end"*—to stop playing over and over in her mind.

Chapter 5

Nothing to Lose

"What?" Simmy asked, breaking eye contact, her cheeks suddenly on fire.

"What? What?" Kyan replied, chuckling.

"You're staring at me. So I'm asking, like, what? Is there something wrong? Do I have a booger in my nose?" Simmy answered sassily, shifting in her seat.

"Nah. I just like staring at that pretty face," he said, reaching across the table and putting his hand on top of hers.

Simmy felt those electric currents shoot up her arm again, but this time she also felt a little something happening between her legs. She had been having long phone conversations with Kyan for over a month now, but they hadn't been able to meet up, and they would only see one another briefly at school each day. After school had become out of the question, since Jayla was picking Simmy up almost every single day to go on their shopping trips. Simmy had finally managed to break away from Jayla for a little bit, and she had met up with Kyan at Sugarcane on Flatbush Avenue.

They sat across from one another at a small table in the back of the restaurant with sexual tension swirling around them like bees over a pot of sweet honey.

"How many other pretty faces have you looked at this week, though?" Simmy came back at him.

He moved his hand and leaned back in his chair. He swiped his hands over his face and exhaled. "C'mon, Simone. You're too pretty and got too much going for yourself. Don't be one of those girls," Kyan responded.

"One of those girls?"

"Yeah, like them insecure chicks who are always accusing a nigga of something they ain't doing," Kyan said, a slight hint of annoyance in his tone.

Simmy lowered her eyes to her coconut shrimp appetizer. "I'm sorry. You're right."

"It's all good. Now, back to you and me. So what was all that mouth you had on the phone about?" Kyan said, flashing his pearly whites and melting Simmy's heart at the same time.

Simmy balled her toes up in her Gucci booties. Her stomach felt like it was doing flips. They'd had a conversation about sex and Simmy had lied through her teeth about what she could do when, in reality, she had never done it.

"I was just talking. I'm—" Simmy started, her words cut short by a girl storming toward them. Simmy's eyebrows dipped as she took in the evil scowl on the girl's face.

"So this is what it is, Kyan?" the girl barked before she could even make it all the way to the table. Kyan's eyes almost popped out of his head, and he shot up from his chair like it suddenly had a spring on it.

"You out here with another bitch when I'm at home waiting for you?" the girl boomed. She was making a scene.

Simmy also stood up. She wasn't trying to be sitting if this clearly angry girl tried to swing on her.

"Who is this, Kyan?" The girl pointed at Simmy and spoke about her like she was an irrelevant, inanimate object. "Who the fuck is this?"

"Yo, Ava. Why you playing right now? For real, you know what it is. I been told you it's over." Kyan gritted his teeth, his face taking on a dark look that Simmy had never seen before.

Simmy's eyebrows shot up into arches. She couldn't believe how much Ava had changed. Her face had dark pockmarks all over it, her hair was thrown back into a ratty ponytail, and she was dressed in a pair of loose-fitting gray sweats and a wrinkled T-shirt like she'd just rolled out of bed. Surely, she was not the gorgeous Nia Long mini me Simmy had seen in the past.

"No. No. What you told me was that you wanted a break and that we would see what it was after the break," Ava spat, her bottom lip trembling. "I haven't been eating or sleeping or nothing because I've been hearing so many rumors about you being with other chicks. I've been in the house waiting for you to tell me we are back together. I can't even function without you, Kyan. Why are you doing this to me?" Ava burst into sobs.

Kyan sighed and shook his head. "Yo. This is not the time or the place."

Simmy had seen enough. She grabbed her Louis Vuitton cherries monogram bag from the back of the chair, dug inside, and tossed three twenty dollar bills onto the table. "Fuck this," she grumbled.

"Simone! Wait!" Kyan grabbed her arm. "It's not like that. Just let me explain."

Simmy wrestled her arm away from his grasp and squinted her eyes into dashes. "You're just like all of the guys out there. Y'all just lie and cheat your way through everything. You ain't nothing but a fucking liar," she said through gritted teeth. She stormed away and couldn't help the tears that involuntarily spilled from her eyes once she was out of his sight.

She took her phone out of her purse and called the only person she felt she could talk to at this time.

"Hey, Jayla," Simmy said as she sniffled and wiped at her tears.

"Hey, cuz! What's up?"

"Can you come get me? I'm walking down Flatbush right now." Simmy wasted no time and got straight to the point.

"Sure thing. I'm on my way." Jayla could tell that her cousin was upset. Instead of asking twenty-one questions, she decided to pick her up as soon as possible and take things on from there.

Jayla took a long pull off of her neatly rolled blunt and blew the thick gray smoke cloud out in Simmy's direction.

"Simmy, I told you already, niggas ain't shit but hoes and tricks. You wanted to believe this one was different and that's okay. I was innocent and naïve like you when I was younger. We all learn the hard way. But you see me? I'm good all by myself. You not gonna see me crying over no man. I don't have faith in none of 'em," Jayla said, extending the blunt to Simmy.

Simmy shook her head no. Jayla reacted like Simmy had spit on her.

"Oh, you too good to smoke a little weed?" Jayla shot.

"No, it's . . . it's just not my thing," Simmy said, taken aback by Jayla's sudden mood swing.

"Well, make it your thing," Jayla said, pushing the blunt farther into Simmy's face. "You sitting up here in my house all messed up and crying about your dude. I'm only trying to ease that little mind of yours. Shit, at this point you ain't got nothing to lose."

Simmy fell in line under Jayla's pressure, as usual. She took a toke off the blunt and immediately started coughing. Jayla snatched the blunt from Simmy's hand before she could drop it. Simmy raised her hands to her throat, bent at the waist until her head was almost between her knees, and hacked and hacked. Jayla was laughing like she was in the front row at a comedy show.

"Same thing happened to me when I got my weed-cherry popped," Jayla said, still laughing. "You'll get used to it. Stick with me and, just like everything, you'll be good at all of this shit."

Simmy finally forced air back into her lungs and caught her breath. Her head felt swimmy, and she couldn't remember what she'd been crying about. She closed her eyes and relaxed against the plush suede of Jayla's couch. A lazy grin spread over her lips. She wanted to say something, but she literally couldn't find the words. Jayla had been right again. The weed had helped her forget all about Ava, Kyan, and her hurt feelings, at least for the moment.

The next day, Jayla was up bright and early as usual. Simmy still couldn't figure out how her cousin could smoke, drink, and party all night and still be up all bright-eyed and bushy-tailed the next day.

"Rise and grind," Jayla sang, snatching open the curtains in her guest bedroom so that the sun beamed right in Simmy's face.

Simmy groaned, but she knew there was no use in fighting it. Jayla wouldn't give up.

"We're making our way upstate today," Jayla announced. "This will be one of the best licks yet."

Simmy pulled the covers back over her head. She was starting to think she'd rather have a full-time job than constantly be in stores stealing. This boosting shit was a lot of work.

***

"Two stacks for three hours of work," Jayla said, handing Simmy twenty one-hundred dollar bills. "Now, you tell me you would rather work for somebody doing a fucking nine-to-five? Shit, not me. Ain't no way a little high school girl like you would be seeing this kind of paper working no regular job right now. There are grown-ass people who don't see this cake for three measly hours of work."

"Thanks, Jay. I really always appreciate it," Simmy said, knowing that Jayla got off on feeling like she had saved her.

Simmy stuffed the cash into her Gucci cross-body bag. The cash didn't have the same effect on her that it used to when she'd started boosting and making money a few months earlier. And, Jayla's constant lessons and pressure were getting to be a little overbearing. Simmy wanted to get back to some semblance of her normal life: reading books, writing poetry, and her schoolwork. She wanted to take some time and think about what moves she wanted to make for herself. She'd been so caught up working with Jayla that she felt like she was losing a lot of herself in it. She felt like she needed a break from working for a little bit. She just had to figure out how to tell Jayla without her getting upset about it.

"I'm heading home," Simmy announced.

Jayla moved her head back like Simmy had just splashed cold water in her face. "Oh, okay. I thought you were going to stay for the weekend. You don't like being here with me?" Jayla said, her jaw going square. Simmy could tell she was offended.

"I do. I do. But I miss Mummy Pat," Simmy replied, cleaning it up real quick. "I want some home-cooked food. Plus, I have a ton of school stuff to do and my library card and my computer are there. Girl, you know I'd much rather be here." She giggled, trying to lighten the mood that, for some reason, had taken a dark turn.

Jayla wasn't smiling or laughing. "A'ight, then go. I'll call you when it's time to go back to work," Jayla said dryly, turning her back on Simmy.

Simmy's stomach clenched. She hated when Jayla was mad at her. She contemplated staying so Jayla wouldn't be upset with her, but she decided she was going to do what she wanted for a change. She loved Jayla and would never want to get her upset, but she couldn't keep doing what Jayla wanted all the time. It was the first small stand she'd taken toward thinking and doing for herself.

"Simone. I'm so glad to see you," Mummy Pat sang after Simmy came up and kissed her on the cheek. "C'mere and taste my stew chicken gravy. Tell me if it is missing something," Mummy Pat said, lifting her metal spoon out of the pot and pushing it out toward Simmy.

Simmy inhaled the rich aroma of the chicken gravy and slurped it up from the spoon. "Mmm. Perfect. I need a plate of that like right now," she said, licking her lips.

Her grandmother laughed. "Same way your father used to tell me he liked my food, by eating it up. I'm glad you're home."

"Me too." Simmy smiled and got a plate.

Simmy ate her belly full and went to her room. As soon as she walked in, she felt claustrophobic. Her mood took an instant dive. The small, cramped space, with the tiny twin bed in the center and the cracked mirror hanging on the wall with chipped paint, was a far cry from Jayla's beautifully painted, expensively furnished, spacious apartment. Simmy rushed over and picked up the picture of her parents. Tears sprang to her eyes, and she flopped down on her bed.

"I miss you, Mommy," Simmy whispered. "I am lost out here without you to tell me things about guys and about life and stuff. I like a boy, but I'm not sure he's a good guy.

He got a lot going on. Jayla is bossy, but I love her. I don't know what to do. I'm doing all right out there working with Jalya and making money, but not the right way. I just feel . . ." Simmy's lips trembled as she whispered to the picture as if her mother could somehow hear her cries.

"Simone?"

Simmy jumped and quickly put her picture under her pillow. She swiped away the tears from her cheeks and backhanded the snot threatening to leak from her nose. She cleared her throat. "Yeah, come in."

Jalissa, her uncle Marcus's stepdaughter, walked into Simmy's room. Simmy moved to the edge of her bed, immediately guarded. Jalissa was five months older than her and had never tried to bond with Simmy before. In fact, in the streets and in school, when Jalissa was with her friends, she would act like she and Simmy didn't even live in the same house. Jalissa had dark skin and coarse hair, which Simmy always thought was beautiful, but Jalissa always had an attitude and would take jabs at Simmy any chance she got. She often gave Simmy a hard time for having lighter skin and long hair. Simmy couldn't tell if Jalissa was jealous, hating on her, or she was just a mean person in general. Simmy couldn't say that Jalissa was one of her favorite people in the house.

"Hey, girl," Jalissa sang, a fake smile curving her lips.

"What's up?" Simmy replied dryly, one of her eyebrows raised.

"How you doing? I missed you around here," Jalissa said.

Simmy breathed out heavily. "You surely didn't come up here to tell me you miss me, Jalissa. I know better. What do you want?"

"I had . . . um, wanted to . . . I, um, need a favor," Jalissa stumbled over her words.

Simmy tilted her head. "Yeah?"

Jalissa made a goofy face. "My friend Tora is having a party and I can't find nothing to wear, girl. I was wondering if I could borrow—"

Simmy threw her hands up. "I don't loan out my clothes, Jalissa. Definitely not. No need to go any further. The answer is no," Simmy said plainly, cutting her off before she could finish.

Jalissa's facial expression flattened. "Okay, well, can you hook me up with your plug then? Maybe I can get some money from my mother and buy stuff."

"My plug?" Simmy froze. "What are you talking about?"

"Everybody knows you got a plug hooking you up with clothes, shoes, and bags. People been seeing you hop in and out of big-time cars after school. People talking, Simone. You ain't just start wearing Gucci and Chanel overnight like that if you don't have a hookup," Jalissa said, her hands on her hips.

Simmy's heart started beating fast. "I don't care what they're saying. I ain't got no plug, and it's nobody's business what cars I get in and out of. I work and I buy my own stuff. Case in point, why I don't loan my stuff out."

Jalissa folded her arms across her chest. "Oh, okay, it's like that. I see you been buying everybody else in here sneakers, jeans, watches, colognes, but never once did you come to my brother or me and offer anything. Why is that? Because your uncle ain't our blood father? Or because you're jealous we still have our mother and she ain't locked up like yours?"

Simmy felt the gut punch of Jalissa's last statement, but she remained cool. She chuckled, although the chuckle contradicted her raging insides.

"No. I don't give y'all anything because when I ain't have nothing, you would walk around with your fancy clothes shitting on me when you was with your little East

New York crew. Did you ever once say, 'Here, Simone, here's a dollar or a pair of jeans'? Anything? You knew I was getting teased at school and all of that. You were down with some of the chicks teasing me, too. I don't forget shit, Jalissa. Now, if you don't mind, I want to lie down. I have a headache." Simmy pointed to her door.

"A'ight. I hear you," Jalissa said, rolling her head. "I hear you loud and clear. You think you all that and your shit don't stink just because you cleaned up and finally learned how to dress and look decent. Just remember, what goes up must come back down."

"Okay, good. Since you heard me, then you heard the part where I said I have a headache and want to lie down. Get out of my room." Simmy pointed to her door again.

Jalissa turned on her heels so hard she almost stumbled over. She stomped out of Simmy's room and slammed the door.

"Some damn nerve," Simmy grumbled. She got up from her bed, grabbed her book from the floor, and took her seat on the long platform in front of her windowsill. Escaping into a book was probably the only thing that could calm her down.

"Finally," she murmured, turning to the dog-eared page in her book.

Simmy fell asleep reading. She was snatched out of her sleep by her name being called out from downstairs.

"Coming," she mumbled, her voice gruff with sleep. She wiped sleep from her eyes and headed toward Mummy Pat's voice.

When Simmy got to the middle of the steps, she paused. Her heartbeat sped up, and her hands curled into fists at her side.

No, he didn't. What is he doing here? This dude is bold. Oh, my God! Simmy shook her head in disbelief. Her face immediately flushed. She folded her arms over her chest, embarrassed that she had on a pair of ratty sweatpants, a T-shirt, and old sneakers. Her hair wasn't exactly perfect, either, since she had just gotten up from a nap.

"Simone, this nice boy ring the bell for you. He bring flowers and all," Mummy Pat said, looking up the stairs at Simmy; then she turned and smiled at Kyan.

Kyan bowed and extended the huge bouquet of roses in front of him. Simmy rolled her eyes and continued to shake her head side to side, but inside she jumped for joy. Kyan smiled coyly. Simmy felt something melt in her core. He was so damn cute!

"Come down here, girl. You nah have nothing to lose with this one here," Mummy Pat said, her accent shining through her words in her excitement.

Simmy squinted and pursed her lips at Kyan. He kept smiling as if to say, "I got you now."

"Boys these days don't come to the house with flowers and ask for permission to date girls like this nice one here did. No more of that. They did that back in my day, but not these days. Ya lucky, Simone. Stop making the young man wait. Come down nuh," Mummy Pat said, waving for Simmy to come all the way down the steps. She patted Kyan on the arm. "What a nice one you are. I'll let you kids talk. I'm going to take these beautiful flowers into the kitchen and put them in fresh water."

"Okay," Simmy said, still giving Kyan the stank eye.

When Mummy Pat disappeared back down the hallway into the kitchen, Simmy stepped close to Kyan. "Why did you come to my house?" she whispered harshly.

"I wanted to apologize about the other day. I tried calling you and left a few messages."

"I know." Simmy rolled her eyes a bit. "I mean, what is there to say? You lied to me and that's that."

"No, but it's not like that at all," Kyan tried to reason with her. "It's not what you think. At least hear me out so I can tell you the whole story, the truth." Kyan looked at Simmy with hope in his eyes.

"Really? Who said I cared enough to want to know the truth. Looks like you had unfinished business with her that had nothing to do with me. That's all I needed to know. At the end of the day, you're not my man and I'm not your girl, so you really don't need to explain anything." Simmy played tough.

"No one said you cared enough to know. I just hope you care enough to hear me out," Kyan replied. "Can we go somewhere and talk, just you and me? Please?" He turned down the edges of his mouth like a sad puppy dog.

Simmy sighed. "I don't know about that, Kyan. Seems like you got a lot of baggage that you haven't unpacked."

"Please," he pleaded, putting his hands together. "C'mon. You going to make me keep on begging?"

Simmy folded her arms across her chest. "I mean, what is there to say? I saw it with my own eyes."

"A lot. I have so much to say, you have no idea. Man, I can't think straight. I ain't made a dollar since that thing happened. I just need you to hear me out," he begged some more.

Simmy rolled her eyes and stuck out her left hip. It didn't seem like Kyan was going to give up anytime soon. She really didn't want to go anywhere with him, though. She glanced over at Kyan, who just stood there looking like one sad case. "I have to change and grab a jacket."

Kyan grabbed her arm. "No. What you have on is fine. You look beautiful to me. And, here, you can wear mine," he said, shrugging out of his jacket and holding it out to her. "You might go up there and not come back."

How did he know that was my plan? Simmy snatched his jacket and put it over her shoulders.

"Mummy, I'm going out with Kyan. I'll be back later," she yelled out to her grandmother. "Can you please lock my bedroom door?"

"Yes, baby. Go on now. Have fun," Simmy heard as she headed out.

"So where are you taking me?" she asked Kyan as they made their way toward his car. Kyan drove a pearl white Honda Civic with charcoal black rims and a black interior to go with it. One thing she appreciated about him was that he wasn't into flashy cars and jewelry. You could tell he had money because he was always decked out in new clothes, hats, and sneakers, but he wasn't the type who went overboard with big gold chains, bracelets, rings, and other flashy things. And even with his new clothes and gear, he was still humble.

Simmy slid on to the seat and immediately was intoxicated with the aroma. His car smelled like fresh Burberry cologne. The car was so clean, it was hard to believe he drove around in it every day.

"You like the way it smells?" Kyan asked as a sly grin crept across his face. Simmy immediately felt herself start blushing. She didn't realize she'd breathed in so hard. She felt dumb for making it so obvious, but she wasn't about to let him see that.

"Yeah, it smells all right." She tried to play it off. "So you're not going to answer my question?"

"What question?

"I asked where you are taking me."

"Oh, that question." Kyan tried to act like he didn't have a clue.

"Yes, that question! Boy, you better stop playing games before I get out this car and go back inside my house." Simmy folded her arms and pouted.

"Oh, so you're making threats now?" Kyan chuckled. Simmy looked over at him, rolled her eyes, and reached for the door handle. "Okay, okay, I'm just playing around with you, lady. Calm down." Kyan reached for her arm and grabbed her hand. "I'm bringing you to my place," he finally admitted as he began to drive.

"So you dragged me out of my house, in my house clothes, just to bring me to your house?" Simmy grumbled, folding her arms across her chest in defiance.

"I wanted us to have a quiet place to talk. That's all. Nothing more," Kyan assured her. "I'll make it worth your while." Kyan winked.

The way he winked at her made Simmy feel all warm and tingly inside. As much as she wanted to stay mad at him, she still liked him a lot. They rode the rest of the way listening to Hot 97 on the radio.

"Welcome to *mi casa*," Kyan announced as he pushed into his apartment.

Simmy walked in slowly, still trying to hold on to her attitude. She couldn't let it go too easily or else he'd think he had her. Once she stepped inside, she didn't want to give him any compliments but, secretly, she admired how neat and well furnished his place was. Simmy looked around at the shiny, blond-wood floors, the gorgeous African artwork on the walls, and the huge flat-screen television. Kyan had good taste for a young dude. But, it was the entire wall of books that had made Simmy's heart pump harder. She hadn't taken Kyan for the reading type, but only a real avid reader would have an entire bookshelf built into one wall of his home like that. It became harder and harder for her to hold on to her attitude with him.

"Make yourself at home," Kyan invited, opening his hand toward the brown leather sectional.

Simmy took a seat at the edge of the couch. She didn't want him to think she was going to get comfortable, although she was already comfortable. It was strange to her that she felt so at ease with Kyan.

"Can I get you anything to drink?"

"Water," Simmy replied. She had to make sure that sleep breath was gone before she tried to speak to him in close quarters. "Thank you."

He disappeared behind the wall that separated his kitchen from his living room. Simmy dug in the corners of her eyes and swiped her hand over her face to make sure she was all good. She was mad she had let him convince her to leave home before she had the chance to clean herself up a little bit.

Kyan handed her a tall glass filled with ice and water. She nodded. He sat down next to her and took off his New York Yankees fitted. He scratched his head and let out a breath.

"That don't sound good," Simmy said, sipping.

"I'ma get right to it, Simone. I don't want to play no more games," he said, his tone serious.

Simmy raised her eyebrows and swallowed hard.

"So, from middle school, I was always feeling you. But, back then you were the flyest girl in school and I was like a nobody. You were definitely out of my league. I used to watch you, and I swore you never wore the same outfit twice. Jewels, furs, the newest kicks as soon as or before they hit the stores. All of that. I was always watching and telling myself I had to step my game up if I wanted to bag you. I knew who your father was and even when people said he had got bagged, he was still a legend in the streets, so I knew what kind of expectations you probably had.

"Then, when we got to ninth grade, you still seemed to be so strong. Everybody knew your mom and pops were both locked down by then but you still walked with your head held high, holding your own, and that made me like you even more. See, for me, as a little nigga out there, I ain't ever have those kind of resources you had growing up. I ain't have no pops lavishing me with shit. I never had nobody coming through with stacks of money to keep me up. What I liked about you the most, though, was that you were the prettiest, best dressed, smartest girl in school but you never acted like you were better than anyone. Facts."

Simmy blushed. Thoughts of her parents and the good old days flashed through her mind. Kyan was right. Her mother and father got locked up when she was fourteen and, up until then, things had always been good for her. Even for the first year or so after her parents were arrested, her father's associates, whom she called uncles, came around and kept her dipped in the best clothes. It didn't last, though. Once her father received that life sentence and her so-called adopted uncles knew he wasn't coming back, the money and the clothes stopped.

She took a big gulp of her water. It was all she could do to stay focused on what Kyan was saying.

"You was one of the reasons I started hustling," Kyan said.

Simmy twisted her lips and sucked her teeth. "So, wait. You blaming me for your not-so-legal activities?"

"Nah, not like that. I just mean you was my motivation for wanting better, for doing better. You and watching my moms struggle, working three jobs just to keep a roof over me and my brothers' heads," Kyan said honestly. "I wanted better for her and my brothers so I started hustling so I could help provide for them. I done good for myself. I'm eighteen, and I helped my mom buy her house, bought her a new car, got my own place, and I give my brothers whatever they need. Everybody thinks I've got it all but the truth is there is one piece missing for me, and that's you. I've always liked you, Simone. To me, you're the most beautiful girl out here, and you're the only girl I want to be with. Real talk." He raised his right hand for emphasis.

"What about Av—"

Kyan put his finger to her lips before she could get the name all the way out. "Shh."

Simmy moved her face away from his finger and closed her eyes. She felt a pang of hurt flit through her chest. She wasn't over what had happened.

"We not saying that name. I promise never to say it in your presence if you promise the same," Kyan said softly.

Simmy nodded and sighed. "That's easy for you to say. I don't know what the story is between you and her, but the way she rolled up on you was crazy. I mean, why would she flip out on you like that if you had already told her it was over between you two? And you brought me here because you said you wanted to explain yourself. Now you trying to brush it off, telling me we won't ever speak her name again. Smells like bullshit to me."

"No, it's not even like that. I promise you I won't ever try to bullshit you about anything," Kyan said as he clasped both hands together. "Truth is I used to date her."

"No shit, Sherlock. Everybody knows that already," Simmy snapped, getting frustrated.

"Okay, but not everyone knows I stopped liking her pretty quick. The more I got to know her, the more I started seeing her through different eyes real quick. She was all beauty, no substance. Cute face. Empty head. It was all about material things with her," Kyan said. "I couldn't have a conversation with her unless it was about the latest clothes, shoes, bags. It started to get on my nerves. There's so much more to life than the material stuff. That's why you don't see me walking around rocking the most expensive stuff. I like my Nikes and a few Jordans here and there, but I don't feel the need to have to go and buy Yeezy's, Gucci belts, and all that extra shit. Most people I know be wasting their money and investing in the wrong shit."

Simmy shifted uncomfortably on the couch. For the past three months, all she'd thought about was material things, how many high-end outfits she could rack up to impress people at school. She felt stupid now.

"So, I had to dead her. I told her I was out. That she wasn't right for me. She ain't want to accept it, but I was very clear about it. Right hand to God," he said, raising his right hand.

Simmy hung on his every word. She didn't know he was so smart and so deep. She'd been shallow to think that being shallow was what he wanted.

"But you, Simone, you are different. I used to see you at lunch with your head always buried in a book. I see you go to class every day when all the other girls spend their time in the bathroom combing weaves and fixing them fake-ass eyelashes and freak 'em dresses they wear. I've always known you are a woman of substance, Simone. I see the ambition in your walk, in your eyes. You're destined for more. You deserve more."

"But you don't really know me," Simmy said, her tone low and soft. "I'm not the same person I was a few years ago. After my parents went away, things became worse and worse for me. Every day was a new struggle, and it still is now." She wanted so badly to really open up to him and tell him about how she felt about things. How much she missed her parents, how much she hated being in that cramped-up house. She wanted to tell Kyan that she had become just like Ava, thinking about clothes and money all of the time. She wanted to vent and talk about how she felt she was losing her drive and desire to do good in school and get a career for herself. She wanted him to know that she had resorted to the easy money life. And, that she was doing all the wrong things just to impress people.

"You ain't telling me nothing I don't know," Kyan interrupted her thoughts. "The struggle is real out there. You think I want to be out in the streets passing poison to my own people? Nah, but the way shit is set up in the world, if you grew up in it, you stuck in it." Kyan kicked more facts. "For real, I'm hustling now, but I got an end goal. All I want is to make enough to invest in a legit business, take my moms out of the hood, and have a woman like you, a smart one with her own goals, by my side."

"But you barely even know me, Kyan. You know my history and what you've seen of me. I'm really not as good as you're making me seem right now." Simmy lowered her head. She didn't want him to see the tears welling up in her eyes right now.

"I know you're smart, funny, and beautiful," Kyan complimented her. " I know you have a mind of your own and you think for yourself. And I know that you and I are meant to be. I've know this since we were in junior high. I've always had feelings for you, Simone." He reached out and gently put both her hands in his. "Simmy, look at me."

Simmy finally looked him deep in his eyes. She felt something inside of her pop loose; her inhibitions floated away like a helium balloon cut from its string. She inched over and grabbed his face and crushed her mouth on top of his. Their tongues intertwined, performing a soft, sensual dance. Kyan moved in closer until he forced Simmy down gently onto her back. She held on to him tight, feeling things happening to her body that she'd never experienced before. Simmy's head spun, and her ears felt clogged. Kyan kissed her deeply, but his hands roamed her body in places no one had ever gone. Simmy didn't fight it. She wanted it.

Kyan moved his mouth from hers and pulled up a little so that he was hovering over her. He looked down into her eyes. "You sure you're ready for this? We don't have to."

Simmy reached up and pulled his face back down to hers. She opened her mouth and accepted his tongue inside. Without another word, she'd given him her answer.

Kyan ran his hands under her shirt and began rubbing her breasts over her bra. Simmy loved the sensation and couldn't help but let out a soft moan. She tugged at his shirt and motioned for him to take it off. He stood up and took his shirt and pants off. Simmy was amazed at how lean and toned he was. He looked like an underwear model, the way he was standing there in just his boxer briefs.

"Your turn," he said as he sat next to her.

Simmy was hesitant about taking her clothes off in front of him. She had never been naked in front of anyone. Kyan noticed her discomfort and decided to help put her more at ease. He pulled her in for another kiss. As they kissed, he guided her arms and pulled the shirt over her head. He reached toward her back and unstrapped her bra while he laid gentle kisses on her neck and shoulders.

Simmy's heart began to race as she felt the bra become loose and her perfectly round breasts were exposed. Kyan slowly laid her on her back again. He grabbed her left breast and gently began to suck on her nipple while his remaining hand slid down her smooth stomach and undid the string on her pants.

Simmy was mesmerized by the sensation. She rested her head and closed her eyes. His hand made his way down, and he slid it in between her legs. He could feel the heat coming from the lady part. He pushed her panties to the side and slid two fingers inside of her. Simmy gasped. She could feel her juices flowing as his fingers came in and out of her.

"Take my pants off," she instructed him barely above a whisper. Simmy no longer felt timid about what he was doing. She wanted to feel him inside of her. If his fingers felt this good, she couldn't wait to see what his dick would feel like. Kyan wasted no time taking her pants and underwear off. As soon as he did that, he took his underwear off too. Simmy saw his member standing at full attention. She sat up, reached out, and put it in her hand. It felt soft and smooth as she ran her hand up and down his shaft. She looked up at Kyan, and their eyes met once again. Without hesitating, Simmy brought her mouth to the tip of his dick and began to suck on it. She ran her tongue up and down as his dick came in and out of her mouth.

Her pussy was throbbing at this point. Simmy lay back down on the couch and spread her legs for Kyan. Kyan leaned over and placed himself in between her legs. Simmy felt his dick begin to enter her tight, wet pussy. The feeling took her breath away. Kyan immediately realized she was a virgin. He took his time making love to her. He wanted to make sure this was an experience she would never forget.

Chapter 6

Things Fall Apart

Simmy felt like she was bouncing on a cloud when she got back home. She rushed into the kitchen and found Mummy Pat at the table going over her lottery tickets. Simmy laughed. "I hope you hit it soon." She kissed her grandmother on the cheek and walked right back out.

Simmy went to her room and realized it was unlocked. *Mummy must have forgotten to lock it.* She flicked on her light and right away she could tell someone had been in there. Simmy rushed over to a group of bags that she had set neatly in the corner of her room and began dumping everything out. Working with Jayla, Simmy had become a pro at taking inventory of things she had. She had also become more observant of her surroundings. She had gotten used to taking note of where things were and leaving them exactly as she'd found them; the slightest deviation caught her attention. Instinct was what Jayla called it.

"For real? I know this chick gotta be out of her mind. Didn't I tell her ass no when she asked me?" Simmy grumbled as she pulled things from the bags. She knew right away who the culprit was. "And she took the best stuff I had at that?"

Simmy's nostrils flared, and her face grew hot. She stormed out of her room, down the stairs, past the kitchen, to the door that led to the basement where her uncle Marcus, his wife Serita, and their kids, including his stepdaughter Jalissa, stayed.

"Jalissa!" Simmy boomed before she even made it all the way down the narrow staircase that led into the basement. "Jalissa!"

Serita rounded the corner from the tiny bedroom she shared with Marcus. "Simone? Why the heck are you yelling like that?" Serita asked, her face crumpled in confusion. "We are in bed."

"Where is she? Where's your daughter?" Simmy barked, the vein in her neck pulsing so fiercely she was sure it could be seen from a distance.

"You better calm down, little girl," Serita shot back. "What the hell is your problem?"

"Jalissa took my brand new stuff and you know it. I want it back. Now." Simmy tapped her foot impatiently, her chest moving up and down like someone was pumping on it.

"First off, she doesn't need your stuff. We give her plenty, and we give our kids plenty," Serita retorted, moving closer to Simmy. "And what stuff are you talking about?"

"Jalissa asked me to borrow an outfit this morning, and I told her no. I left my door unlocked by accident, and now my stuff is gone. There's no one else in here who would take it. The boys sure can't wear it. It's no coincidence that she asked me, I said no, and now it's all missing." Simmy argued.

Serita laughed at her like she was a big joke. "Listen, crazy child. My daughter doesn't steal. Furthermore, she doesn't even like the stuff you wear. And, she can't fit into your clothes. If you haven't noticed, Jalissa has a much more shapely body than yours. Now please get out of our apartment acting crazy before I do something that you and me will regret," Serita said firmly.

Simmy's body temperature went up at least ten degrees. She felt like her blood was boiling in her veins and something throbbed behind her eye sockets. "I'm not going nowhere until I get my stuff back. Where's my stuff?" Simmy yelled, pushing past Serita and storming farther into the basement space. Simmy pushed over the standing, foldable partition wall they used to make a makeshift bedroom for Jalissa. She threw open Jalissa's drawers and plastic bins and began pulling stuff from them and tossing it onto the floor. "I want my stuff! She's nothing but a snooty little thief! I want my stuff now!"

"Simone! I'm telling you, you better stop right all this before you regret it!"

"What's going on?" Marcus seemed to appear out of nowhere as Simmy went through Jalissa's room like a cyclone.

"You better get her, Marcus. I'm telling you if I put my hands on that girl . . ." Serita threatened.

"Simone, what are you doing?" Marcus yelled, grabbing Simmy, halting her movement. He clamped down on her arm until it was painful, but that didn't seem to faze her.

"Your thief of a daughter stole my Gucci jacket, my Chanel boots, and a Givenchy skirt that I just bought. All of it still had tags on it. She asked me to borrow my clothes, and I told her no! She still went in my stuff and took it! She's a thief!" Simmy screamed, angry tears in her eyes.

"She didn't take it," Marcus said firmly. "Now get out." He pulled Simmy toward the steps. She tried to resist, but she was no match for his strength. He released her in front of the steps with a shove.

"And don't bring no noise down here again," Marcus grumbled.

Reluctantly, Simmy went stomping up each step. She stormed past the kitchen and out of the doors. This wasn't the end of it. *This bitch is gonna come home eventually.*

Jalissa didn't arrive home until three o'clock in the morning. Her rowdy group of friends pulled up in a raggedy Honda Accord, and she climbed out being just as raucous. Jalissa laughed loudly and screamed profanities at her friends jokingly, but not for long.

"Ow!" Jalissa shrieked. Her hands flew up to her head. She clearly didn't know what had hit her.

Simmy gripped Jalissa's weave so tight it rendered her powerless. Simmy had been waiting all night for Jalissa to get home.

"I asked you not to touch my stuff," Simmy said through gritted teeth, dragging Jalissa down to the ground by her stitched-in hair. Jalissa tried to scream, but a fist to the mouth sent the sound back down her throat.

Jalissa's friends exited the car and started screaming and jeering. They were trying to encourage Jalissa to get up and fight, but she couldn't get up. Simmy's anger had given her brute strength that even she didn't recognize she had. Simmy grabbed her Gucci jacket with one hand and began yanking it off of Jalissa's back.

Jalissa finally managed to scream. And scream she did. The way she was yelling out someone would have thought she was being murdered. Simmy kicked Jalissa in the stomach and wound her other hand tighter into Jalissa's hair. When the jacket was off, Simmy began tugging on the Givenchy skirt. Simmy didn't care if the clothes ripped at this point. She was more pissed off at the fact that Jalissa had the nerve to steal from her. That kind of disrespect was unforgivable.

"Fucking thief." Simmy gritted her teeth. "I'ma leave your bum ass out here naked."

Jalissa continued shrieking like she was being slaughtered. Not one of her ratchet friends dared to try to help her. As late as it was, in Brooklyn there were always people outside, so it didn't take long before a big crowd had gathered to watch. Simmy heard people screaming, "WorldStar!"

By the time Simmy was done, Jalissa had nothing left on but her bra and one shoe. She had obviously worn Simmy's skirt without panties underneath. Jalissa's weave was ripped out in patches and lay scattered on the ground. Some stray pieces blew down the block like tumbleweed in the desert.

Jalissa ran screaming into the house. "She attacked me! She attacked me for nothing!" she screeched, holding her head.

Simmy followed her inside but stomped up to her bedroom. She paced the floor, trying to will herself to calm down. Even she didn't recognize the person she was at that moment: chest heaving, eyes wild and roving, nostrils flaring like a bull on the charge. Simmy couldn't decipher if the blind fit of rage was about the clothes, the principle of the matter, or just pent-up anger for everything coming down at once.

"Don't try to take shit from me. I told you no, and I meant it. That stuff was mine. Don't take my stuff. They already took everything I had." Simmy gritted her teeth through tears, raising both of her hands to either side of her head, tugging hard on her hair as she walked in circles grumbling.

"Simone!" Mummy Pat burst into Simmy's room, her usually butter-colored face the color of cooked beets, her eyes hooded over. "Did you leave Jalissa naked outside in front of all those people? Did you attack her like a stranger in the street?"

"She took my stuff, Mummy!"

"I don't care!" Mummy Pat boomed, walking into Simmy with the force of a wrecking ball. Simmy fell flat on her butt. Pain shot straight up her back. "We are a family! You don't attack your own family over material things!" Mummy Pat boomed, throwing wild slaps at Simmy's face and head.

Simmy threw her arms up to shield her head from her grandmother's blows. With each slap and punch she took, Simmy felt her heart breaking more and more. Her grandmother had never raised a hand to her like that. The shock of it all made Simmy feel like her heart would explode. She imagined this was what dying felt like.

"If you can't get along in my house with my family then find yourself on the streets," Mummy Pat said with finality, ending her assault. Her words exploded like small bombs in Simmy's ears.

Simmy cried so hard she couldn't catch her breath. She kept her head covered and rocked back and forth on the floor.

"Mummy! You're wrong!" Sheryl burst into the room and stepped right in Mummy Pat's path.

"Move." Mummy Pat gritted her teeth. "I'm in no mood for you this morning, Sheryl."

"No! You're going to hear me out!" Sheryl barked, pushing Mummy Pat hard in her chest. Mummy Pat stumbled backward a few steps.

Simmy sat up. "Forget it, Sheryl," Simmy cried out. "I'll just leave. If she wants me gone, then I'll go!"

"It's not right, Mummy! That girl stole Simone's things. You told me yourself that Simone is working hard for her stuff. Why is it okay for Jalissa to take her things like that? Why? I'll tell you why. Because she's Marcus's stepdaughter, that's why! Right, Mummy? He and his devil spawns can't do no wrong in your eyes, right? Right? You're going to toss this poor girl on the streets over the likes of them?" Sheryl preached, her voice so loud it sounded like she was speaking through a microphone. Simmy couldn't believe her aunt, who usually gave her a hard time, was taking up for her.

"You know what, Sheryl? Anybody who don't like what I do in my house can leave, including you. If Simone can't keep her hands to herself, then yes, she has to leave. It don't have nothing to do with Marcus," Mummy Pat exclaimed in her heavy Jamaican Patois.

"It has everything to do with Marcus! You've been babying him since we were kids and that's why he's a no *bumbaclot* good now!"

Mummy Pat lurched back and slapped Sheryl across the face. The sound was so loud, Simmy sprang to her feet and rushed between them. The tension was so thick it was like a thick, stifling cloud of polluted air surrounding them, choking them.

"Now. If you both want to leave, then leave." Mummy Pat gritted her teeth. Simmy saw a fire flashing in her eyes that she'd never seen in her life.

"You don't know what you just did," Sheryl huffed, holding her cheek. "You just don't know."

Mummy Pat walked out of the room and left Sheryl and Simmy standing there in silence.

"I'm sorry, Simone. I know you've always thought that I don't like you but that is far from the truth. And I know I come off like a bitch and I've said some messed-up things to you. But, the truth is, I've been hurt all my life, and I don't know any other way to talk but with pain. You're gonna leave now but be careful what you get into. Your cousin Jayla is bad news, Simone. If you take anything of what I am saying to you right now, take this: stay away from Jayla. She is going to bring you down." Having said that, Sheryl walked out of the room.

***

Simmy could not stop the tears from running in streams down her cheeks as she paced outside, her bags at the curb, waiting for Jayla to pick her up. She had thought about calling Kyan but decided Jayla was the better choice. She'd heard everything her aunt said to her in the room, but she couldn't understand why her aunt was so against Jayla. Jayla was the only one who really looked out for her, and she hadn't given Simmy a reason not to trust her.

Jayla pulled up to the curb, tires squealing. She scrambled out of the car in a fury, her face drawn tight into a frown.

"Where the fuck is that little bum bitch?" Jayla gritted her teeth, heading for the house. "This shit ain't over."

Simmy grabbed her arm before she could make it to Mummy Pat's stoop. "It's not even worth it, Jay. I don't want you to get involved. I'm just going to leave and never come back. They showed me where I stand today," Simmy said, her voice cracking with pain.

"Ew, that makes me so fucking mad." Jayla punched at the air. "Ain't shit change in that fucking house but the day and year. Same shit, different day. Mummy Pat always did have her fucking favorites. For some reason that bitch Serita—who, mind you, hasn't fucking worked or brought a dime in that house in twelve fucking years—always gets a pass. And, forget about Marcus's weed-head, shiftless, ten-illegitimate-kids-having ass. He can't do no wrong in the eyes of Patricia Jones. Oh, not her baby fucking boy," Jayla ranted as she snatched up Simmy's bags from the curb and tossed them into the trunk.

"I'm so hurt," Simmy cried, burying her face in her hands. "I'm just so hurt." Jayla grabbed her around the shoulders and pulled her into a tight embrace. "I know, boo. I know," Jayla comforted her, her jaw rocking feverishly against Simmy's shoulder as they hugged. "But, in life, things fall apart. You just got to always be ready to put shit back together when they do."

"She was supposed to be there for me and love me while Mommy and Daddy are gone." Simmy hiccupped a sob. The pain was evident behind every one of her shaky words. "She actually hit me. She hit me, Jay. She took that girl's side. She's not even her blood, and she still took her side. It was my stuff. She took my stuff."

"Oh, I know how shit goes up in that hell hole, little cousin. Why do you think I've been gone? Same thing they used to do to me for years. Just jealous shit. I love Mummy Pat, but she's definitely got her favorites. That shit will never change, either. You and me, we can't do no right in their eyes. We are not the chosen ones. Never have and never will be. That's why we have to make our own way in the world."

That made Simmy cry harder. Without her parents, her grandmother was really all she had, and now she was gone too.

"Okay. Okay." Jayla patted her back. "C'mon. Get in. You're coming to live with me. My house is your house, Simmy. You already know this," Jayla comforted her. She opened the car door and helped Simmy into the passenger seat.

Simmy swiped hard at her tears and cleared her vision for a few seconds. She looked out of the window at the brownstone one last time before Jayla sped away from the curb.

"You ain't never coming back here. Fuck that," Jayla said.

Simmy felt a void open up inside of her like a gaping sinkhole on a street in a Midwestern state. She felt like she'd left a big part of herself behind. She knew from here on out, things would never be the same for her.

Chapter 7

Alone

A fresh coat of snow had blanketed New York City, and the view outside of Jayla's apartment window resembled a Christmas card. Simmy stood at the window in Jayla's guestroom, which had become her room for the month and half she'd been staying there. She watched all of the snowflakes fall, wishing she was outside so she could open her mouth and catch a few on her tongue like she used to as a kid. Winter had always been her favorite season. When she was little, her father would take her snow sledding in the large open field at the side of their house. Simmy could remember falling over into the snow and feeling it, cold and wet, against her face.

Simmy also loved winter fashion. She loved fur coats and warm, chunky sweaters, too. But, she hated being stuck in the house. She was missing Kyan something terrible. He'd been upset to learn that she'd moved all the way to Harlem. They definitely couldn't see each other as much as they did when she was in Brooklyn; and since Simmy had been missing more and more school after the move, Kyan wasn't happy about that, either. He was concerned that she might not graduate if she kept up like this. She was worried about how much school she'd missed too. And she didn't like how mad Kyan was about it, but she just couldn't say no to Jayla. Jayla had done so much to help her out. She felt like she owed it to her to do all the jobs Jayla would have her do.

Her relationship with Jayla had changed since she'd gone to live with her, though. It was a little different now that they shared an apartment and were around each other twenty-four hours a day. When Simmy had first gotten there, Jayla had indulged her, introducing her to the big girl life. Every night they'd hit up a different club in the city. Simmy didn't know people even partied on Monday and Tuesday nights like that. But the partying got old fast for Simmy. She wasn't into the partying and drinking all the time. She was more of a homebody. She preferred to just stay in, curl up in a blanket, and read a good book. Whenever she'd get a chance to go see Kyan, they would order takeout and watch movies. She loved that he was homebody too.

Kyan had been trying to convince her to move in with him so she'd be able to make it school, but she didn't feel comfortable doing that. Jayla was always warning Simmy about not giving a man too much power over her. Jayla told her if she moved in with Kyan, he was most likely going to change up on her and start telling her what to do.

"He's already doing it to you, and you don't even see it," Jayla exclaimed. The two cousins had just come home from doing another job and were sitting in the living room eating pizza.

"No, he's not," Simmy replied defensively. She had just revealed to Jayla that Kyan asked her to move in with him.

"Simmy, you need to open your eyes, baby cousin. He asked you to move in because he wants to be able to see everything you're doing. Didn't you tell me he's already riding you about going to school and shit?"

"Yes. But that's different," Simmy tried to defend her man.

"No, it ain't. It's all the same shit, Simmy. He's trying to tell you what to do with your life. Last time I checked,

you only had one daddy, and he's locked up, so why is Kyan trying to act like he's your daddy telling you what to do?"

Simmy was at a loss for words. What her cousin was saying made sense. She didn't want to believe that Kyan was the controlling type but, for the most part, Jayla was right about the things she spoke about.

"Your best bet is to just keep working to get your paper up and keep doing you," she'd told Simmy.

"Hey," Jayla called from the doorway. "Going stir crazy?"

Simmy turned toward her cousin. "Pretty much." She eyed Jayla suspiciously and then brushed her own nose: a signal. Jayla was too high to even catch on.

"Chick, me too. Hate being in this house. Can't go make no money. Nothing," Jayla said, although she was grinning.

Simmy cleared her throat. "You have something on your nose," Simmy said, slightly annoyed.

Embarrassment flashed across Jayla's face. She brushed her nose vigorously and chuckled nervously. "A little something to chase away the boredom. Completely under control," she said.

Simmy just nodded, but she didn't return Jayla's guilty smile. The cocaine use was just one of many things Simmy had learned about Jayla since being there. The constant parade of different men was another thing that bothered Simmy. Every night there was someone different in Jayla's bed. It didn't sit right with Simmy at all. Some nights she was so uneasy about it, she'd just lie awake until she heard Jayla letting the flavor of the night out the apartment door. It shocked Simmy to learn just how much of a mess Jayla was. Simmy had always held her in such high esteem and thought she wanted to be just like Jayla. That had definitely changed.

Simmy was powerless. Until she could save up enough money for a place, she would have to bite her tongue and deal with Jayla's lifestyle. She'd thought about asking Kyan to help her get a place, but that would just be another thing to make him think he had power over her. It was bad enough he'd found out from one of Jalissa's friends that Simmy was a high-end booster. He wasn't happy about it, either. Simmy had gotten defensive and told him not to judge her, just like she hadn't judged him for selling drugs.

"We about to make some good money," Jayla changed the subject. "Holiday season is here, girl. Christmastime is busy and we can rack up."

"Really? I thought the opposite," Simmy replied, tilting her head. "Don't they hire much more security for Christmas time than normally? Won't it be much more risky now?"

Jayla's eyes lowered, and she pursed her lips like she always did when she felt Simmy was being ungrateful. "So what if they hire more security? We are professionals. Or, wait, I'm a professional; maybe you're still an amateur," Jayla snapped, taking a dig at Simmy that she knew would usually bother her.

Simmy set her jaw. "Amateur or professional, I still think holiday time is more risky," she said, turning back to the window.

"Well, either way, we're going out there. Period. End of story." With that, Jayla disappeared from the doorway.

When Jayla swung her newest Range Rover into the parking lot of the Mall at Short Hills in New Jersey, Simmy looked over at her.

"We never go to Jersey," Simmy said, her eyes wide. "I didn't know we were going to Jersey."

"Ugh," Jayla grumbled. "You're getting on my nerves with all of these questions. That negative vibe is fucking bad juju, Simmy."

"I'm just asking because you always bypass Jersey. We've been to Connecticut, Delaware, Maryland, Pennsylvania, upstate, but never Jersey. I just always assumed there was a reason for that. That's why I asked," Simmy said.

"Well, don't ask. This is my business, and I make the decisions where we go. We in Jersey today and that's that," Jayla shot back. She sniffled and backhanded her wet nostrils. "Now, since we got that bullshit out of the way, you ready?" Jayla picked up her pocketbook and went to pull on her door handle.

"Wait, what about our look?" Simmy asked, panic in her tone. Was Jayla slipping or what? She hadn't told Simmy what type of mall they were hitting up. She hadn't figured out what look was right for them for the day. Simmy hadn't seen the list of things they needed to focus on getting so that they had a direction when they went into the stores. Nothing. No game plan. Jayla had failed to plan for the day's work. It made Simmy uneasy. Very uneasy. She felt nauseated.

Jayla fidgeted impatiently and seemed unable to keep still. Nothing about the day was right. Simmy didn't like what she was seeing at all. Simmy was racking her brain trying to remember if Jayla was always like this and she was just too enamored with her to see it. Simmy didn't like the feeling trampling through her gut. Was this what was meant when she'd always heard older people say they had a gut feeling?

"It's Jersey, Simone. We don't need a look," Jayla said, sucking her teeth. "Everybody and their mother come out here so no need to put on airs. Now, let's go before you really blow my high and fuck up my vibe. You've been acting real stink lately and, for all that I do for you, I'm not really digging that vibe."

Simmy fell silent. She could see that Jayla was getting angry with her and she hated when that happened. Maybe Jayla was right. Maybe out of frustration for her own situation, Simmy had an attitude with Jayla for nothing. Simmy began second-guessing herself and scolding herself silently for coming across as ungrateful. Out of respect for Jayla and to keep arguments down, Simmy bit her tongue and didn't ask any more questions. She dug into her Louis Vuitton monogrammed never-full tote and pulled out her silver Dior mirrored-front shades. Respect was one thing, but stupidity was a whole other story in Simmy's eyes. And, just because Jayla wanted to be stupid, this was one time Simmy wasn't going to follow her lead.

With no list and no plan, Simmy and Jayla entered Neiman Marcus first. The store was packed with holiday shoppers who, like Simmy and Jayla, did not let the snow stop them from coming out. There were huddles of people at the jewelry counters and perfume counters. There seemed to be droves of women invading the handbags sections. Even the special salon brands, like Gucci, Louis Vuitton, and Céline, which had their own separate rooms, had crowds gathered inside.

Simmy was loving the beautiful silver, red, and green sparkly Christmas decorations that the store had chosen. It kind of made her sad. This was usually the time of year her father loved most. He'd take her around to different malls to shop, but really to see all of the lights and decorations. Simmy hadn't even gone back to the big tree in Rockefeller Center since her father had gotten locked up. She just couldn't bring herself to visit it without him.

Simmy tried to shake off the foreboding feeling that had crept over her, but it didn't work. Although Simmy and Jayla always acted like they weren't together when they went on their trips, this time, Simmy felt like everyone in the store was watching her and Jayla. She tried again to shake off the dark feeling and the paranoia that was plaguing her, but she could swear each time Jayla passed, hushed murmurs and whispers rose and fell among some of the store associates. Even with the crowds, Simmy felt like all eyes were on them.

Get your mind right, Simmy. It's just your mind. You're bugging. It's nothing. She gave herself a pep talk. It was all she could do to keep from following her mind and bolting from the store.

Simmy felt relieved when Jayla gave her the signal to split up into different areas of the store. It was their usual course of action; except, without their game plan mapped out like usual, Simmy had no idea where to meet Jayla at the end. And, she didn't even ask.

Simmy clutched her kitted-out bag, her shoulder bag, and a cute little stylish Louis Vuitton backpack, and she headed to the women's shoes. Shoes were the easiest things to get. The crowded store would make it even easier.

Simmy finished getting a few things she liked and rushed through the store for the escalators. Still feeling like she was being watched, sweat dripped down her back and soaked the waistband of her jeans. As she rode down, she heard it. At first, it sounded like arguing but the closer Simmy got to the bottom of the escalator, the more she recognized the voice.

"Get off of me! Get the fuck off of me! She's a liar! Y'all can't fucking do this to me! Get off of me!"

It was Jayla! Simmy's entire body grew hot. She looked over her shoulder to see if she could escape back up. She was trapped on the escalator, people in front of her and people behind her. As the escalator continued its slow descent, Simmy felt like she was on a ride down to the fiery pits of hell. She felt lightheaded. She fanned her face with her hands in an attempt to keep herself from fainting. It was over. Simmy just knew they were going to come for her next.

"Get off of me! I didn't do anything!" Simmy could hear Jayla still fighting.

Simmy stepped off the escalator and froze watching the nightmarish scene. Two store security guards dragged Jayla, kicking and screaming, through the store. The entire store seemed to be suspended in time, nothing moving. Everyone watched. Some people whispered. Others pointed. Some laughed. Simmy felt like all of the sounds were extra loud in her ears. Her brain was screaming, *run! Run! You're next! Run.* She couldn't move. It was as if her feet had suddenly grown roots and planted themselves into the floor. Her eyes were so wide she could feel her eyeballs drying out. Her heart jammed into her chest bone, and she could feel vomit creeping up her esophagus.

"Always happens at this time of the year."

Simmy jumped at the sound of a girl's voice. The girl was standing right next to her.

"You better get out of here. You're so close. Take that as a sign and run for those doors," the strange girl said.

Simmy snapped out of her trance. She rolled her eyes at the girl and sped for the doors. When Simmy got outside, she didn't have time to stop and process what had just happened. She sprinted toward Jayla's car but, as she approached it, she noticed two cop cars parked in front of it. Two officers circled the car and shined their flashlights into the windows.

How did they know that was Jayla's car? And, that fast?

Simmy sucked in her breath and made a U-turn. She slowed down her pace and hoped she hadn't brought any attention to herself. She couldn't process what was happening. Her head pounded, and she trembled so hard her teeth chattered uncontrollably. Simmy had to think fast. There was no time to feel sorry for herself or Jayla.

Finally, her brain started working a little better. She dipped into Nordstrom and found the bathroom. In a huff, she rushed into the bathroom, raced down the long line of stalls, and pushed into the last stall at the end. Once inside, she locked the door and rested her back on the inside of the door. She exhaled loudly. It felt like the weight of the world had literally just fallen onto her shoulders.

She closed her eyes and began to cry. She clasped her hand over her mouth and sobbed like she had just experienced death. That was exactly how she felt, like the chasm of a huge void had just opened up inside of her. Simmy had never thought about or planned for this day. She and Jayla had never made any contingency plans just in case one of them got caught. Simmy bit down on her bottom lip so hard she broke the skin. Reality was hitting her so hard she didn't even feel the pain. The reality that, for the first time since she and Jayla had started boosting together, Simmy was alone.

Chapter 8

Wrong Path

When Kyan pulled up, Simmy nearly bolted into a full run to get to his car. Her legs moved so fast. She didn't know a person could walk so fast without actually running. Her lips were white from breathing so hard through her mouth, and her hands still wouldn't stop shaking. She looked around frantically before she snatched the door open and rushed into the car.

"Thank you," she huffed, as she flopped down heavily into the passenger seat. "I . . . really appreciate you coming all the way out here to get me." Simmy was speaking, but she stared straight ahead, unable to look at Kyan. The shame of what happened was almost too much to bear. She knew Kyan was mad because, no matter what, he opened his car door for her, but this time he hadn't. Simmy could feel the heat of his gaze on her face, but she still would not look at him.

"So?" Kyan said, reaching down and turning his music down. "What do you have to say?"

Simmy pinched the bridge of her nose and exhaled a windstorm of breath. She knew the lecture would be coming. She felt too mentally exhausted to argue with him. "Kyan, you already know what it is. We talked about this. This is how I've been surviving. I don't have a choice. You can't believe that I want to be out here stealing shit and being put in situations like this. Stuff happens. I didn't have any control over it."

"But, now you see where it could lead, right? You think your cousin hasn't been bagged before? You dodged a bullet and by a real slim margin, Simone. You definitely ain't cut out to be locked up, especially all the way out here," he said, his tone preachy.

Simmy bit down into her jaw. "I'm not a little kid who doesn't know right from wrong, Kyan. Yes, I always knew where it could lead but, like you with your hustle, it's what I do to eat. Please don't judge me," Simmy said, annoyed and on the brink of more tears. She thought he had some nerve. Still, she wouldn't get too mouthy with him because she was grateful he'd come all the way out there when she called.

There was a long, awkward silence. Simmy's mind raced with a million thoughts: *how am I going to get Jayla out? Where did they take her car? Can they even do that? Did anyone know I was with Jayla? Where am I going to stay? Will she get right out? They can't really keep her that long, right?*

"So what exactly happened? How she let herself get bagged like that?" Kyan broke the silence and Simmy's train of thought.

"Ugh. It was so bad." Simmy sighed. "It's just so crazy. I feel like it is my fault. I should've just followed my first instinct," Simmy said, her words coming out on a long exhale of breath.

"First instinct?"

"Yeah. From the gate, when Jayla said we was going out, I felt leery about today. It is the holidays, for one. I know this is a time when the stores really ramp up their security. She argued with me about that. Then, I could see that Jayla wasn't her usual, sharp self. Since I been staying with her, I've noticed that she has a bit of an alcohol and powder problem," Simmy said, touching her nose for emphasis.

Kyan's eyebrows shot up into arches, and he shook his head like a disappointed father.

"We ain't have no direction, no plan, nothing. I should've known that was a bad sign. I should've fought her on it and insisted that we go another day. Like I said, I should've followed my first instinct or, like the old people say, my gut feeling," Simmy lamented, shaking her head.

"So why did you go?" Kyan pressed.

Simmy shrugged. She had asked herself that same question at least fifty times while she hid out in the Nordstrom bathroom waiting for Kyan's call after Jayla's arrest. She'd come up short on an intelligent answer every time. How would she look saying that she ignored her instincts and went all because she hated when Jayla was mad at her? All because she wanted to always be on Jayla's good side because, up until that moment, Jayla was the only person she looked up to? Instead, Simmy closed her eyes and leaned back on the headrest, her head pounding with a migraine.

"Well, why did you go?" Kyan asked again, this time more bass in his voice.

"Because I always feel obligated and indebted to my cousin. She looked out when no one else did. She helped me put money in my pocket and in the process I was able to shit on a few chicks with my wears. So, I have a hard time telling her no. Even when I am not feeling the situation, like today, " Simmy confessed. She told him half of the truth.

"So, in other words, you gave in to her peer pressure?" Kyan replied, his statement more of a question. "When you don't even have to do that? You got such mad resources available to you, me for one, that you don't have to ever give in to anyone's peer pressure, Simone."

Simmy sucked her teeth. Was he serious? Kyan's apparent unwillingness to understand frustrated Simmy.

"It wasn't peer pressure, Kyan. It was loyalty. Trust. Respect. Love. You know anything about those things? Probably not. You probably never felt indebted to anyone, so you wouldn't understand it," she snapped.

"Nah, being a fool ain't the same as loyalty, trust, respect, and love. You can have all that without following somebody down the wrong path. I mean, how much loyalty, trust, respect, and love does she have for you if she taking you down that same wrong path? Think about that, Simone. As a big cousin, Jayla shouldn't even want you to be out here getting it like this. I say you got too much going for yourself to waste it on some bullshit clothes. You get arrested for grand larceny and get a record, then what? What happens to all of that reading and studying you been doing over the years? It goes to waste; that's what happens. Then you'll really be like Jayla, with a rap sheet and can't get a job, forced to boost clothes for a living for the rest of your life. Always wondering where your next dollar coming from. C'mon, man, that ain't the life you want. I swear, I miss coming on the block and seeing you on your grandmother's stoop with your nose in a book. Who cares about wears, when I've already told you I thought you were beautiful then and now?"

"You thought I was beautiful but never really said a word to me until I started dressing better," she grumbled. Even after all Kyan had said, that was Simmy's flimsy response. She knew he was right and she hated to admit it.

"I didn't step to you then because I knew you were a good girl and I didn't want to corrupt you. But, I couldn't shake the feelings, so I decided to finally do it. I love you, Simone," Kyan said sincerely.

Simmy squeezed her eyes shut, but the tears still came hard and fast. "I'm not the same person you used to see, Kyan. I'm not the so-called good girl you think I am," she whimpered.

"You are the same good girl; you just got caught up. I don't want that type of girl. I want that smart, always-reading, always-focused girl back."

Simmy swallowed hard. She didn't know what to say to that. It wasn't often that she was at a loss for words; but, this time, she was. She didn't know if that old girl lived inside of her anymore. She just didn't know.

"You're going back to my crib," Kyan announced, breaking another long silence that had settled in the car.

"No. I really need to go back to Jayla's. I have to figure this all out."

"Ain't nothing to figure out. You're out of that business, and I'm going to take care of you. You're going to start going back to school every day and concentrate on graduating. Period. End of story."

Simmy didn't say another word, nor did she protest. She didn't have many options at this time. Maybe having someone take care of her was what she needed.

When they arrived at his place, it felt like forever since Simmy had been there. She looked around, trying to see if she spotted any long hairs, lipstick-stained glasses, or any other remnants of a recent female guest. There was nothing.

"You looking around like you a DT," Kyan chuckled. "You ain't gonna find nothing, Sherlock Holmes. You keep trying to make me the bad guy. I'm the good guy," he said, coming up and hugging her from behind. "And I fucking missed you like crazy."

Simmy blushed. "I wasn't looking for nothing," she lied. She inhaled his scent and closed her eyes. A smile spread over her lips and, for the first time in the hours since Jayla's arrest, Simmy relaxed a little bit.

"Yeah, right, that's why your eyes moving a mile a minute around the room?" He squeezed her tighter. "C'mere, Detective Jones." He turned her around so he could hug her from the front. He swallowed her body with his embrace. "I can't say enough how much I fucking missed you," he whispered into the top of her head. "I don't ever want us to be apart for that long again. Fuck staying in Harlem. You a Brooklyn girl. You belong in Brooklyn."

"Always will be a Brooklyn girl," she whispered.

Simmy melted against him, and her pulse quickened. The throbbing between her legs matched her heartbeat thump for thump. She'd forgotten how good it felt to be in Kyan's arms. He hadn't touched her in weeks. With all of the partying and running around with Jayla, Simmy had totally lost sight of how much she missed him too. She closed her eyes, inhaled his cologne, and felt his heart beat against her.

"Don't ever leave me," Simmy said, being the most vulnerable she'd ever been around him. "I'm so scared to be all alone, Kyan. Please don't leave me."

"I won't. I ain't going nowhere, and neither are you," Kyan said, holding her a little tighter. "I'll never leave you, Simone. I swear."

Simmy's mind raced. She was thinking about Jayla and the uncertainty of her situation. She was thinking about how Brooklyn reminded her of how much she missed Mummy Pat and her parents. Simmy was petrified of being all alone. She wanted to hold on to Kyan forever and never let him go.

With thoughts of being abandoned controlling her actions, Simmy reached up, grabbed Kyan's head, and pulled him close to her face. He followed her lead and put his hot mouth over hers. Simmy parted her lips and allowed his tongue between them. She sucked on it softly, which caused the petals of her flower to open up. The pulsing between her legs was so intense she squeezed her thighs together.

"Damn, I missed you," Kyan whispered into her mouth. He gently held each side of her face as they kissed passionately. Simmy let out a soft moan and moved her body against his, her nipples so erect the friction sent stabs of heated sparks down her spine. Within a few minutes, she could also feel his iron-stiff erection pressing against the top of her pelvis. She wanted him. She let her hands travel below his belt line so that he knew she wanted him, needed him.

"You feel so fucking good, Simone," Kyan whispered in her ear. Then he gently bit it. A hot feeling tingled through Simmy's body. She wasn't going to fight it. She wanted to be all his forever. She wanted to be the best he'd ever had. Most of all, she just wanted to be wanted.

"C'mon," Kyan said softly, moving his body apart from hers. He grabbed her hand and led her through his apartment to his bedroom. Simmy didn't bother to take her bag or her cell phone. She was lost in lust, and even thoughts of Jayla had faded out of her mind for that moment.

Kyan led her to his bed. He grabbed the bottom of her shirt and slipped it over her head before he eased her down onto his bed. Simmy lay there watching as he slid out of his sweater and then his wife beater, exposing his six pack abs and slim but muscular chest. His smooth brown skin seemed to glow against the faint beam from the streetlights coming through the slats in his blinds.

"Did you miss me?" Kyan asked as he climbed onto the bed and then on top of her.

Simmy shook her head and bit down on her bottom lip. They shared more deep, passionate kisses. Simmy made the first blatant move and slid her hand down to Kyan's pants. She pushed at his belt line, letting him know she didn't want to wait another minute. She needed him. She wanted him. She was demanding him.

Kyan took her cue and eased up from the bed. He smiled at her as he slowly unhooked his belt, unbuttoned his jeans, and let them fall to the floor. Simmy smiled back. "Take it all off," she said sexily. She didn't want to play any more games.

"Okay. Okay." He chuckled. With that, he eased his boxers down and freed his long, thick love muscle. It was standing up like a snake being charmed by a snake charmer. Simmy didn't mind being the snake charmer.

"Damn," she huffed. "You're so perfect. Damn right I missed you."

"Nah, I'm not the one who's perfect; that would be you," Kyan said, his voice gruff with lust. He rushed to the bed and grabbed at the waist of her pants. With the skill of a craftsman, he had her out of her pants and panties in a flash.

Simmy's thighs trembled, but she didn't let that stop her from taking control.

"Lie down," she said. "I want to show you how much I've missed you."

Surprise flashed in Kyan's eyes. She could tell he was a little taken aback by her newfound sexual confidence and prowess. Simmy let her inhibitions fall away; she wanted Kyan to understand that she was his.

"I love you, Simone," he whispered. It was the second time he'd said it, and she still hadn't said it back. Simmy's stomach quivered at the sound of those words. When she first started out talking to him on the phone and seeing him occasionally, falling in love wasn't part of the plan, but she couldn't help it or hide it anymore. Fear and reservations were all tossed away at that moment.

Without another word, Simmy climbed onto Kyan and straddled him. She leaned over his face and looked right into his eyes. "I love you too, Kyan." Something exploded inside of her. She began licking his neck, then moved a little farther down, her tongue trailing down to his pecks, and she gently bit each one.

"Fuck." Kyan breathed out heavily, his voice thick with lusty pleasure. With every noise he made, Simmy gained more confidence. She wanted him to feel good. She wanted to feel good. She continued down his abdomen, taking special care to run her tongue over every ridge on his sexy, firm six pack. Kyan groaned. When Simmy got to his manhood, she looked up at his face. She parted a mischievous smile and bit her bottom lip seductively. She grabbed his thick rod and, with the skill of a professional, she opened her mouth and took him inside.

Kyan let out a long puff of air and grunted. Simmy could feel his muscles tense each time she bobbed her head up and then down. She ran her hand up and down over it as she moved her head at the same time.

Kyan was making noises that sounded like growling. He couldn't take it any longer. "I fucking need to feel you. I want to feel you now." He sat up abruptly and flipped Simmy over onto her back before she could even react or protest.

"Take it," she whispered. A pang of anticipation flitted through her chest. She kind of liked the feeling of Kyan being in command. She was on her back watching him now. She put her hands on the top of his head.

Kyan kissed her stomach as he inched down. "Mmmm," he moaned. Simmy's chest rose and fell in anticipation of what was coming. Kyan moved back up and kissed her, while at the same time he used his knee to gently part her legs. Simmy lifted her knees willingly to help him.

Kyan slowly guided his manhood into her deep, wet center. Simmy let out a song of soft moans and groans as he ground into her.

"Gotdamn," he growled, his eyes closed and his nostrils open wide. He planted his hands on the bed at either side of Simmy's head for leverage.

"Oh, God," she cooed. Kyan felt so good. They were a perfect match. He filled her up just right.

"Oh, shit. Oh, shit!" Kyan belted out, picking up speed from the excitement of feeling her tightness suck him in. Simmy had tears in her eyes; not from pain, but because it was so good.

"Let me ride it," she panted. Jayla had always told her that riding it was a sure way to take the control from the man, to let him know you could take over if needed. *"Strong bitches always ride the dick,"* Jayla had told her.

Before Kyan could protest or say anything, Simmy had him on his back. She climbed over his stiff tool and lowered herself down on it slowly while swirling her hips at the same time.

"Ahh," she called out as his ramrod pole penetrated her insides until she felt like it was hitting her cervix. Kyan put his hands on her waist and guided her up and down. Within minutes, Simmy picked up on his rhythm and began bouncing on his thick pole with each pump of his hips. They were making their own beat, their own music.

"Mmmm!" she yelled. "Oh, shit! I . . . I . . ." Simmy was stuttering because she had never felt the fireworks exploding in her loins that she was experiencing right then. She quickly figured out that this was what an orgasm must feel like. She felt like she was having an out-of-body experience and the feeling made her bounce up and down on Kyan harder and faster.

"Gotdamn, Simone. Your shit so fucking good," he growled, clutching two handfuls of her ass cheeks. Simmy was feeling good now. She had him and she knew it. She rocked back and forth and then swirled her hips, grinding hard.

"Ohhhh! Ahhhh!" she screamed out. She fell down onto Kyan's chest, letting her breasts brush against his pecks. A lightshow of fireworks exploded in her head and squirms of light filled her eyesight. She rocked harder and faster now. She had leaned down enough for Kyan to be able to urge her mouth over his. He sucked on her tongue. Another explosion erupted in her loins.

"Kyan!" Simmy belted out. Her entire body shook like she was in the center of an earthquake and all of a sudden she was weak. Her legs trembled fiercely, and she went completely still, unable to move. It was only a few seconds later that Kyan's body tensed up and he had his climax, holding on to Simmy's ass as he busted.

Simmy collapsed on top of Kyan, and they both tried to calm their rapid breathing. He stroked her hair gently.

"Promise me that you'll be with me for good," he said. "None of that leaving for weeks at a time."

She closed her eyes. "I promise," she said softly. "Now you."

"You already know. But, I swear, I promise. I'll always be here for you, Simone."

Simmy slid off of him and lay next to him. She put her head on his chest and listened to the beat of his heart. At that moment, she decided it was there that she wanted to be. Forever.

Chapter 9

Spiraling

Jayla finally called Simmy's cell phone from jail early the next morning. Simmy unhooked Kyan's arm from her waist, eased out of the bed, and rushed out of his bedroom to speak to Jayla.

"Jay?" Simmy had gasped. "Are you all right? Oh, my God, I've been waiting for your call."

"Listen, little cousin. I don't have a lot of time. You going to have to help me out. This shit pretty serious. They had me on a wanted poster for some old charge, something about fifty thousand in stolen furs. Some old, trumped-up shit. They trying to say I was part of some network and all this bullshit. I ain't do that shit, Simmy. I promise you, I ain't do it. I wouldn't have taken you out there if I thought you'd be at risk. But listen to me carefully, okay? This is why I always told you to save for a rainy day. You gotta be strong and hold it down. Take care of the bills and the rent. I'm gonna need you to go and talk to my lawyer. I need you to go to the apartment and . . ."

Simmy closed her eyes and hung on Jayla's every word: *rainy day, lawyer, fifty thousand in stolen fur, rent, bills, apartment, hold it down.*

With Simmy's understanding of each sentence, each word, each syllable Jayla had uttered, Simmy's heart had sunk further and further into the pit of her stomach. She may not have been a criminal justice system expert, but Jayla's situation didn't sound promising at all. It made sense to Simmy now why in the beginning Jayla never went to New Jersey to boost. Simmy had a feeling that Jayla knew she was being sought in New Jersey. But, Simmy couldn't understand why Jayla had decided to go back if she knew shit was hot for her out there. It had to be that Jayla was too high to think things through, too desperate for a quick buck. Jayla had always been so careful and on point with their trips. Simmy wished she would have protested harder, stood up to Jayla once and for all; but now it was too late. All she could do was be strong and do as much as she could to help her cousin out of this situation.

Simmy sat on the hard wooden courtroom bench six rows behind the defendant table. Her legs swung in and out nervously. She'd sat and watched person after person be led into the courtroom, stand before the judge, hear their fate, and taken away again. Not one person was released. It was chilling.

Simmy looked around at the people on the benches with hope and desperation glinting in their eyes, just like her. It was heartbreaking. She was surrounded by mothers with crunched-up Kleenex fisted so tight their knuckles paled, and women with small children laid across their laps, anticipation arching their brows when they saw their baby fathers, boyfriends, or husbands paraded in front of the judge, only to have those same brows dip low with disappointment and sadness after hearing their man's fate. There were street dudes there, hunched forward, arms resting on knees, trying to play it cool and show their support for a fallen street brother.

Simmy's stomach ached, and her palms were slick with sweat as she watched. She wondered what each defendant thought as they stood before the judge, hands shackled, their freedom hanging in the balance while prosecutors rambled on about their mistakes and added on all of the charges they could find in the books.

Simmy thought about her parents. What had been running through their minds when they'd stood before a judge and heard their fate: life in prison for her father and twenty-five years in prison for her mother? Had her mother cried knowing Simmy would be all grown up the next time she saw her outside of the walls of a prison? Had her father, who'd always been so strong, finally cracked when he learned he would never, ever get to share another Christmas, his favorite holiday, with Simmy? The thought made her want to cry. She bit down into her jaw and swallowed the hard lump that had formed in the back of her throat. At least she was old enough to be there for Jayla.

Simmy hadn't been allowed at her mother and father's court appearances, not even their sentencing. Mummy Pat had said it would be too traumatizing for her at fourteen years old seeing her parents shackled and in bondage like violent criminals. But now, Simmy regretted not being there. She imagined that her parents would've wanted to see her for the last time before having to submit to controlled visits in a prison visitation room. Simmy shivered and wanted to cry and just let it all out despite her being in a courtroom. But she knew better than to cause a scene right now.

Get it together, Simmy. You can do this. Her thoughts were interrupted. She used her thumb and pointer finger to wipe away the wetness from her eyes before it fell. She told herself to be strong. She had to be strong for herself and for Jayla.

"Next up on the docket: State of New Jersey versus Jayla Dion Massey."

Simmy sat up straight at the sound of Jayla's name. Simmy's eyes stretched as Jayla was led in through a side door that looked like the dark wood wall had simply opened up. Jayla's hands were cuffed in front of her, her hair wild and unkempt like a haphazard bird's nest atop her head. Even from a distance, Simmy could see the swollen puffs of flesh under Jayla's eyes and her busted bottom lip. Simmy sucked in her breath. Someone had beat Jayla up, badly. A flash of heat settled over Simmy like a wool blanket had been thrown over her head on a ninety-degree summer day. Her hands curled into fists on their own, and she pursed her lips. She wished she could just rush up to the front, punch all of the court officers in the face, grab Jayla, and run away with her. The rustle of clothing in the courtroom sent an unsettling chill down Simmy's back. She watched as a slender, young white woman stood up from the table on the opposite side of the room.

"Your Honor, the state is asking that Ms. Massey remain in custody as she is already known to this court and is considered a repeat no-show risk. She has been before this court numerous times for the same crimes: grand larceny, theft, and aggravated identity theft. Yet, Ms. Massey continues to come to the state of New Jersey, from her domicile in the state of New York, to victimize our establishments and our residents. The state is asking that Ms. Massey be remanded until the preliminary hearing and thereafter for all proceedings to prevent her disappearance back into the big city of New York. We cannot risk her disappearing and costing the state of New Jersey unnecessary use of time and resources to establish and execute a warrant for Ms. Massey's future arrest. The state cannot risk that cost. We have been looking for her for a very long time, and it is in the state's best interest that we do not let her go this time."

A wave of nausea washed through Simmy's gut as she watched the white female prosecutor with her Brooks Brothers women's suit on speak about Jayla with a familiarity that made Simmy want to throw up.

"She has been before this court numerous times for the same crimes: grand larceny, theft, and aggravated identity theft." Simmy replayed the prosecutor's words in her head over and over.

These people know Jayla! Simmy screamed in her head.

"Ms. Katz, we might be getting ahead of ourselves here," the judge said, looking over the rim of her wireframe glasses. "We will first appoint Ms. Massey an attorney if she can't afford one. We won't even talk about release or bail until I have set a date for a hearing. Slow down. I had no intentions of letting Ms. Massey just walk out of here today. I do realize this is not her first offense in the state of New Jersey, counselor. We all went to law school, just like you."

Simmy cheered a little bit inside, feeling like the young prosecutor had gotten a slap from the judge. But, maybe it was just that Simmy didn't understand what was really going on. Her quick moment of excitement faded fast.

"Ms. Massey, do you have an attorney?" the judge asked, turning her beady-eyed gaze to Jayla.

Jayla, flanked by two court officers, cleared her throat. "No, ma'am. Not yet."

"Do you wish the court to appoint you an attorney?"

"You can appoint one for now, ma'am. My family is currently in the process of hiring a lawyer for me." With that, Jayla made a quick glance over her shoulder at Simmy. "I believe that is in the works right now, ma'am. In the meantime, I would very much appreciate a court-appointed lawyer." She gave another quick, telling glance back at Simmy.

Simmy's stomach clenched, and she tried a halfhearted smile at Jayla. It probably came across more like a look of panic since that was exactly what Simmy felt at that moment. She wanted to shake her head no and tell Jayla that the attorney wasn't in the works and that she had better stick with the one the court would appoint to her. But, Simmy just kept that silly smile on her face, although the vein at her right temple throbbed with worry.

After Jayla's call, Simmy had done like Jayla said and gone back to the apartment to find her stash. There was about $8,000 there, but every attorney Simmy had contacted, once they heard "$50,000 in theft" and all of the charges, wanted a $10,000 retainer to represent Jayla.

"And that will go up if we have to go to trial," several of them had told Simmy. There was no way Simmy could pay an attorney, put money on Jayla's books, pay Jayla's $2,500 monthly rent, hold some just in case bail was set, pay Jayla's utility bills, and stay afloat with the small stash.

Before Simmy knew it, she locked eyes with her cousin one last time before Jayla was led back out of the courtroom. That was it. All of those hours of waiting and Simmy was left feeling worse about Jayla's situation than she had when she first walked into court.

Simmy's mind raced as she made her way back to Brooklyn. She needed to figure out how she was going to take care of everything her cousin needed. Jayla had always been there for her so she would have to find a way to do right by her cousin.

"Ky, I need to ask you . . . No. No. Um, hey, Ky, can I borrow . . ." Simmy mumbled, rehearsing how she would ask Kyan for the money she needed to help Jayla.

Simmy exhaled loudly and swiped her hands over her face as she exited the train station. She hated asking anyone for anything, especially Kyan. Although he had told her he would always be there for her, she wanted to prove to him that she could hold her own. Her father had preached that she should never ask any other man but him for anything.

"Nothing in life is free. If a man who is not your father gives you something, trust me, he wants something in return. I am the only man you ever ask for anything. If I can't give it to you, go without."

Simmy scoffed at her father's words now. "If you can't give it to me, go without? Well, where are you now, Daddy? Huh? Am I just supposed to go without forever?" Simmy grumbled under her breath as she thought about the audacity of her father's words. He wasn't around to give her shit so was she just expected to go without forever? That made a small ball of anger build up inside of her.

Simmy rounded the corner onto Kyan's block, still trying to build up the courage to ask Kyan for money although her father's words still haunted her. She made it a few steps in and froze. She tugged her earbuds from her ears and let them fall onto her shoulders. Her mouth went slack, and her heart instantly banged so hard she felt like it would burst through her chest. Simmy's head moved side to side, and her eyes roved frantically as she took in the scene: flashing red, white, and blue lights on top of blue and white police cars; black unmarked police vans; hundreds of uniformed and plainclothes officers. They were all in front of Kyan's building.

"Ky," Simmy gasped, breaking into a run. Her mind had already started thinking the worst.

"Ma'am, you can't go past here," a young, fresh-faced uniformed NYPD officer told her, pushing her back from the blue wooden barricades that read NYPD POLICE LINE DO NOT CROSS.

"But . . . but my, um, I live there," Simmy stammered, her tongue and brain seeming to be on separate brainwaves.

"Once the building is cleared and everything is cleared up, you'll be allowed back inside if you have proof you live there," the officer droned like he'd said the same line more times than he would've liked.

"Who . . . what happened?" she asked, barely able to speak.

"Drug bust," the officer said like it was nothing.

His words made Simmy's ears burn. *Drug bust. Drug bust. Drug bust.* Suddenly she couldn't breathe. She placed her hand over her chest, a sudden sharp pain stabbing through it.

"Miss? Are you all right?" the officer asked.

Just then, Simmy saw her worst nightmare materialize into real life. Her eyebrows shot up into arches and her mouth opened into a wide O.

"Ky! Kyan!" she screeched, as she tried to run toward him. His hands had been forced behind his back and his wrists locked in handcuffs. He hung his head, nothing but a wife beater covering his chest and a pair of his house sweats on his bottom half. It was freezing outside, and they hadn't even let him get dressed. Simmy could feel her heart breaking.

"Y'all can't take him! No!" Simmy screamed so hard the back of her throat burned. The scene was like something out of a movie. Cops with long guns, short guns, helmets, and black bulletproof vests surrounded Kyan like he had committed mass murder.

"No! Kyan! No!"

Simmy didn't even realize she was kicking and screaming as the officer at the barricade line held her around the waist. She watched in horror as they forced Kyan's head down and shoved him roughly into an unmarked black van.

"No! Please! Y'all can't take him! Please. No!" Simmy let out a guttural scream, her hands flailing so wildly she hit the officer across the face. She was scooped off of her feet like a little ragdoll and slammed back down to the ground on her feet. The impact sent a ripple of pain up her legs, but she didn't care. She continued to fight to get to her man.

"Listen, miss. If you don't want to get arrested, you need to calm down!" the uniform police officer chastised her, finally releasing her with a rough shove.

Simmy collapsed to the ground and sobbed uncontrollably. How could this all happen? First, Jayla. Now, Kyan. The people she cared about the most—her parents, Jayla, and Kyan—were all caught up in the system now. Things were spiraling out of control. And, faster than Simmy could keep up.

"Why? Why?" she cried. The more she cried, the harder it became for her to breathe. She started gasping for air but, as much as she tried, she just couldn't seem to get any oxygen into her lungs. She lay on her back and could see everything around her spinning out of control as she tried to breath. She kept closing and opening her eyes in hopes that everything would stop spinning. Then, in one last blink, everything went dark. She was suddenly thrust back to the tragic day that had changed her life forever.

Crash! Bang! Simmy had been snatched out of her sleep by the loud noises. With her mind fuzzy with sleep, she made out the sounds of crashing glass and wood smashing. There were more noises, like voices, but she couldn't make out what they were saying. She sprang out of her bed, out of her room, and rushed down the long hallways of their sprawling home toward her parents' room.

"What the fuck?" Simmy heard her father screaming before she could even see him. "Fuck is this?" he cursed

out loud. The sounds around Simmy grew louder and louder. She couldn't move. The loud sound of feet thundering in every direction around her caused her heart to pound so hard it moved the material of her nightgown. There was more screaming, and immediately Simmy recognized her mother's voice. The person screaming was her mother. Simmy's mind was not foggy with sleep anymore; she was wide awake and on alert.

"Hey! There's someone else up here!" Simmy heard someone yell.

Simmy blinked rapidly, but still she didn't move. The pounding and banging around her sounded like an earthquake was happening right there in her house. She hadn't heard them say, "Police!" but as soon as her mind finally processed the scene, she knew that there were what seemed to be at least ten or fifteen police officers trampling throughout her home.

"Get on the floor! Get the fuck on the floor!" Simmy heard the commands being barked at her parents. That spurred her into motion. She ran to their bedroom door just as her father was roughly pushed down to the floor and about five police officers dropped their knees into his back. Her father's arms were yanked behind his back, and he was handcuffed and made to lie face down on his own bedroom floor. There were cops swarming like flies around a pile of freshly dropped cow manure. Simmy's head whipped around; she was trying to take in their white faces. They were all over her father as if they were trying to subdue a wild animal. She didn't understand why it was taking so many of them to cuff him.

"Punk bitches. Don't do this in front of my daughter. Don't do this shit in front of my kid, man," her father yelled out when he spotted her standing there watching everything.

It was then that she heard her mother's cries again. She was on the other side of their bedroom. Several officers had her surrounded, and they were yelling at her. "You better tell us! You better talk, or you'll go down with him. You better give it up, or you'll never see your daughter again," one cop yelled out. That same cop then pointed to Simmy.

"Get the girl. Call CPS," he yelled out.

Simmy saw her mother lose it. "No! Don't you dare take her away!"

"Simone Jones, I'm going to need you to come with me." One of the uniformed officers startled her when he approached her from behind.

"No. I'm not going anywhere with you," she protested.

"I'm afraid you have no choice, young lady. Your parents are being arrested, and legally we cannot leave you on the property."

"I don't care what you say. I'm not going."

"All right, have it your way," the officer said as he proceeded to grab her by force.

As Simmy was being forced out of the bedroom, she started screaming and reaching out for her mother as she tried to free herself from the officer's grip. "Mom! Mom!"

The cops didn't care. She was carried down the long, winding staircase, kicking and screaming.

"Sit down right here and don't you dare move," the officer said to her while pointing to the couch. Then he turned to another officer and told him to watch her. Simmy just sat there watching on as they ransacked the house. It felt like forever just sitting there watching people destroy her home. She heard a large commotion from the top of the stairs.

She looked up just as the officers dragged her father down the stairs.

"Daddy!" Simmy called out.

"Why the fuck is this girl still here? I thought Williams was on her way to get her," one of the officers in charge screamed at the others.

"Daddy!"

"It's okay, princess. Daddy is fine," Simmy's father tried to comfort her as they dragged him past her.

Simmy threw her hands up to her head and covered her ears. She tried in vain to drown out the sound of those horrible officers destroying their beautiful home and treating her father like he was an animal. She rocked back and forth and bit into her cheek until she drew blood

"Bring down the wife. She ain't cooperating so lock her stupid ass up too," Simmy heard someone bark.

"These stupid ghetto bitches never tell. They'd rather leave their kids behind than give up their men. Look at this poor girl; warrant says she's fourteen and her mother's willing to leave her out here just to cover for her piece of shit husband. Fucking shame," another officer replied.

Simmy bounded off the couch when she saw her mother being forced down the stairs, but the officer quickly restrained her and Simmy had no choice but to sit back down. Her mother started squirming around with the handcuffs biting into her skin when she saw Simmy.

"Mom!" Simmy rushed toward the stairs, hoping to reach her this time. She didn't make it very far. She was hoisted up into the air, her legs swinging like a doll's.

"Sit down before I cuff you up and send you to juvie!" the officer warned her.

"Simmy, baby! I love you! Don't you ever forget it! I love you!" her mother screamed until two officers pushed her forward. Finally, she disappeared from Simmy's sight.

It seemed to Simmy like the officers were searching through her house for days. She had no idea what they were looking for. She kept hearing different detectives bark out commands.

"Take out that wall! Tear this fuckin' place up until we find all of the shit!" an officer yelled. Then he looked over at Simmy and smirked. "Your daddy is in a whole lot of trouble," he said with a sinister grin.

Simmy squeezed her eyes tight. She didn't want to look at his devilish blue eyes. To add to that, his shocking red hair made her think of a monster.

When she heard the officers axing down walls and cabinets to her left, her eyes popped right back open. All she could do was look on as they tore the house apart. The house her parents had worked so hard to get.

"Bingo, motherfuckers! We fucking got 'em! I knew we would find something. We always fucking do!" All the officers stopped and broke out in applause.

"All right, roll out!"

"Sir, Williams never showed up to get the girl," the cop who had been assigned to Simmy informed one of the detectives.

"All right, put her in the back of my car. I'll bring her to the precinct myself and make sure she gets placed in foster."

Once they had her in the back of the detective's police car, Simmy started sobbing to herself. She couldn't believe everything that had just happened.

Two days later, Mummy Pat was allowed to pick Simmy up from the foster care place, and they were allowed to make one last trip to Simmy's Long Island home to gather a few things. When Marcus pulled his car up to the house, Mummy Pat gasped and put her hands over her mouth. The front door was splintered like it had been hit a million times with an ax, or blown up with twenty sticks of dynamite. There were no locks left on it. When they walked up, and Mummy Pat gently pushed the door open, it practically came apart with pieces of wood falling. Simmy put her hands up to shield herself, and her uncle shoved Mummy Pat just in time to avoid the wood that dropped in her place. Marcus helped his mother through the doorway, being careful that she didn't slip or step on everything that was on the floor. There was glass, wall debris, and sheetrock all throughout the house. Mummy Pat put her hand over her mouth and clutched her chest like she couldn't breathe. She grabbed on to Marcus to keep herself up. Simmy's entire body became numb. Despite having witnessed the cops destroying the house, it still felt devastating to see it in the daylight.

"I can't believe they did all of this. I swear Mummy, them pigs is the biggest gang in America," Marcus had said.

"Oh, my God. They destroyed all of Chris's hard work and belongings. I mean, these evil people have left him with nothing," Mummy Pat said, tears running down her face. Mummy Pat reached out and grabbed Simmy's hand.

"My life is over!" Simmy screamed out, breaking free of her grandmother's grip and running through the mess toward the stairs. It looked like a tornado had hit the inside of her house. All of the furniture was either chopped up or thrown over. Simmy could hardly get up the steps; the entire winding banister had been broken into pieces, and wood splinters littered the carpeted stairs.

"What am I going to do without my parents!" Simmy screamed louder although she knew it was in vain. She slid on wood as she scrambled up the stairs. Her grandmother and uncle called after her, but she kept on going.

When she finally got up the stairs and ran through all of the sheetrock and plaster in the long hallway, she ran into the bathroom. She climbed into the only thing that seemed to have been left untouched: the Jacuzzi bathtub. She climbed into it and let all of the tears flow freely down her face like a river. Her pulse was racing so hard it felt like it was beating in the back of her throat. She decided she needed to see everything.

"Come here, Simone. It might be dangerous!" Mummy Pat called behind Simmy as she walked in and out of every room. Simmy didn't stop, though.

The family room was in an even worse condition than the rest of the house. The artwork that usually adorned their walls was sliced up, and the expensive gold and silver frames her mother had picked out were shattered into tiny shards. The wall right before you entered the bathroom had a huge hole in the center like someone had taken a sledgehammer to it.

She walked into the custom-built expansive closets her parents had designed, and she took in the scene. All of their clothes were on the floor of the walk-in closets. Their dresser drawers were emptied onto the floor, and the dresser had been hit down the middle and completely split in two. The dresser mirror lay shattered on the carpet in a million pieces. Two small pictures of Simmy were crumpled up nearby. Simmy stepped back out of the closet and walked around the room. She couldn't stop crying.

The mattress and box springs from her mother and father's bed were on the floor and cotton spilled from the middles like a gutted pig. Simmy had witnessed the total destruction of her house, her parents, and her entire life.

"Come here." Mummy Pat had finally grabbed Simmy into a tight embrace. "It's okay. I am here," she had comforted her.

"I'm going to find the safe. Chris said it had their life savings and all of the money you needed in case something ever happened to him," Marcus told Mummy Pat. Simmy had heard her parents talk about the safe when her father first had it installed. She remembered him saying something to her mother about putting in the safe and having his "attorney stash" in it.

Simmy watched Marcus scramble toward the closet for the safe. She could hear him kicking through debris, and she imagined him climbing through the piles of clothes and shoeboxes that littered the floor. She could literally hear her uncle falling and pushing stuff aside trying to locate the safe.

"Damn!" Marcus yelled from the closet.

Mummy Pat stood up and rushed to the doorway of the closet. Simmy was right behind her. They both watched as Marcus stood there shaking his head. Simmy could clearly see that the carpet had already been peeled back and the big hole in the floor that usually contained the safe was empty. The electronic hoist that controlled the safe coming up out of the floor was smashed to pieces, and the large Picasso painting that usually covered the switch for the hoist was also destroyed.

"Oh, Lord! What will happen to Chris now? If there's no money left, what will happen?" Mummy Pat cried, holding her chest again. Simmy couldn't stop herself from crying. Marcus just stood there shaking his head from side to side.

"Simmy, baby. Shh. It's going to be all right. Shhh," Mummy Pat walked over to her granddaughter and held her in a tight embrace.

Simmy and her grandmother stood there sobbing together for what seemed like an eternity. It seemed like a lifetime had passed before they'd finally gathered a few of Simmy's things. There wasn't much left, but they grabbed what they could: her favorite doll, some of her clothes, and a locket her father had given her.

By the time Marcus had pulled away from the house, Simmy's eyes were swollen, and her throat was sore. The house became smaller and smaller as her uncle drove farther down the street. Simone knew it would probably be the last time she'd ever see her house again.

"Wait! Stop! Stop the car!" she yelled out.

"We have to go, Simmy. There's nothing left there for you," her uncle explained.

"I can't go! I don't want to go! Stop the car! Please stop! Stop!"

"Stop! Please stop!" Simmy was flailing her arms wildly.

"Hey, hey! It's okay. Deep breaths."

Simmy opened her eyes and was face to face with a tan lady with honey blond hair. Simmy saw kindness in her eyes.

"Deep breaths, sweetie. Breathe in, and breathe out."

Simmy felt herself calming down. The lady's voice was peaceful and soothing. She realized she was in an ambulance. The back doors to the ambulance were open, and she could still see all of the commotion going on outside of the building.

"You passed out, and my partner carried you in here. You must have been having quite a dream." The lady smiled at Simmy, "I'm Jennifer. How are you feeling, sweetheart?"

"I'm feeling okay," Simmy replied. Her throat felt sore, probably from the screaming and crying she was doing before she passed out. She blinked away the horrible memories and hugged herself tightly. "Thank you for helping me, Jennifer. I really need to get going, though."

"Oh, sweetie, you really shouldn't get up just yet. Plus, I need your information so I can make a report for you."

"No, no, I don't need a report. Thank you. I must get going, or my mom will be worried sick about me," she lied.

The paramedic could tell something was up. "Look, sweetie, I don't know who you are or even what your name is, but something tells me that you have something to do with the mess going on over here with that drug bust. Is that your friend, or boyfriend who just got picked up?"

Simmy was somewhat listening to the paramedic. Her eyes were set on the van holding Kyan. She noticed that it was filled with more guys, some of whom Simmy recognized as Kyan's people.

"I'm sorry, Miss Jennifer." Simmy locked eyes with the paramedic.

"That's all right. This must be hard on you." She looked around to make sure no one was listening to their conversation before speaking again. "Not that you asked for my advice, but I'm going to give it to you anyway. You seem like a nice young lady, and you should be careful not to get caught up in all that mess. Now, I'm going to go grab something from my first aid kit that's over there by the tree. If you're not here when I get back, then I will have nothing to report to the police when they come." Jennifer winked at Simmy and walked over to the tree just as she had said she would.

Simmy got the hint and jumped out of the ambulance and ran without looking back. She ran until she was blocks away from Kyan's building. She was out of breath from running, and her heart was racing. She looked around trying to decide which direction to go in. She had no clue where to go from here.

What now? she asked herself. *What the fuck am I going to do now?*

Chapter 10

Out in the World

Simmy couldn't stop crying as she sat across from Kyan in the Rikers Island visit room, almost a week to the day after his arrest. She had found out that twelve of Kyan's people had been arrested the same day he was picked up. She couldn't care less about them, though. All she cared about was Kyan.

He put his hands on top of hers for the few seconds of physical contact allowed by the correction officers. "Shh. Don't cry, baby. It's all going to work out. Just trust me on this," Kyan comforted her, smiling although Simmy could see that it was a struggle.

She shook her head in despair. "I don't know. I just don't know. It's all over the newspapers, Kyan," Simmy cried, looking across the table at him. He averted his eyes like it was too hard to look at her.

"They're saying it's like some big conspiracy you're caught up in and that people were locked up in Brooklyn, Manhattan, and Queens. Like, twenty other people. They wrote something about RICO charges and criminal enterprises and black mafia groups. They said it was like some big drug network and that everybody is looking at a lot of time," Simmy said, her voice rising and falling with grief.

Kyan sighed. "Don't believe all that, Simone. I'ma be a'ight. They putting all that stuff out there in the media trying to scare people into snitching. That's all a mind game being played by the cops using the papers. That shit ain't gonna work. Our team is pretty solid. We have a plan for if this shit ever happened. Plus, we ain't do shit," Kyan said firmly. He said the end of his sentence a little louder hoping that the undercover officers the Department of Corrections usually planted in the visit rooms to listen in on inmates would hear his words, "We ain't do shit."

"What about a lawyer? Money? Your place? Do you need—"

Kyan put his hand up and smiled again. "Listen, baby. Didn't I just say for you to trust me? I haven't ever led you wrong. I got this. I'm good on all those fronts. I got people taking care of all of that. I want you to go see my man, the paper I gave you. He got it all covered." Kyan nodded toward her bag where she'd dropped his note.

Understanding washed over Simmy's expression. She wiped her tears away. She felt a little better when Kyan said he had people taking care of everything. She wished Jayla had been as prepared as Kyan was.

"My dude got you for a little bit. I want you to take what he gives you. Continue going to school, and make something good out of that beautiful mind of yours," Kyan said. "Plus, I'ma be home in a flash to pick up right where we left off."

Simmy started crying again. She couldn't even speak. She could see that he was trying to hold on to his optimism but, to her, something about his words and his tone seemed so final. It was like he knew something that she didn't know.

"When? When will you be home, Kyan?" Simmy cried.

"Soon. All I'm asking for is your loyalty, Simone. While you out in the world, just make sure you do the little things: take my calls, visit me until I get out of this, and check in on my moms and brothers, hit them off with some of what my man give you. I hear too many horror stories of dudes being abandoned in these situations. Just promise me you won't—"

"I won't," Simmy interrupted him. "I promise I won't abandon you. I promise on everything I love, Kyan. As long as I have breath in my body, I will be here for you."

Simmy waited five days and still hadn't heard anything back from Kyan's man, Doc. According to Kyan, Doc had the information Simmy needed to access Kyan's emergency stash, which, Kyan had said, in total should've been around a hundred stacks in several different places. Doc also had the information about the lawyer and all Simmy was supposed to do was take some of the cash and get it to the lawyer.

Simmy picked up the burner phone she'd purchased like Kyan had instructed, and she dialed Doc's number, for what seemed like the one hundredth time that week. Simmy took the phone from her ear and crinkled her face when an automated message said, "The number or code you've dialed is no longer in service."

"Fuck!" Simmy screamed, throwing her burner phone into the wall in Jayla's guestroom. "This dude got rid of his phone. He probably took Ky's money and bounced. How the hell am I supposed to find him now? I don't even know his real name," Simmy spoke out loud to herself. She felt like she was losing her mind. She paced in circles. Her eyes landed on the bed where a rent notice for the apartment, several more lawyers' names for Jayla, and Jayla's commissary information lay spread out. Simmy lifted her hands to her head at either side and squeezed her scalp. She had to think hard and fast.

"I can't keep sitting around here like this. I have to make some money," she grumbled, pacing again. With no Jayla and no Kyan, Simmy quickly realized that she'd been totally dependent on others to survive all of her life. She had gone from depending on her parents to Mummy Pat, to Jayla, and then to Kyan, but never on herself. Simmy felt like a failure in every sense of the word. Her shoulders slumped, and she hung her head. She was three weeks away from her eighteenth birthday, and it was time she grew up and started acting like an independent adult. She hadn't listened to Jayla when she had told her to save money, either. Simmy now regretted not having saved. In her defense, though, she didn't think she'd ever be in a position where she would need to rely on emergency money. Boy, was she wrong.

Simmy stormed out of the guestroom and into Jayla's bedroom. She yanked open Jayla's nightstand drawer and began frantically rummaging through it. Her hand landed on a Baggie. Simmy paused and picked it up. She held it up in front of her face and shook her head. "This fucking girl was really doing this shit on a regular," Simmy grumbled. She tossed the cocaine into the small garbage pail next to Jayla's bed. Then she rushed over and started searching through the nightstand on the other side of the bed and then Jayla's dresser.

"Argh!" Simmy yelled, frustrated when she didn't find any money. She walked over to the mirror connected to Jayla's dresser and looked at her reflection. She looked a mess. She had dark rings cropping up under her eyes, and her hair was in desperate need of a wash and set. Simmy stared at herself for a few seconds until something caught her eye. Stuck in the side of the mirror was a card. Simmy snatched it down and read it out loud.

"Luxury Babe High-end Consignment." Simmy flipped the card over. It read on the back of it: SEE CASSANDRA FOR PRICING. Simmy's heart jerked.

"This has to be who Jayla gets the list from. Cassandra is the one who pays for the stuff after we get it. She owns a consignment shop where she sells it. Makes perfect fucking sense," Simmy said to herself.

She rushed back into the guestroom and slid on her jeans, a Givenchy sweatshirt, and her Hunter tall rubber snow boots. She grabbed Jayla's long down North Face coat and her favorite of Jayla's Chanel boy bags.

Satisfied she looked the part, Simmy rushed out of the apartment. She was headed to see Cassandra. Simmy wanted her to know that she would be taking Jayla's place for a while.

Simmy was utterly shocked to find that Cassandra was a white woman. When the chubby, cherub-faced, Pillsbury Dough-woman wobbled from the back of the small store to meet her, Simmy couldn't get her mouth to close all the way. She even had to blink a few times to make sure she was seeing correctly. Simmy had assumed, based on the list requests, that Cassandra was some black chick who sold the items hot in the hood to all the girls and guys who wanted to be fly but couldn't really afford it.

"Hi. I'm Simone," Simmy introduced herself, and she extended her hand, but Cassandra didn't shake it. From the minute Cassandra laid eyes on Simmy, she seemed overly suspicious and cautious of her, like she suspected Simmy of being an undercover cop or a stick-up kid.

"So, tell me this again, Jayla sent you here to see me? Is that what you said when you called earlier?" Cassandra said, rubbing her double chin, while her eyes and eyebrows moved up and down seemingly on their own.

Simmy shifted her weight from one foot to the other and shoved her sweaty palms deep into the pockets of Jayla's down coat. It didn't matter how cold it was outside, Simmy's entire body was burning hot at that moment. "Um, yeah. She's, um . . . Jayla is a little sick. So that's why, um, she couldn't . . . I mean, she sent me. But, she said . . ." Simmy stuttered so badly even she couldn't keep track of what she was trying to say. She was kicking herself inside, knowing she sounded like a complete idiot. She'd always been a terrible liar, especially without Jayla there like usual to feed her the lines she needed to say.

"I don't do business with anyone but Jayla," Cassandra said flatly, set to turn her back on Simmy.

"Wait!" Simmy tightly grabbed Cassandra's thick, chunky arm, her fingers sinking into the woman's soft, meaty flesh. "Please. Please just hear me out." Simmy softened her tone, realizing from the look of terror on the woman's face what she'd done. Simmy quickly snatched her hand back and released her grip on Cassandra's arm.

"I'm sorry," Simmy said, putting her hands up to show she didn't mean any harm. "Listen. I'm really sorry. But, please just hear me out," Simmy said, lowering her eyes to her wringing hands. She swallowed hard. "You're right to be suspicious. And, you're right; Jayla didn't send me. Well, not exactly," Simmy said, coming clean.

Cassandra made a grunting nose and twisted her lips as if to say, "I knew it."

"But, Jayla is my cousin. That's the truth. And, I've been working with her. For months now. I was the one helping her get the stuff off the lists. The lists you give her with the orders. I don't think she would've been able to fill such big orders without me. I'm really good. I learned everything I know from Jayla."

Cassandra's scowl eased a bit, and one of her eyebrows went up. She stepped a few paces closer to Simmy like she wanted to hear more.

"The truth is, Jayla got locked up in New Jersey almost two months ago, and I need to work. I need to make money to help her get a lawyer and to keep her apartment until she gets out," Simmy said, choosing full disclosure over the deceit that had gotten her nowhere in the beginning. "I mean, I could go out there and boost the stuff.

I'm just as good at it as Jayla, but I wouldn't know the first thing about fencing it for cash. I don't need clothes, right now. I need cash. If you give me a chance, you will see. I can make good on my word."

"I don't know," Cassandra said tentatively. "You know, my lists are not easy. It's always the requests of some of my most well-off customers that I would give to Jayla. Most of what they request is high end, very high end," Cassandra said. "Anything else would be a waste of my time. I don't deal in petty stuff because it doesn't pay well. And, if the consignment customers don't pay me well, then I damn sure can't pay you well."

Simmy shook her head vigorously. "That's all I get when I go out there. All high end. All big names. Just like Jayla. I swear," she agreed, a bit too excited.

Cassandra seemed to contemplate what Simmy was saying. She sighed so hard, Simmy thought she'd blow her down.

"I'll give you this one chance to see how you do. But, if you don't deliver you'll be all out of chances with me. I definitely don't do second chances," Cassandra said firmly.

"I will deliver. I promise you I'll deliver and you will be very satisfied," Simmy swore, making a commitment even she wasn't sure she could keep.

Chapter 11

Stranger of Savior

Simmy got off the Long Island Railroad and caught an Uber to the Roosevelt Field Mall. It was the best she could do to get out there. She didn't have a license to rent a car and hike it all the way to Connecticut or Delaware, and she'd been too spooked to return to Short Hills, New Jersey. Jayla had taken Simmy to Roosevelt Field the very first time she'd taken her shopping. They hadn't stolen anything that day, but Simmy remembered the mall having nice high-end stuff, since she'd bought a bunch of things that trip.

"Can you be back around here in about an hour?" Simmy asked her Uber driver. "I'll pay extra for a ride out to Brooklyn. Whatever your price."

The driver assured Simmy that he could pick her back up in an hour, but he'd have to go off the call so it would be a few extra dollars. Simmy agreed. She was down to the last $1,500 of Jayla's money, all of which she had in a knot in her Gucci bag, just like Jayla had taught her.

"Just in case any of those store clerk bitches try to front on you, you can pull this out and make them feel like shit for hawking you. Once they see you really do have money, they'll leave you alone and run away, too scared they might get pulled up for harassing a legit, paying customer. I've had to set more than a few bitches straight in my time doing this." Jayla's exact words played in Simmy's head. She was ready.

Simmy exited the Uber car with her dark Chanel shades on, her head draped with a monogram Louis Vuitton scarf, and her kitted-out booster bags with the shoeboxes and demagnetizer she needed for the store alarms. She'd chosen a Gucci tote bag, just in case she came across something small she could slip into it.

Simmy had nearly memorized Cassandra's list: two Gucci ghost T-shirts, two pair of Christian Louboutin So Kates, any color, and a Valentino rock-stud clutch. The list seemed easy enough. Cassandra had said she wanted to start Simmy out with a short list to see how she'd do.

As soon as Simmy walked into Neiman Marcus, she went to work. She didn't have time to waste. Simmy walked into the Gucci section for the T-shirt first. She spent a little time browsing the handbags, then the shoes, before she traveled over to the clothes.

"Can I see these?" Simmy had summoned the salesgirl. She looked at Simmy's expensive clothes, her bag, and shades, and smiled at Simmy.

"Sure. They are our hottest new item," the salesgirl said as she rushed over to unlock the chain alarm that ran through the shirts and connected them to the rack. Simmy examined the shirts for a few minutes and, as soon as the salesgirl got distracted by another customer—a pretty girl Simmy couldn't help but notice—Simmy slipped the shirts into her bags and headed out of that section of the store.

Simmy shivered once she was in the clear. She couldn't lie; a funny feeling came over her at how easy it was to get those shirts. Almost too easy. It seemed like the pretty girl had just materialized out of nowhere to distract the salesclerk, just like Simmy and Jayla would've planned to do it. Simmy shook off the feeling. Maybe it was just a very lucky coincidence, she told herself. Simmy moved through the rest of the store on a mission.

***

She was almost finished getting everything on the list. She rode down the escalator clutching her bags, feeling good that she was almost done. Simmy was going to make Cassandra proud and be her new go-to girl.

Simmy stepped off the escalator, smiling. Her smile quickly faded when she heard it. It sounded like a stampede of wild elephants coming straight for her. "You! Don't move!" Then she felt hands grabbing on her bags and tugging her in different directions. Before Simmy could react, her bags had been snatched from her hands, and she was being wrestled to the floor.

"Wait. I didn't . . . I didn't do anything," Simmy cried out as she was roughly thrown down. No one said another word. Not even to tell her what she'd done wrong. She was pulled up from the floor. Her cheeks flamed over the gawking crowd of shoppers who had stopped shopping to see her get bagged.

"You have the wrong person. I have money," Simmy pleaded. "Just look in my pocketbook. I have money! I didn't do anything!"

"Well, you should've used it to buy all the merchandise you snuck into those bags," a fat white man dressed in plain clothes said snidely.

"Let me guess, you're here from the Brooklyn Zoo?" another man said, holding on to Simmy's left arm while a female held on to her right.

"That's usually who we get out here stealing. All of the animals from Brooklyn. Can't stay in your own fucking hood. Always got to come out here and fuck up our peaceful neighborhoods, don't you?"

Simmy hung her head. "I didn't do anything. I have money," she whimpered. No one listened. No one cared. It was all over now. She was no better than Jayla or Kyan, and now neither of them would have her on the outside to help them. She had failed them both.

"Jones!"

The correction officer's booming voice startled Simmy. She stood up from the floor where she'd taken up residence sitting in a corner with her knees to her chest for the seven hours since she'd been transported to the Nassau County central booking lockup cell. Simmy stretched and tried to work the kinks out of her numb butt cheeks and her stiff legs.

"Let's go, Jones," the officer demanded, using his keys to open the cell.

Simmy stepped out, her eyes wide and wild. "Where?"

"Be quiet and don't ask no gotdamn questions," the officer barked.

Simmy snapped her lips shut.

The officer grabbed her arm roughly. "Follow me and don't talk. I got a headache, and I don't want to hear your fucking mouth."

Simmy was led through a series of doors and hallways until finally, she was standing in a small room in front of a video monitor watching a judge.

"Are you Simone Jones? Date of birth, February 27, 1998?" the judge asked.

Simmy nodded her head. She looked over her shoulder and then at the ceiling, wondering how the judge knew she was there.

"No, Miss Jones, you have to speak your answers and loud enough for the monitor's speakers and the court reporter to pick it up. So, no nodding. I need to hear your answers loud and clear," the judge chastised her.

"Yes, I . . . I'm Simone Jones," Simmy said, still bewildered.

"I am a magistrate, which is different from a judge. I am the person who determines if your charges are serious enough to keep you or let you go before such time as you'd see a district judge. Do you understand that, Ms. Jones?"

Simmy didn't really know what the hell it all meant, but she wanted to go home, so she just agreed. "Yes," Simmy spoke up this time.

"It is my understanding you've been arrested and charged with grand larceny. It is also my understanding this is your first offense and that you are younger than eighteen; however, you are seventeen and just weeks away from your eighteenth birthday, which is old enough to be seen as an adult in the County of Nassau, should we so choose to move forward with the charges," the judge droned on in a monotone voice, like she'd said those same lines a million times.

"Um, I guess. I mean, sorry. Yes," Simmy agreed.

"It is my understanding that someone has come forward and offered to pay the County of Nassau a fine amount equal to or greater than the sum total of the merchandise you stole. That fine amount is $5,692."

What? Someone came forward to pay a fine? Simmy repeated in her head. Simmy didn't know what to say to that. But, something told her to just say, "Yes."

"Ms. Jones, I will accept the fine payment as sufficient enough to let you go today. But, I will do so only on one condition," the judge said.

Simmy stared at the screen.

"I am warning you never to come back to the County of Nassau to steal again, Ms. Jones. We will place your picture in the establishment you stole from, and you are banned from their property for a term of three years. Which means you are not allowed back, not even if you're just there to browse. Do you understand that if you return to the County of Nassau and commit a crime, you will be arrested and held without the option to simply pay a fine and walk like you're doing today?"

"Yes."

"Released with final payment of the fine. Next."

Simmy's shoulders slumped with relief, and she let out a long, cleansing breath. The anticipation of getting out of there had her knees knocking together.

The officer led Simmy back through another maze of doors and hallways until they came to a large room crowded with desks and chairs. There were several women behind the desks, some typing, some on the phone, some speaking to people in front of their desks.

"Sit down and wait for someone to call you to process you out," the officer told her, pushing her down into a hard waiting room chair. "And stay the fuck out of Nassau County, idiot."

Simmy shook her head. Those officers acted so tough when they were behind those walls, but they were really little bitch-ass punks when that uniform came off.

Simmy looked around trying to figure out how, out of the blue, her fine had gotten paid. Her mind raced with several possibilities. Maybe Doc had finally come through? No. That didn't make sense. He hadn't even called her back to give her Kyan's stash; plus, he wouldn't know she was out there anyway. It couldn't have been Cassandra either. Simmy hadn't told Cassandra where she was going to get the stuff from and, besides, as mean as that lady was, she would not be paying to get Simmy out. Kyan was locked up still, and so was Jayla. They had no way of knowing she was out on a mission. No one in Mummy Pat's house cared enough about Simmy to put up that kind of money knowing they'd never get it back. Besides, she hadn't spoken to any of her family since the Jalissa incident.

Finally, an older black woman with long blond crochet braids and smooth mocha skin called Simmy to her desk.

"Have a seat," the lady said, pointing to another waiting room–style chair at the side of the desk. "Date of birth. Address. Phone number."

Simmy gave the woman Jayla's address and her own cell phone number. The woman pecked a few keys on her computer keyboard and tapped her front tooth with her pen as she waited for something to print from the small, boxy printer sitting on the far left corner of her desk.

"Sign here. This is your receipt for payment of the fine. Page two is stating that you agree to the terms of this release."

Simmy picked up a pen and scanned over the paperwork. She didn't want to take too long and risk them pulling it back and taking her back to jail. Even after Simmy had signed the papers and given them back to the woman, she still hadn't been able to see who'd paid the money.

"I am going to return your property now," the woman said, pulling out the tagged bags that held Simmy's things. The woman set them on the desk, and Simmy reached for them. The woman put her hand on top of Simmy's.

"It is none of my business, sweetheart," the woman said.

Simmy paused and looked deep into the woman's eyes.

"But, you should consider yourself lucky. You are a beautiful young girl with your whole future ahead of you. Don't waste it like this. I see them start off young and pretty like you and they come through here over and over again until they look horrible and have no other choice but to stay stuck in the system. That's what these white folks want, honey. They want us to have records so we can't get ahead. Be smart. Go to school. This stuff, it ain't worth it." She gave Simmy a warm, motherly smile.

Simmy smiled back. "Thank you." That was all she could say. She knew that the woman was right. The paramedic who helped her the day Kyan was arrested sprang to mind. She had pretty much told her the same thing as this lady. She wondered if maybe God was trying to tell her something.

As much as she wanted to lead normal life, that just wasn't something she could do right now. Her desire didn't change the fact that she needed money to survive on her own and to help Kyan and Jayla. There was no way she would walk away from them and leave them caught up in the system. The system had already claimed her parents and left her feeling like an orphan. What other way was she supposed to survive? Simmy guessed that was all part of the white folks' plans too: devastate the black family by removing the parents and you leave entire communities failing. In her case, it was definitely ringing true.

After Simmy got her property back, the first thing she did was dig down into her bag. She closed her eyes and whispered, "Thank you," when she verified that Jayla's money was still there just like she'd left it.

"That's all, Miss Jones. Good luck," the lady said, finally dismissing Simmy.

Simmy stepped through the door and into a crowded hallway. She was dazed and confused, and she was sure she probably resembled a baby deer standing in oncoming traffic.

There were people posted up around the walls, people on cell phones sounding like they were trying to figure things out for their locked-up loved ones, and some just sitting, wearing that desperate look of misery.

Simmy wanted to get home. This, just like her entire life lately, had played out like her worst nightmare. Simmy headed for the exit but paused when she heard her name.

"Simone? Simone Jones?"

Simmy spun around so fast she almost toppled over. Her eyebrows dipped into the center of her face as her head whipped around. Who would know her out there to be calling her name?

"Right here. Over here."

Simmy's face really contorted in confusion now when she saw who had called out her name. A tall, gorgeous dude with smooth caramel skin, a close-cut fade that was perfectly lined up, and a neatly trimmed goatee was walking toward her wearing a smooth grin like he'd known her all of their lives.

"Simone Jones." He chuckled.

"Do I know you?" Simmy asked, her tone so low she was half whispering.

"Not yet. But you will soon," the dude said, extending his hand to her. "I'm Alex. Nice to meet you in person."

Simmy squinted, and suddenly she remembered seeing him in the store before she got bagged. He had been walking with the pretty girl who'd helped Simmy get those Gucci T-shirts.

"Simone," Simmy said, shaking his hand weakly. "But, I guess you already know that since you screamed out my whole government just now."

Alex laughed. "I was the one who paid your fine for you, sweetheart. I definitely know your name."

"But why? Why did you pay it? You don't even know me," Simmy said, suspicion in her tone. She didn't know whether to regard him as a stranger or a savior.

"Well, let's just say I knew of you for a while," Alex told her. "I know people you know and people who know you," he said cryptically, then laughed. It was a weasel laugh that you'd expect a conman to have. It definitely didn't go with Alex's handsome face.

Simmy tilted her head. "Know me?" She chuckled nervously, although she didn't find it funny. She shook her head side to side. "That's impossible. I don't know many people."

"Well, I know your cousin Jayla," Alex finally revealed. "So I guess you could say I know you by association. I'm surprised she never mentioned me. We kind of go way back." Alex smiled and looked like he was recalling some wonderful memories in his mind.

Simmy's scowl eased, and her shoulders relaxed. "But, Jayla didn't know I got bagged. So how did you?"

"I just happened to be around today, and I recognized you. Y'all came to the club a few times, and I could never forget a gorgeous face like yours. I guess it's a lucky thing for you that I always remember a pretty face."

Simmy relaxed even more now. Any friend of Jayla's could definitely be a friend of hers, especially at a time like this. Simmy's eyes drank Alex in. He was older than her; she estimated he had to be in his mid to late twenties. She settled on twenty-seven as his age. She took a quick inventory of his wears: Rolex watch, Balmain jeans, Buschemi boots, Moncler coat. Definitely somebody who might run in the same circles as Jayla.

"Thank you for paying that fine. I swear, I'll pay you back," Simmy said.

"Nah, I'm not looking for you to pay me back. Take that as a gift," Alex said, parting a sly grin.

Simmy blushed and shifted on her feet. She couldn't help but be attracted to him. Any woman with eyes would've been.

"I tell you what; let me give you a ride back to the city. We can agree to stay in touch. You know, so I can check up on Jayla from time to time."

"That's cool," Simmy agreed. Right away a pang of guilt stabbed through her gut and Kyan's handsome face popped into her mind. Simmy tried to convince herself she wasn't really attracted to Alex and that she was just being polite since he'd done her a big favor.

"Good. Then let's get the hell out of this prejudiced-ass Nassau County," Alex said, pushing the door open for her.

Simmy tried not to look too impressed with Alex's gleaming white 2015 Range Rover, but she couldn't lie; the vehicle was the epitome of luxury. The huge low-profile tires with the matching white rims inside gave the vehicle that extra something that said, "I'm lit. Notice me."

Alex was a perfect gentleman and opened the passenger side door for Simmy. Kyan always opened the door for her too. Unbeknownst to both men, the gesture struck a chord with her because it was something else her father had always warned her about. *"If a man doesn't open the car door for you to get in and out, don't you ever think of dating him. It means he doesn't value you or women in general."* Her father had preached that from the time she was a little girl. Simmy was secretly happy that Alex had opened the car door for her.

"So, you just go around paying fines for girls and getting them out of lockup?" Simmy asked, laughing. "I mean, I'm not being ungrateful or anything, but I'm just saying, it is kind of strange."

Alex got comfortable behind the steering wheel of his ride and exhaled.

He laughed too. "Here you go again, looking a gift horse in the mouth," he said, shaking his head, still smiling. "Nah, I don't go around trolling jails for pretty girls like you who get themselves knocked but, like I said before, it was lucky for you I peeped game and saw those plainclothes mu'fuckas tailing you through the store all day. I don't know how you ain't notice them. You must've been on a crazy mission, too focused on getting your shit that you did not see them. Either that or you're just that much of an amateur. They were obvious as shit. Man, I wanted to tell you before they got you, but I guess I wasn't fast enough," Alex said smoothly. "When I saw them running toward you, I was like, 'Damn, baby girl got pinched. Now I'm gonna have to help a sister out.'

They even gave me a hard time with that. I had to do a bunch of paying just to find out your information to pay the damn fine."

Simmy was quiet for a few minutes. She thought about what he said. Simmy didn't know if she was lucky or if it wasn't a coincidence at all. She shook off the suspicious thoughts. She was just grateful she was out. She couldn't imagine what Kyan would think if he had to hear that she'd been locked up for boosting after he'd warned her about going back to doing that.

"It was my first time being out there by myself. Me and Jayla usually tag team and work off of each other. But, I guess you already know Jayla ain't around right now. I needed money, so I took the chance," Simmy confessed, immediately feeling like she'd said too much.

"Yeah, I could tell you wasn't used to being alone. I could also tell you still fucking with Jayla's style and that old-fashioned shit she be on. I tried to tell that girl there's a whole new world of hustle out there. But Jayla is hard-headed," Alex said. He looked over at Simmy, seemingly gauging her reaction.

"Old-fashioned? You think having bags that disable the sensors is old-fashioned? Jayla got that stuff down to a science. Trust me, she may be hardheaded like you said, but she's the best at her craft."

"Baby girl, let me tell you something. Boosting is old-fashioned. Period. I'm saying, why be sneaking and putting shit up your back, down your pants, and in foil-lined bags—one of the oldest tricks in the book, by the way—when you can just walk right up to the counters and buy shit like them white folks do it?"

Simmy crinkled her brow. "Well, that takes money."

"Or credit cards," Alex said. "C'mon, young'un, there's another way to get your hustle on. It's much easier, smoother, and pays a hell of a lot better. Shit, there's a few different ways to make real money out here these days, but that's just an example of how easy it could be," Alex said.

Simmy sat up a little straighter in the passenger seat and turned slightly toward Alex. Her ears were tuned in to his every word. Especially if he was talking about a way to make money.

"Ah. Now you're getting interested. I'm glad I finally have your attention."

"Hell, yeah," Simmy answered a little too quickly. All she could think about was making money to stay afloat and help her people out. Alex didn't have to know all of that, though. Besides, she didn't know him like that anyway.

"A'ight. If you really interested, come to the club tomorrow night and we'll talk. Ain't no better way to get to know someone than to party with them a little bit. That's how I got to know Jayla so well," Alex said, then he smiled and bopped his head. "Good ol' Jayla. Mmm. Mmmm. Mmm."

Simmy didn't ask any questions about his dealings with Jayla. She didn't really care. Right now she was in a situation, and he sounded like the person who could turn that situation around. Simmy promised herself that once she found out the details from Alex, made a little money, and paid him back for the fine amount, she would tell Alex that she had a boyfriend. Then she'd walk away. Free and clear. That was her plan, anyway. Simmy didn't know it then, but even the best thought-out plans sometimes go left.

Chapter 12

Part of the Family

Simmy looked over her shoulder at her reflection in Jayla's silver-trimmed standing floor mirror. "Stomach looks fat? Hmm. I don't know about this dress," she mumbled, switching positions so she could look at herself from another angle. She turned around and eyed all of the expensive outfits she had laid out on Jayla's bed. Some of the high-end pieces belonged to Simmy, but most belonged to Jayla.

Simmy sighed. She turned and looked at her ass in the turquoise Hervé Léger bandage dress one more time. "Nah, this is not the right one for me for tonight. Too 'come fuck me'-ish," she said before she slid out of the turquoise dress.

She walked over to the bed and scanned the items. "Maybe this one." She picked up a white deep-plunge Roberto Cavalli dress that still had the tags on it. She held it up to her body and turned to the mirror.

"This might be the one," Simmy said, liking how the white glowed against her skin. She put the dress on, and it fit her so perfect. It looked as if it were tailor-made for her the way it hugged her in all the right places. She was finally satisfied she looked old enough and sexy enough to hang with Alex.

Simmy had gone a few hours earlier and spent money to have her face professionally beat at the MAC counter down on 125th Street. She leaned closer to the mirror to apply another coat of deep burgundy lipstick. She smacked her lips together and stood back to examine herself again. Simmy loved a dark lip. There was something sophisticated about it. Simmy touched her loose curls to make sure they framed her face just right. She was stunning and she knew it. Over the past months that she'd been spending time with Jayla, she had learned to appreciate her body and embrace her curves. It was like she had finally snapped out of her ugly duckling syndrome. She now had a confidence about her, and she felt good about herself.

"Kyan would fucking kill you if he knew you were out here primping like this for the next man. This shit ain't right, Simmy," she scolded herself; then she smiled. "Oh, well. You gotta do what you gotta do to make that paper. If he were here, you wouldn't have to be out here impressing another nigga to get put on. Or if his fake-ass man Doc had come through you would've never met the next man. How about that shit?"

All of that talking and Simmy still couldn't shake the guilty feeling that had crept into her mood. She knew why she was going to meet up with Alex at the club: to find out how she could make money. But something still felt sinister about it all. She still felt like she was somehow being disloyal to Kyan.

"I'm doing this all for you, baby," she said as she adjusted the dress to make sure it would all stay in place. She blew a kiss in the wind as she thought of Kyan.

Simmy slid into a pair of Jayla's purple, aqua green, and silver peacock feather vintage Gucci stilettos. It was great that they had the same shoe size and were the same size in clothes, too. Both cousins had that Coke-bottle shape that their grandmother had blessed them with. She grabbed Jayla's deep purple and silver python-skin

Chanel classic jumbo bag. She turned around and examined herself one last time in the mirror. She shook her head up and down.

"You are a bad bitch, Simone Jones. Who knew you could put it together like this?"

Simmy knew Jayla would've been proud of her for the ensemble. It was, as Jayla would say, just the right amount of classy and flashy. Simmy thought she could get used to dressing up like this just to hang out. But, she also knew that these types of wears took a steady flow of funds.

Simmy looked down at Jayla's diamond-encrusted Rolex gleaming from her wrist. "Shit." She rushed through the apartment. She had about six minutes to get downstairs. Alex said he was sending a car to pick her up so that she wouldn't have to take an Uber and, more importantly, so she wouldn't have to stand in line outside of the club. Alex had promised her that everything with him was straight VIP treatment. Simmy couldn't wait to find out if everything he'd said was true.

Just then, her phone rang. She looked down and saw that it was Alex. "Hello?" she answered inquisitively.

"Hi, beautiful. You ready?" Alex said into the phone.

Simmy couldn't help but take notice of how sexy he sounded over the phone. And, again, that pang of guilt struck her in the back of her mind. "Yes, I am ready." She took a deep breath. "As ready as I'll ever be."

"Excellent. I have a car waiting for you outside already. I'll see you soon." He hung up before Simmy even had a chance to respond to anything.

She grabbed her purse and headed downstairs. *Destiny awaits.*

"Damn," Simmy gasped as the car pulled up outside of the club. It was absolutely packed out there with people.

There was a big crowd in front of the club but also a line snaking along the side of the building and wrapping around the corner. "It's serious out here tonight. Who the hell gonna be here? Jay-Z and Beyoncé? This place is packed out." She was talking to the driver, but he didn't say a word to her.

Simmy spotted Alex in front, posted up outside of his Range Rover with a group of dudes and small clique of chicks. Even from a distance, Simmy could see that Alex looked good as hell in a deep blue suede jacket, a simple white Balmain T-shirt, a pair of neat, fitted jeans, and a pair of dark blue suede Louboutin hard bottoms. Alex's row of thick solid-gold Cuban link chains gave him a street edge although he was dressed up.

The car pulled up, and the driver got out, walked around the car, and opened the door to let Simmy out. As she put one leg out of the car and eased the rest of her body out sexily, she felt all eyes on her. Simmy wasn't used to this caliber of a crowd giving her that type of attention. Her cheeks burned under all of the gazes. Her nerves and the freezing cold air slapping at her bare legs had all of the hairs on her body standing at attention. Jayla's short chinchilla fur wrap wasn't helping Simmy's freezing legs and feet. Simmy was learning that the price of being beautiful was steep these days.

"You got this. You got this, Simmy. You're a bad bitch tonight. Don't act nervous. Act grown up." She gave herself a pep talk as she walked over, teeth chattering, to where Alex stood looking fine as hell.

"Hey," Simmy said, a completely involuntary goofy grin spreading over her trembling lips. She felt like an awkward school nerd walking up to a crowd of cool kids to ask if she could hang out with them.

"Ay, Simone. You made it," Alex said cheerfully. He opened his arms. Simmy stepped closer and, to her surprise, he pulled her in for a hug. It was awkward but, still, she smiled and reminded herself that this was what she had to do to get the money.

"Everybody, this is Simone," Alex introduced her. He pushed her forward like she was a prized possession he was bragging about. Simmy knew that her cheeks were red because she could feel her face filling with blood. The dudes in Alex's entourage, of course, smiled at her and welcomed her warmly. Some eyed her up and down like she was a piece of meat they were ready to eat. But, the chicks with Alex's group barely spoke. They eyed her up and down too, but in a way that said they wanted to see what she was wearing so that they could hate on her. A few of them even whispered and rolled their eyes at her.

"C'mon. Let's go inside. I was just waiting out here for my special guest," Alex said, throwing his arm around Simmy's shoulders.

Simmy couldn't lie to herself. Getting inside with that kind of special treatment felt hella good. She already liked everything about this new situation with Alex. She just hoped that the money was as good as the treatment.

Once they were inside, Simmy saw that, just like outside, the inside of the club was packed and jumping. There were two floors, and each floor had a DJ. The crowd wasn't afraid to dance, either. Simmy loved seeing how the dance floor downstairs was packed with swaying bodies. Alex reached his arm back, grabbed Simmy's hand, and pulled her along as she followed him through the sea of people. Simmy couldn't say that having him hold her hand didn't kind of make her feel special. Especially since, as they walked through, there were so many chicks trying to get his attention. Simmy fielded their glares and knew they all wished they could be in her place at that moment.

Once Alex stopped at the entrance to the VIP section, it was like the president or some important dignitary had arrived. The security smiled and exchanged daps with Alex and moved aside so that he, Simmy, and his entire entourage were allowed beyond the velvet ropes. The waitresses inside the VIP section seemed to have been awaiting Alex's arrival. They all rushed toward him wearing smiles so big their teeth glowed in the dim purple lights. Alex and Simmy were escorted over to the biggest of the seats inside. When Simmy stepped up to Alex's specially reserved table, she tried to play it cool, but it wasn't working very well. She had never had the privilege of hanging out in VIP, so this was all new to her, and she was awestruck. She always had fun when she went clubbing with Jayla, but they had never partied in VIP. This was all new to Simmy, and she'd be lying if she said she wasn't liking it so far.

Simmy's eyes stayed wide like a kid at Christmas as Alex invited her to get comfortable on the beautiful white leather wraparound couch that he called his "personal seat." It was probably her young age, but Simmy wanted to take out her iPhone and snap pictures of everything. She didn't think anyone her age would believe her otherwise. From the tables filled with at least twenty expensive bottles of premium liquors and champagnes—gold bottles of Ace of Spades, the top-shelf Luc Belaire Rare Rose, Moët, and Dom Pérignon to name a few—to the extremely well dressed, beautiful, exotic women who shared the space with them, to the handfuls of cash being moved around right under Simmy's nose, she was overwhelmingly impressed. She cheered herself on silently that she'd been smart enough to take Alex up on his offer.

"Here, have a drink," Alex offered and handed Simmy a flute filled with Ace of Spades. Simmy became nervous thinking of what excuse she was going to tell him. She didn't feel comfortable drinking without Jayla. Her cousin was the only person she had ever drunk around. She started to refuse and tell him that she didn't drink, but she didn't want to be viewed as a party pooper or, worse, she didn't want Alex to think she was a stupid little girl. She smiled and took the flute. "Thank you." She raised it in the air and smiled. She took a sip and wanted to spit it out but, instead, she forced the nasty liquid down. It burned her throat. Simmy didn't know how people drank that stuff.

"You having a good time so far?" Alex asked her.

"Yeah. Thanks for inviting me. It's really nice," Simmy yelled into his ear over the music. "I'm definitely impressed."

Just then three bottle service girls wearing black lace leotards and black fishnet stockings sauntered into the section carrying six more expensive bottles of liquor with sparklers lit up at the tops. Simmy's eye lit up. Jayla had told her that buying bottles in the club started at $300 for the cheapest bottle and could go all the way up to $1,000 per bottle. Everything Simmy had heard about in rap songs and saw in rap videos she was living at that moment.

Alex slid his hand down, put it on her knee, and squeezed. "I'm glad you came. I love showing you a good time. You can enjoy this all of the time," he said, moving his hand a little farther up her leg until it rested on her inner thigh.

Simmy's stomach clenched, and she squeezed her legs together. She acted like she was getting something from her bag and shifted away a few inches so that Alex's hand fell off of her leg.

"Sorry, excuse me," Simmy said awkwardly. Moving didn't stop Alex. He inched closer to her and this time threw his arm around her shoulders and forced her even closer to him. He leaned his face close to her ear. "You look fucking amazing tonight. All grown up and sexy as shit," he whispered in her ear.

His hot breath sent an uncomfortable tingle down Simmy's back. She swallowed the hard lump that had suddenly lodged in her throat. "Tha . . . thank you," she stammered, shifting in the seat. This definitely wasn't what she'd come there for.

Simmy could see a few of the beautiful women across from where she and Alex sat leaning over to one another and whispering and then glaring in her direction. Simmy shifted some more, again trying to get out from under Alex's hold. She didn't like him touching her like that. She thought about Kyan again, and her heart started racing. She needed to get the information and get the hell out of there.

"So, about that thing we talked about," Simmy said, moving a little farther away from Alex, pretending she moved so she could look at his face to talk to him. She kind of wanted to get to the point now.

"What?" Alex seemed to play dumb at first.

"The thing you invited me here to talk about. You know, the change in the way I do things, changing my old-fashioned way of getting money," Simmy reminded him, a hint of annoyance in her tone.

"Oh, you mean, how we talked about using credit cards instead of stuffing shit into booster bags? Yes, we need to talk about how you could be going to the register and hitting them with a credit card and straight paying for your shit," Alex said, laughing. He picked up his flute of expensive champagne. "Ain't nothing special about it, baby girl. You just do it." He raised his glass at her and then put it to his mouth and drank the flute clean in one gulp.

"Are the cards stolen or something?" Simmy pressed. She tapped her foot impatiently. She didn't like that Alex wasn't getting to the point. He knew why she'd come there, so why was he playing games?

Alex picked up another flute full of champagne. "Look, why don't you just have a good time tonight? Enjoy the party, the free liquor, and the company—my company. If you're really down, I'll send you out with some of the girls in my network tomorrow. Trust me, they'll break it down to you and show you how to work all angles. You'll be making money in no time," Alex said.

Simmy's shoulders flopped, and her corners of her mouth turned down with disappointment.

"Stop being so uptight. Relax and enjoy this lifestyle, young'un. Isn't your birthday coming up in less than two weeks?"

"Yes, it is," Simmy replied, surprised that he knew that much.

"Well, consider this an early birthday present from me to celebrate you turning eighteen. You only live once. YOLO," Alex told her. Then he laughed. There was the weasel laugh again. This time it made Simmy cringe. With everything going on, her birthday was the last thing on her mind right now, and she was a little irked that Alex was making her wait on getting the job information.

"A'ight, tomorrow then," Simmy relented, still uncomfortable with how close he was to her. "I need to go to the restroom," Simmy said, unhooking his arm from around her shoulders. She didn't really have to go, but she did want to get from under Alex.

"Dina!" Alex called to one of the scowling chicks across the room. The pretty girl said something to her clique and then sauntered over.

"This is Simmy. She's a part of the family now. Show her to the restroom. I need to make sure she's good at all times. She got a lot of potential. I wouldn't want her to forget her way back to us," Alex said. He was talking to the girl, Dina, but looking directly at Simmy.

Dina nodded like an obedient soldier. "I'll show you," Dina said to Simmy.

Simmy laughed a little. "It's okay. I'm a big girl. I think I'm okay to go to the bathroom alone," Simmy said, more to Alex than the girl.

"Just go with her," Alex told Dina, totally ignoring what Simmy had just said.

Simmy thought that the whole master and servant type of scene with Dina and Alex was strange. Simmy also thought his comment about her forgetting her way back to them, like she was going to run away, was strange. The fact that he thought she needed to be watched made her a little uneasy. But, once again, Simmy chose to ignore her gut feelings. She was desperate to make quick money, so she had to roll with the punches at this point. She just kept telling herself this was something she had to do. This was the only chance she had at making some real money.

At the end of the night, Alex said his good-byes and made his rounds through the VIP section, slapping fives and chest bumping with dudes and getting pecks on the cheeks from chicks. Simmy stood aside and watched. She wanted to be home and in her own bed already. Simmy had tried to leave at least six times that night, but Alex wasn't having it. He'd told Simmy to wait for him and he would give her a ride back to Jayla's place. He used her safety as a ploy to keep her there, and since Simmy had never been to the club alone or had to go home alone at the end of a night, she took his word for it.

When he was done acting like a movie star waving and kissing his way toward the exit, Alex led Simmy out of the club to his waiting SUV out front. He opened the passenger side door for her and, just as she was about to get in, she heard someone yelling out to Alex.

"Alex! Alex! Wait a damn minute, Alex!"

Simmy heard a woman's booming voice coming from her left. She paused and turned around. *Not this again.* A quick flash of that crazy day with Kyan and Ava went through Simmy's mind.

A beautiful girl stormed toward Alex and Simmy, her face folded into an evil grimace. She was coming fast and furious. Simmy squinted. She hadn't remembered seeing this girl in the club or with Alex's network of chicks. The girl was dressed in a pretty sequined minidress and a pair of Sophia Webster Chiara butterfly sandals like she had just left the party. But, Simmy was sure she hadn't seen her inside. She would've definitely remembered this girl.

Simmy stared at her as she got closer, dumbfounded for a minute. *Damn. She looks like she could be my older sister,* Simmy thought as the girl got right up on her and Alex. The girl bore a striking resemblance to Simmy. In fact, she had the exact honey complexion, long, dark hair, and hourglass build. She looked like an older version of Simmy.

"Alex! Are you serious right now? This is the thanks I get? I've been trying to reach you all night! I'm out here working for you and you out here doing this?"

Simmy clutched her bag and was immediately on the defensive. Clearly, the girl had the wrong idea, and she looked like she came to fight. If confronted directly, Simmy was prepared to tell this chick that she wasn't trying to get with Alex if that's what she was thinking and that this was all about business for her. Simmy would let the girl know she simply wanted to get to the money. She didn't want to have to take out her pepper spray and go to work.

"Ay. Vee, what's up?" Alex sang nonchalantly like he didn't notice that the girl appeared ready to attack. "I thought you would've been here earlier. You must've been working hard. I missed you tonight."

"Don't fucking try to play me, Alex! What is this?" the girl asked, pointing at Simmy like she was a thing and not a person.

Simmy wanted so badly to tell the girl that she was a woman, not a "this." She thought better of making an already contentious situation worse. Besides, Simmy found it amusing that this older chick was feeling insecure or threatened by her. It kind of made her feel powerful.

"Veronica, don't start this bullshit. I already told you about her. This is Simone. Last week, Nassau County," Alex said like the girl was dumb for not remembering.

Wait, they talked about me?

The girl's face didn't ease any. "Oh, really, Alex? You made it seem like she was some desperate, young girl, not this," Veronica snapped, looking Simmy up and down again.

She got one more time to refer to me as "this," Simmy thought, tapping her foot and blowing out heavily. She climbed into Alex's passenger seat and closed the door. She didn't want to hear or see anything else going on with Alex and his girl or whatever she was to him. Their issue had nothing to do with her and was none of her business. She thought it'd be best for her to just get in the car and wait to be taken home before she heard that woman say one more rude thing about her. She knew she was liable to punch Veronica in the face if she didn't remove herself from the situation. Unfortunately, though, Simmy could still hear everything Alex and Veronica were barking at one another.

"C'mon, Vee. Get off this already. You always acting jealous when a pretty one comes in the family. That shit is getting old now. Stop bugging," Alex said, waving at Veronica like she was being stupid.

Veronica folded her arms across her heaving chest. "Just remember who made me like this, Alex. Just fucking remember how much I've been through with you. I'm always the one who gets played in the fucking end, Alex," she pouted.

Simmy thought Veronica looked on the verge of tears. She would never let herself be made to look crazy in front of a crowd like that. She would never be that girl looking stupid chasing down her man at all hours of the night. Simmy shook her head in disgust. *Better her than me.*

"Man, listen. Get over the past. Stop holding on to that shit. It's giving you wrinkles," Alex said facetiously. "Now. Come over here," he said, tugging on his passenger door and opening it, "and meet Simone. She's part of the family now, and you're going to teach her everything she needs to know about the business. Like I told you already, she got a lot of potential." Alex grinned.

Then he turned toward Simmy and winked. "Simone, this is Veronica. She's one of my more seasoned workers and very good at what she does. She's going to train you and show you the ropes of the business, inside and out. And, Don't worry, you'll get used to her attitude and her antics. She's a little jealous because she's an old head now and young girls like you make her feel threatened." Alex laughed, but Simmy and Veronica didn't. The two women stared at each other for a few uncomfortable seconds.

"Nice to meet you, Veronica," Simmy said, nodding.

Veronica didn't say anything. She turned toward Alex and squinted her eyes. "You're going to get enough of using me. One of these days you're going to turn around and I'll be fucking gone," Veronica spat.

Alex laughed. "Yeah, a'ight, Vee, whatever you say. Until that day you work for me. Remember that. Be ready to start training this young'un very soon. I'll hit your phone with instructions." With that, Alex walked around to the driver's side and climbed into his SUV, leaving Veronica standing there brooding.

Simmy hoped this chance meeting hadn't set the tone for the rest of her dealings with Veronica, especially if she would have to depend on Veronica to get her to the money.

Chapter 13

Training Day

It took Alex two days to call Simmy. She spent two uncomfortable days of worrying, pacing, and going crazy about whether he'd call so that she could learn his method of making money. When he finally contacted her, Simmy had tossed and turned all night, anxious. She was ready bright and early the next day waiting for him. When Alex pulled up in front of Jayla's building to pick her up, Simmy's smile faded when she saw Veronica perched in the front passenger seat. *Not this crazy chick again.* She respectfully climbed into the back and played her position.

"Hey," Simmy said with fake cheerfulness as she got into the car.

"What's up, young'un?" Alex greeted her. "You looking bright-eyed and bushy-tailed this fine day," he said, smiling as he winked at her through the rearview mirror.

Veronica didn't say a word. Simmy shifted uncomfortably in the seat as Alex pulled out from where he was parked. She could already tell it was starting off to be a rough day.

"First, I'm going to take you to get some pictures taken by my man in Brooklyn," Alex announced. "He's my ID guy. He's the fucking best."

"Okay," Simmy replied apprehensively. *Pictures? ID guy?* Her mind raced. She didn't ask any questions, though. She would not rock the boat at all. She was there to learn.

"Then, you'll be ready to hit the ground running. How much money you make out there depends on how well you do, how smart you are, and how much you can level up. I think you're smart, Simone. So, I think you'll do fine."

Simmy just nodded. She sure hoped Alex was right.

Alex, Simmy, and Veronica rode to Brooklyn without saying another word to each other. When they pulled up in East New York, Simmy looked out of the window at the run-down little house they'd parked in front of, confused.

"This is it," Alex said. "I know it don't look like much, but that's the point," he said, noticing Simmy's crumpled facial expression. "Niggas gotta stay low-key to make it out here. Feel me?"

"Now you gotta explain everything to her?" Veronica grumbled.

They all exited the car and walked up to the little ramshackle house. Alex pounded on the dirty white door like he was the police. When the door swung open, Simmy was surprised to find a young kid standing on the other side. The boy looked to be no older than Simmy. He had a boney chest, a protruding Adam's apple that bobbed when he spoke, and the longest, skinniest arms Simmy had ever seen. Simmy thought he was more suited to be a water boy for a basketball team than anything else.

"Jeff," Alex sang, rushing into the skinny kid for a hug. "What it do, baby? You good? You know why I'm here. As usual, I need the hookup," Alex continued with his slick lingo as the kid allowed them all inside.

He's the ID guy? He looks like he's seventeen! Simmy couldn't believe it.

Jeff led the way, and Alex, Veronica, and Simmy trailed in a line down a long, dark hallway until they reached a door.

"Don't mind the mess," Jeff said, pushing the door in.

"Man, you say that same shit every time I come here." Alex laughed. "You're one of the smartest kids I know, but damn if your ass ain't junky as hell. That's from all that homeschooling. Shit, your mother turned you into a genius with these computers but a complete hoarding-ass hermit."

Jeff shrugged.

Simmy paused when she stepped inside. The space was cluttered from floor to ceiling with boxes, papers, magazines, books, and probably every type of computer and digital equipment that had ever been sold. There had to be at least fifty Apple computers set up on a back wall. There were big screens, smaller screens, and all sizes of laptops. There were digital cameras, high-resolution printers, professional-grade scanners, color copiers, video equipment, and even a plotter. You name it, Jeff had it in that little apartment. Even the kitchen had computer monitors set up. Simmy didn't even see a bed or a space that Jeff might have used to eat a decent meal in there. Jeff was clearly a computer geek who could probably hack into computers all over the world.

"So, what can I do for you, Alex?" Jeff asked.

"My man. Good ol' WikiLeaks," Alex sang, clapping his hand on Jeff's boney shoulder. "I need a driver's license and six new cards for my new girl Simone here. She's the newest member of the family."

Simmy couldn't stop gawking. She was literally in awe of what she was seeing. There were stacks of credit cards, passports, driver's licenses, Social Security cards, paystubs, and even college IDs on a long folding table against a wall. Simmy thought stuff like this only existed in the movies and on TV. Someone could literally come there and buy an entirely new identity. It was fascinating and scary at the same time.

"C'mon over," Jeff said to Simmy. He pointed to a white wall with a small piece of square blue material taped on it. "Stand in front of the blue square," Jeff instructed. "Don't smile." He took four pictures of Simmy.

"Okay, now sign here," Jeff said, passing Simmy a small, flat black machine with a tiny rectangular digital screen and a special pen to use to sign on the screen. Simmy scribbled her signature in the designated space.

"Okay, she's all set," Jeff told Alex.

"How long? And don't forget to apply my family discount. Shit, I been giving you mad business lately," Alex said all in the same breath.

"About thirty minutes," Jeff replied. "I would tell you to make yourself at home, but the way my clutter is set up . . ." he joked, emitting a snorting nerd laugh after.

Alex laughed. "That's all right, man. Just get that ID and them cards right. We'll be back in thirty. I'll have your money, too, with the discount applied."

Simmy had so many questions floating around in her head. *How old is Jeff? How did he become a counterfeit ID guy? How much does he charge? What if I get stopped with the fake stuff? Will the cops be able to tell?* But, she didn't dare ask one.

She listened to Veronica and Alex speak about which mall she would take Simmy to, how she would have Simmy dress, what names they would assign her, and how things would go. Simmy didn't utter a word. She felt like she was training with Jayla all over again with someone showing her how to dress, act, and get items. Despite how uncomfortable she felt though, again, she kept convincing herself that she was just trying to get to the money and this seemingly weird crew was going to help her get there.

Alex dropped Simmy and Veronica at Veronica's smoke gray Mercedes-Benz C350.

"Take care of her, Vee. I know you don't like her, but this benefits all of us," Alex whispered to Veronica. Simmy heard him.

Once inside the car, Simmy tried to lighten the tension between her and Veronica with small talk. "This is a really nice ride. I love this car," Simmy said in a soft voice.

"I'm sure you do," Veronica grumbled in response.

"How long have you been doing this stuff with the cards and IDs and stuff?" Simmy asked, ignoring Veronica's snide reply.

"Look, little girl. We don't have to do this. I don't need you trying to be friendly with me. I'm here to show you the job because Alex is forcing me to and I don't have much of a choice or say in it. This is a job for me so I can continue to feed myself. Outside of that, I don't want to get to know you. I have friends, and I don't need new ones," Veronica said flatly. Veronica had never been one to beat around the bush. She was a straight shooter.

Simmy sighed. At first, she was going to just shut up, but the little ticking time bomb of anger that was building inside of her finally went off.

"You're right, Veronica. We don't have to be friendly, but I was trying to be cordial because it's the mature thing to do. I don't know what your problem is with me considering you just met me but, to me, this whole being mad at me for no reason other than your own insecurity is stupid."

Veronica grunted. "No. Me having to take some little girl out, to me, is stupid."

"You don't even know why you don't like me. You don't know me. And, just so you know, I don't want Alex. If that's what you were thinking, you have it all wrong. I have a boyfriend. He's locked up right now, and I took this job so I can support myself and make money so I can help him. This is all about making money for me. I'm not here to take your place, Veronica. I can tell you love Alex. I don't know your story, but I plan on riding out my man's bid with him. Besides, Alex is way older than me from what I can tell. He probably sees me as a little sister anyways."

Veronica seemed to soften a tiny bit after listening to what Simmy said. "Okay, I can respect that. Look, Simone, I've been doing this for years. Money keeps you in this life like a locked box that you don't have the keys to. Every time you try to walk away, you get sucked back in because the thought of not having it makes you crazy. It becomes an addiction, all of it, especially being in love with the wrong person. That fucks you over every time. So, if there is one thing you learn from me let it be this: don't plan to stay in this business longer than you need to. And, never let the fear of being broke keep you chained to a situation that leaves you broken in the end."

Simmy nodded. She turned her head and looked out of the window, letting Veronica's words sink in. She made a silent promise to herself not to get caught up with the money and to stay true to herself.

Just like with boosting, Simmy and Veronica ended up in a department store. This time it was the Saks Fifth Avenue flagship store on Fifth Avenue in Manhattan. They didn't put on disguises or shades. In fact, when they walked in, the sales associates rushed over to Veronica like they knew her very well.

"Ms. Brim, you came back to see us," a tall, anorexic white chick sang, smiling brightly at Veronica.

"Yes, and today I have my baby sister with me. She's home from college for a weekend and Daddy said she can have whatever she wants," Veronica replied, suddenly speaking such proper English, Simmy had to do a double take.

"It's nice to meet you." The white chick extended her hand to Simmy.

"Tia," Veronica filled in the name.

"Tia," the white chick repeated. "Oh, my God! That is such a unique name!" the bubbly girl exclaimed.

Simmy just smiled like Veronica had instructed.

After three hours in Saks, Simmy and Veronica had been served fresh fruit, wine, and imported chocolate while they shopped. Simmy was amazed when Veronica sat back in a lounge area, handed her credit card to the white chick, and just waited for the chick to return with a receipt on a silver tray. Veronica quickly scribbled her signature and waited. After about fifteen minutes, several other store clerks returned with about twelve huge bags with bows tied on the handles, and they set the bags at Veronica and Simmy's feet.

"Will you be needing us to call you ladies a taxi?" the original one asked Veronica.

"Oh, no. You know my father always has a car waiting for me," Veronica replied, using her same proper English voice.

"Wonderful. I'll see to it that your bags make it outside to the car."

Once Simmy and Veronica were settled into their awaiting car, and all doors were closed, Simmy let out a long exhale.

"Oh, my God. That was so fucking boss," Simmy said excitedly. "I have never experienced anything like that."

"Shh," Veronica hushed her and nodded toward the front of the car at the driver. "We'll talk once we get out of here."

Simmy snapped her lips shut. Her insides were exploding. She would've never imagined that she would have an experience like that in her lifetime. It was like being a celebrity or a rich person. With Jayla, she only got to pretend for a little bit until the clerk was distracted and they could take what they needed. But with Veronica, she had been able to get the full treatment.

Simmy had been given an American Express plum card with the name Tia Brim on it. The card looked and felt authentic. For the rest of the ride back, Veronica took the time to teach Simmy how the business worked. She explained to her that the strip on the back was the important thing. The strip was tied back to the credit card of a real person. Simmy had learned fast that one of Alex's businesses was using authentic-looking counterfeit credit cards with high limits. Alex would send his crew of girls out with the cards, and they'd buy expensive high-end clothes, electronics, jewelry, and gift cards from the most sought-after stores. They'd also use other people's identities to obtain store credit accounts in high-end and big box stores. This was so they could service all types of clients, high-end and hood clients alike. Simmy thought Alex was a genius.

Chapter 14

In Deep

Simmy sat on Jayla's bed, where she'd been sleeping since fully taking over the apartment, and she counted up the money she'd made in a week. $8,000 was nothing to sneeze at for the easy work of using fake credit cards. She stuffed a few dollars into her pockets, grabbed her newest Chanel purse, and headed out the door.

When Simmy saw Kyan being led into the visit room her heart sped up until it was galloping in her chest. Aside from being in terrible need of a haircut and a shave, Kyan was still fine as hell.

"Hey, baby." Simmy stood up and hugged him.

Kyan kept his arms down at his side, not bothering to return her embrace.

"What's wrong?" Simmy asked, her eyebrows furrowed.

"I guess if you don't know, then I don't know either," Kyan replied dryly.

Taken aback, Simmy leaned back in the chair across from him and stared at him strangely. "I put money on your books. I contacted a lawyer, and he said he would take your case. I went and gave your mother some money and checked in on your brothers. What's the problem?" Simmy said, her tone firm. She didn't expect to get attitude from him when she'd been out there working so hard to help him.

Kyan sighed. "It's nothing, man. For real. I appreciate what you been doing," he said.

Simmy still felt like there was something he wasn't saying, but she hadn't come all the way to Rikers Island to argue. "Oh, okay. Well, like I told you on the phone before, Doc never came through. I guess he bounced with your paper." Simmy didn't want to stress Kyan out but, at the same time, she wanted to subtly point out that she was the one hustling to help him out.

"So how were you able to put money on books and do everything else?"

"Oh, I used some of Jayla's money." Simmy thought on her feet. "I have to make sure to put it all back, though, because she's still going through her case, so I'm sure I'm gonna have to pay some stuff for her too."

"I got it," Kyan said, bopping his head. "So how are you otherwise?" he asked, looking her up and down. "You look like you're doing great. New bag. New bling."

Simmy's face got hot. She knew better than to tell Kyan what she'd been doing to make money. "I'm managing. All this stuff, it belongs to Jayla. I'm just using it to impress you on visits," Simmy lied again. She'd been getting better and better with lying and thinking on her feet, another new thing she'd picked up from Alex and his crew. Simmy had become much more comfortable with making stuff up as she went along.

Kyan rubbed his chin. "A'ight, if you say so. I'm real happy to see you, Simone. For real. And again, thank you for checking in on my family." He stood up and motioned for the guards to come and take him back to his cell.

"Wait, why are you leaving?" She was surprised that he had ended his visitation with her so soon. In the past, he would sit and talk with Simmy down to the very last second he had before the guards made the announcement that visitation time was over.

"I'm sorry, Simmy. I'm just not feeling too well today," he said just as the guard came to get him.

"Okay, Kyan. I understand. Get some rest and feel better."

Simmy smiled at him but, inside, she felt the phoniness of their interaction. She looked on as her man disappeared behind the bars. Something was happening to them, and Simmy knew there was probably nothing she could do about it.

Over the next two weeks, in between making money, Simmy had convinced Veronica to take her back to see Jeff. With all the computers and access to names he had, she was sure he'd be able to get Simmy information on her mother. Just yesterday, Jeff had given her the news that he found out where she was. Turned out, Simmy's mom was in a prison in New Jersey, not far from where Jayla was staying.

This morning, Simmy had her stomach in knots just thinking about what she was going to say when she finally saw her mother after all these years. The ride to New Jersey felt like forever, but they finally reached the prison that held the most important person in Simmy's life.

She took a deep breath as she stood in line waiting to walk through the metal detectors. Her mind was in overdrive just thinking about all the things she wanted to say to her mom. She was excited to finally get to see her mom. She was looking forward to hearing her voice, hugging her, and just being able to see her.

"Please state the inmate you are here to see," a tall, heavyset guard said to Simmy without bothering to look up at her.

"Carla. Carla Jones."

"Please sign the visitor log and show me your identification."

Simmy signed the log and gave the guard what he had requested.

"Okay, have a seat in the visiting room. You will hear an announcement and then a buzzer. That is when the inmates will be brought out."

"Okay, thank you," Simmy replied.

Simmy found an empty table and took a seat, anxiously waiting to see her mom. When she heard the announcement and the buzzer, her palms became sweaty, and her mouth went completely dry. She kept looking out for her mother as ladies kept making their way out. When the last woman came out, Simmy's heart skipped a beat. There she was, walking toward her. Her hair was still long and shiny. Simmy took notice of her mother's aging face. She saw the wrinkles that had started to form near her eyes.

"Hi, Mom," she said as she stood up to hug her.

"Hi, baby," Carla said with tears filling her big brown eyes. "You look beautiful," she said as she leaned in and embraced her daughter for the first time in years. The two ladies held on to each other until one of the guards instructed them to separate.

"I can't believe my baby girl is all grown up," Carla said as she admired her daughter sitting across from her. "I'm proud of you," she said.

Simmy felt guilty hearing those words come out of her mother's mouth. Her mother might not be so proud once Simmy told her about what she'd been up to the last six or so months. She took a deep breath before filling her mother in on everything. Simmy was getting used to lying, but lying to her mother was not something she could ever do.

"I'm sorry to disappoint you, Mom, but I can't give you many reasons for you to be proud of me right now," Simmy said, unable to look her mother in the eyes. For the entire hour that they had together, Simmy filled her in on everything that had happened to her ever since Jayla came into her life. She didn't leave a single thing out. She even admitted to losing her virginity to Kyan. The entire time, her mother just sat there and listened. She never once interrupted, scolded, or judged her. When Simmy finally finished she felt like she'd gotten so much of her shoulders. It felt liberating.

"Wow," Carla said. "I'm sorry that you're going through all of this, Simmy. I would have never wanted you to suffer or have to resort to boosting and using fake credit cards to survive out there. I don't agree with Mummy Pat taking Jalissa's side, but that's her house, and you have to respect her rules. This Kyan boy doesn't sound too bad. From the way you described him, he kind of reminds me of how your father was at that age."

Carla chuckled. "From what you told me, it sounds like he really cares about you; but, Simmy, love and feelings don't mean nothing if you end up getting locked up in here. If that boy is to ever get out, he needs to get out of this dealing business and go legit. And that goes for you too, Simmy. I understand right now you're doing what you have to do to help out our cousin and your man, but you need to get out of that as fast as you can before you get sucked in so deep you won't know how to get out of it, or even want to get out of it."

Simmy hung on to every word her mother said. She was absorbing everything like a sponge does to water.

"Now, listen up, baby. I want you to finish up with this illegal cards business you're in as fast as you can. At this rate, you not gonna graduate in June but that doesn't mean it's not too late for you to sign up for night classes so you can work on your GED. I know you're a smart girl and I want to see you do big things. You understand?"

"Yes, Mommy." Simmy smiled up at her mom as if she were a little girl again. "I missed you so much," she said as tears welled up in her eyes. She wished she could hug her mother again, but she knew the guards wouldn't allow it.

"I've missed you too, baby girl. I love you." Just as Carla said this, the announcement was made that visiting hours were over. Carla stood up and blew a kiss to her daughter.

Originally, Simmy had planned on going to see her mom and then heading over to visit Jayla, but seeing her mom and having that intense conversation left her emotionally drained. She did not have the energy to visit Jayla this week. Instead, she called an Uber to take her to a Starbucks, where she sat for almost two hours going over everything her mom said. As she sipped her Green Tea Frappuccino, Simmy contemplated what her next move should be. She wanted to do what her mom said and stop doing all the illegal stuff; but, at the same time, she knew this was the only way she'd ever make enough money to be able to support Kyan and Jayla.

It had made her feel good being able to provide for her boyfriend and cousin. But wanting to heed her mother's warning, Simmy was left feeling confused about what the right thing to do was. It had actually left her depressed and questioning what she was doing.

"What's wrong with you, young'un?" Alex had asked Simmy as she sat across from him at a diner in Brooklyn.

"Just feeling down. My grandmother's birthday is tomorrow, and I'm just thinking about her," Simmy admitted, pushing her food around on the plate with her fork.

"Oh, shit. I ain't know you even had family like that. You've never mentioned anyone before. C'mon, young'un. Ain't nothing to be down about."

"I haven't seen her in months," Simmy admitted to him. "She put me out of the house because I beat my cousin Jalissa's ass for taking some of my stuff."

"Damn, and she didn't do nothing to your cousin?" Alex asked.

"Nope."

"That's pretty fucked up then. Family doesn't do each other like that," Alex affirmed. "But look, Simmy, me and the family your people now," Alex said.

Simmy smiled a little bit. "True. Y'all have been good to me."

"Here, look. Take this and buy something nice. We gon' take you out so you could get your mind off of things. Shit,we gonna do this big time," Alex said, digging into his pocket and handing her a thick wad of cash.

Simmy's eyes lit up. She had learned quick never to refuse free money. "Thanks, Alex."

"That ain't about shit, young'un. Anything for you. You know how I do. I get that back in a few hours, as soon as I hear from my girls," he said, grinning slyly. "Yup, my girls got me."

The next night, Simmy was surprised to find Veronica sitting outside of her building instead of Alex. Simmy rushed to the car trying to get out of the rain. It had been raining cats and dogs all day.

"Hey," she huffed as she flopped into Veronica's passenger seat. "Where's Alex?" Simmy didn't waste any time asking since he'd said he would be the one picking her up.

Veronica sucked her teeth, seemingly offended. "What? You his keeper now?" Veronica snapped. Simmy knew that meant Veronica was in one of her bipolar, "insecure about Alex" moods.

Veronica pulled up to Tao restaurant uptown on Fifty-eighth Street. Simmy looked around, confused. "Oh, I thought we were going to the club," Simmy said.

"Just get out. Damn. You are so annoying with all of your questions all of the time. Shit," Veronica snapped.

The valet opened Simmy's door and she exited. Simmy waited a few seconds for Veronica to come around and meet her since, clearly, she didn't know anything about coming to this place.

"C'mon, nosey," Veronica snapped, leading the way.

Simmy followed her inside. Veronica whispered something to the girl standing at the hostess podium in the foyer. The girl said something into a tiny black microphone clipped to her shirt, and two waiters appeared.

"Right this way, ladies," one of the waiters said.

Simmy thought it was so amazing how Veronica received super VIP treatment everywhere she went. Money talked and bullshit definitely walked in Veronica's case.

Simmy followed until Veronica stopped and stepped aside.

"Surprise!" a crowd screamed.

Simmy threw her hand up to her mouth, and her eyes stretched wide. She gasped. "Oh, my God! Oh, my God!" she kept saying over and over.

Within seconds, Alex rushed into her and pulled her close to him. "Surprise, young'un. I told you that your family was gonna come through. Now we here to celebrate you officially becoming a member of the family. Today we celebrate you!" he exclaimed. Right after, he whispered in her ear as he held her close, "I got you now and forever. Don't you ever forget that. You're in deep with me now, young'un, in real deep."

Simmy had a smile from ear to ear. She completely ignored what Alex had just whispered to her. She returned Alex's embrace and scanned the crowd that had gathered for her. When her eyes landed on Veronica, the look on Veronica's face sent a cold chill down Simmy's spine. Simmy realized right then that if looks could kill, she would've dropped dead on the spot from the way Veronica was looking at her.

***

Simmy got sloppy drunk at her surprise party, so drunk that Alex had to throw her over his shoulder and into the back seat of his SUV just to be able to take her back to his house.

"I can't trust you to be alone tonight," Alex said.

"Me? Man, I'm grown," Simmy slurred from the back seat. It was the last thing she said before falling into a deep sleep. She was so drunk she didn't feel Alex's hands roaming all over her body later.

When Simmy finally awoke the next day, she struggled to open her eyes. Every time she tried, pain daggered through her skull. Her entire body ached like she'd worked out for twenty hours straight.

She groaned, "Where am I?" She fought to get her eyes to focus. It was definitely not Jayla's apartment. Simmy bolted upright. The sudden motion caused her head to spin. She put her hands up to her aching head and looked to her left. Alex was sprawled on his stomach, naked and snoring. Simmy's eyes bulged. She looked down, and she was buck-naked too. Then, she became painfully aware of the nagging ache between her legs. Even with her head pounding and the room spinning, Simmy jumped out of Alex's bed like she'd woken up next to a poisonous snake.

"Oh, my God," she gasped, gathering her dress up from the floor and rushing out of his bedroom. She stopped in the hallway and looked around for the bathroom. She tried a door, but it was another bedroom, and inside was one of Alex's boys and a girl, both naked and sprawled out too. Simmy hurriedly closed the door and tried another. She rushed into the bathroom, locked the door, and flopped down on the toilet.

"What the fuck?" she whispered, her hand trailing down to her crotch. She felt the sticky wetness. "Oh, God." She lowered her face into her hands. Alex had had sex with her, and it was unprotected at that.

Simmy didn't know whether to cry, scream, kick, fight, or curse. She wanted to do it all. Kyan's face the last time she'd visited him trampled through her brain. Then, she pictured the evil glare Veronica had shot at her last night when Alex had hugged her. It was betrayal all the way around. This wasn't supposed to happen.

A knock on the door startled Simmy so bad she almost fell off the seat.

"Ay, young'un, you a'ight?" Alex called from the other side of the door, his voice still gruff with sleep.

Simmy closed her eyes and bit down into her bottom lip. "Um, yeah. I just had to pee," Simmy replied, fighting back tears.

"A'ight. Come back to bed. I miss you," he said.

That was it. Simmy couldn't hold in the tears any longer. She covered her face with her hands and cried as silently as she could into them. What the hell was she going to do now? What the hell had just happened? She felt violated in the worst way possible. She never thought this would or could ever happen to her. But she knew better than to make a fuss to Alex about it. She needed this job, and she didn't want to say anything and risk losing it.

Simmy was able to convince Alex that she was too hung over and sick to come back to bed. She told him she really needed to get home. After quite a bit of pleading on her part, he finally relented. As Simmy and Alex exited his building together, she tried to walk a few paces behind him. It didn't matter. Simmy didn't know it then, but she would find out later that someone had been watching them leave together and knew that she had spent the night with him.

Chapter 15

Turned Out

Simmy didn't answer Alex's calls for days after the morning of her celebration. She needed to refocus on the things that were important to her.

"So what's next?" Simmy asked as she handed $10,000 to Kyan's new attorney, Mr. Levitz.

"Well, I will speak to the prosecutor and see what can be worked out before we jump out there and scream, 'Trial.' I've reviewed everything about the case and, I'll tell you, a plea might be your boyfriend's best bet," Mr. Levitz said.

Simmy left the lawyer's office feeling worse and less hopeful than when she'd first arrived. She spent almost two hours on the train and buses, something she hadn't done in a while. She was feeling better now that she would see Kyan and tell him that she'd finally fully secured a lawyer for him.

"You getting big being up in here," Simmy joked as soon as Kyan sat down across from her.

"Nothing to do but work out in here," he replied. Again, she found his demeanor ungrateful and his tone flat.

"I paid this Jewish lawyer. He's supposed to be the best at handling your type of case," Simmy said, forcing fake cheeriness into her tone.

"I appreciate it," Kyan said, still dry and flat.

Simmy sighed. "Look, Ky. I know you're stressed but it takes me a few hours to get here, and I don't want to sit across from you with you treating me like this," she said.

"Like this how? What do you mean?" Kyan tried to act like he didn't have a clue.

"Like I'm a bother to you. Like you don't really want to see me here."

"A'ight, then stop coming," he said in a monotone voice.

Simmy's head jerked like he had slapped her across her face. "What?"

"You don't come like you used to anyways. I guess it's all that partying you been doing with that dude Alex," Kyan shot.

Simmy's body grew hot, and she sat up straight in the chair. Her heart throttled up. She let a dumb, nervous smile curl on her lips. "What? What are you talking about?" she played it off.

"Oh, now it's funny?" Kyan grumbled. "You right. It's funny that I'm locked up in here, and all I asked from you was loyalty, trust, and respect. That's real funny."

"Kyan, please stop. You have no idea what you're—"

Kyan slammed his fist on the table, garnering a stern look from the correction officers and stares from other visit room guests. "Shut the fuck up. I know you be lying, Simone. You don't think I got people out there? You don't think the fucking streets is talking about how Alex got this bad, young bitch he bragging he turned out? And, then my man sees that the bad, young bitch Alex bragging on is you, my fucking girl. You," Kyan said through clenched teeth.

Simmy had never seen him this angry. She immediately started to cry and shake her head no. She opened her mouth, but he wouldn't let her speak.

"Save whatever you have to say for that nigga," Kyan cut her off. He let out a long windstorm of breath. He looked over at the correction officers who were staring at him and Simmy.

Suddenly Kyan changed his tone to eerily calm. "You know what? I'm cool with you moving on, Simone," he said, throwing his hands up in surrender. "But, I know you. You're a naïve girl who don't know shit about them streets. You'll get chewed up and spit back out if you keep your head in the clouds. You better be careful with that nigga Alex. There's a whole lot more to ol' boy than you could ever know. You think he just dealing in clothes and shit, but living like he lives? Nah. You may look down on me as a hustler, but at least I'm real. That nigga is faker than a three dollar bill. And, he trappin' and pimpin' more than he's doing anything else. Don't think I'm hating, either. I just know what it is. Do you, but you better be careful of the company you keeping," Kyan warned.

Simmy swiped angrily at her tears. "I did it all for you, Kyan. Everything I fucking did was all for you. So that's how it is? You didn't even say happy fucking birthday to me and my birthday was weeks ago. But I still come. I still make sure you're taken care of. It's all good, Ky. You can turn me away to the next man but, just remember, if you were out there with me, if my parents were out there with me, if Jayla were out there with me, I wouldn't be, as you say, getting turned out by the next fucking man. Fuck you. Fuck all of you," Simmy cried. With that, she stood up and stormed away without giving Kyan another look or a chance to say another hurtful word.

"I'm hurt," Alex said, twirling a skinny wooden toothpick sticking out the side of his mouth. He hovered over Simmy as he spoke.

Simmy kept her head down and stared at her hands like a child in trouble with her father. She didn't even have to look at him to picture the disappointment on his face.

"That's the thanks I get for helping you? No calls. Ignoring my calls. You not even going out there and working?" Alex asked, laying the guilt on thick. He started pacing in front of her.

His movements unnerved her. It was the first time she'd seem him upset. "I had a lot on my mind. I'm sorry," Simmy said softly, still looking down at her hands. After Kyan's dismissal at their last visit, Simmy had decided sticking to making her own money with Alex was the only thing she had left. She reached back out to Alex that same day.

"I thought I had eased all your problems when I invited you into my family," Alex said, offended. "I guess we ain't good enough, then."

"No. No." Simmy jerked her head up. She finally looked at him. He wore a hurt puppy dog, sad-eyed expression. "Don't take it like that. I am truly grateful for everything, Alex. Real talk, nobody has really ever looked out for me like you have. I love being in the family. I'm just stressed. My boyfriend, he broke up with me," Simmy came clean. "It was so unexpected. I didn't want to come around all sad and depressed."

A sly grin spread across Alex's mouth. "Is that what got your mind so gone?" Alex asked, waving his hand. "Any nigga who break up with your fine ass don't deserve you in the first place." He pulled Simmy up from his couch and pulled her into him.

"Don't you leave me like that again. You hear me?" Alex said, embracing her while his hands trailed slowly down her back to her ass.

"I'm sorry," Simmy whispered. She didn't stop him. She didn't protest. She didn't think about Kyan or Veronica or even Jayla. Simmy had her own survival on her mind.

At that moment, in that space, she felt like Alex was the only person she had, the only one who cared about her.

Alex grasped her face and crushed his mouth over hers. "You're so fucking sexy," Alex moaned the words into her mouth. "I fucking want you so bad. I've wanted you from the first time I laid eyes on you." His hands moved over her body now.

"Me too," she breathed heavily, her words hot on his lips. "I want you too." Simmy thought about Kyan as she said the words and a stabbing pain shot through her heart.

"I missed you," Alex panted.

The room spun around Simmy as she tried to lose herself. She closed her eyes as Alex worked the buttons on her shirt. She forced the images of Kyan out of her head. She shook away thoughts of Veronica's potential wrath. She was glad to be back in Alex's good graces. Not all alone and sad.

"I missed you too," she groaned, throwing her head back as his tongue trailed down the ladder of her throat. Simmy inhaled his scent. Now that Kyan had turned his back on her, she didn't have to lie to herself anymore. Everything about Alex was intoxicating: his swagger, his money, his power. She didn't have to fight against her own feelings anymore. Simmy reached up and touched his face, feeling the fine sheen of sweat as it dampened her fingers. Alex continued kissing and licking until he got to her breasts. Simmy hissed when he lowered his hot mouth over the rigid skin of her erect nipples.

"Oh," Simmy cried out.

Alex chuckled. "You like that, young'un?" Alex asked in between sucks on her. Simmy shook her head up and down motioning yes to him. She loved it. Alex walked her backward a few steps, and she fell back onto his couch.

"Talk to me," Alex commanded.

"I don't want you to stop," she said, her breath catching in her throat.

"Shit, I ain't stopping, baby girl. I been wanting this since the night of your celebration when I tasted that sweet young pussy," Alex said, dropping down in front of her. He tugged her pants off and took a few minutes to look at her. "Gotdamn, you're sexy as shit," he grunted. Then he pulled her panties off. He held them up to his nose and inhaled deeply. "Mmm. That pussy smells fresh and young," he said.

Simmy's thighs trembled. She was looking forward to having sex with Alex and being awake to experience it this time. Up until today, she'd only known what sex was with Kyan and he never really got too freaky with her. It was more romantic, clean lovemaking.

Alex moved between her legs and starting kissing her stomach. Simmy could barely breathe when he began licking her inner thighs. She let out a long song of moans as he took his time and licked the insides of each thigh gently.

"Open up for me," Alex whispered. "Open all the way up for you new daddy," he said.

Simmy moved her thighs apart wider, giving him full access. Alex wasted no time. He took his long tongue and drove it right between her soft petals.

"Ahh," Simmy belted out, arching her back. She had never experienced this feeling. She had never had this done to her before.

Alex lifted his head so he could see her reaction.

"Don't stop. Please," Simmy begged, her hips writhing.

Alex put his mouth back down there, but this time he just blew on her gently.

"Oh, my God," Simmy screamed out, her voice thick with wanting. Sparks that felt like electricity rippled through her entire body. Her heart was racing, and her thighs quaked. Simmy could barely keep enough air in her lungs to breathe as her body became engulfed in the heat of desire. This must've been what it meant to have someone take your breath away.

As Alex lapped up her juices, he reached up and pinched her erect nipples, sending an even stronger electric sensation flooding all over her body.

"Fuck," she whispered, swirling her hips against his mouth. Alex continued to thrust his long, wet tongue deeper into her warm, gushy center.

"You ready to feel me?" Alex asked, wiping his soaking wet face and chin with his hands.

"Yes, daddy, I want to feel you," Simmy whispered. Even she didn't recognize the sex kitten voice that was suddenly coming out of her mouth.

Alex stood up and took off his clothes. He lowered himself down in between her legs.

"Ow. Ow." Simmy winced as Alex used his rock-hard member to fill her up. The pressure and his girth hurt so good. Tiny sharp pains shot through her loins. Simmy dug her nails into his back, which spurred him on. Her body was on fire. She lifted her pelvis in response to his forceful, grinding thrusts. Their bodies moved in sync.

"Fuck!" Alex grunted as he plowed into her harder.

Simmy's inner thighs vibrated from the explosion of pleasure filling her body. She could feel the pressure building up. She thought only Kyan could do that to her. Finally, she screamed out in ecstasy. Her screams seemed to turn Alex on more and more. He ground into her pelvis with longer, deeper strokes. Her super-slippery walls responded immediately, pulsating and squeezing him tight. Alex grunted like an animal.

"This pussy mine?" he huffed in Simmy's ear.

"Yes. Yes," she cried out.

"You better mean it," he growled. "Ah!" he screamed out as he came hard. He collapsed on top of Simmy.

She reached down and stroked his head gently. She closed her eyes and this time Kyan didn't appear. Maybe Alex had turned her out.

"You got some good-ass pussy, young'un. Don't you ever take it away from me again, or next time, I won't be so nice," Alex said before turning over and falling asleep.

Chapter 16

This Here Lifestyle

For the next two months, Simmy stayed at Alex's place almost every night. She had heard from Kyan's lawyer, Mr. Levitz, and found out that Kyan took a plea deal and was sentenced to two to four years. Simmy didn't even have time to be sad, between being wooed by Alex's constant gifts—so far, a pair of diamond-encrusted signature Cartier bracelets, two exclusive waitlisted Chanel purses, and numerous pairs of high-end designer shoes, sneakers, and boots—and his little impromptu vacation getaways to Hawaii and Puerto Rico. Simmy didn't think much about Kyan at all anymore. She didn't have time. As far as she was concerned Kyan deaded her for working with someone so she could pay for his freedom. He was the one who was fucked up, not her. All she had tried to do was be a good girlfriend and do what she had to do to pay for his lawyer and take care of him.

Veronica was a whole other story. She seemed to be buzzing around and all up in Simmy's face even when they weren't working. It seemed like Simmy couldn't shake her. Simmy may have been younger, but she could tell that Veronica was suspicious that something was going on between her and Alex. Veronica never let up. She was constantly harassing Simmy with a million questions about her whereabouts at different times, about where Simmy got certain pieces of clothing or jewelry from, and she was always trying to listen to who Simmy was speaking to on the phone. Veronica was like a sore pimple on Simmy's ass that just wouldn't go away. Whenever Simmy had to work with Veronica, Simmy would sneak back to Jayla's place and let Veronica pick her up from there. The more Simmy stayed with Alex, the deeper she fell for him.

"Ay, young'un." Alex shook Simmy's shoulder.

Simmy pulled his Egyptian cotton duvet up over her head and groaned. "It's not my day to work," Simmy grumbled, hiding her head.

"But is it your day to go to Jamaica?" Alex asked. He yanked the cover off of Simmy's naked body.

She popped up in the bed like she suddenly had a spring underneath her. "Jamaica? What?"

Alex laughed. "I knew that would get your sexy ass up," he said. He threw down a booklet with JAMAICA printed on the front. "Plane tickets will be printed. Resort information inside. Need to get that passport. Let a real nigga show you how to live."

Simmy bounded out of the bed and jumped on him, her legs straddling him and her arms around his neck. "Thank you, daddy! Thank you!"

Alex laughed and wrapped Simmy up in his arms. "Did a lot to live this here lifestyle," he sang, mimicking the popular rap song by Rich Gang.

Simmy giggled. "You're so silly. But for real, I'm loving this here lifestyle." Simmy sang it out too.

Alex cracked up. "Oh, yeah. How much you loving this here lifestyle? How you gonna repay ya daddy for introducing you to this here lifestyle?"

"I've never been out of the country. That's so big for me. And, to Jamaica where my grandmother and my father were born," Simmy said, excited. "You are the best!" Simmy had a quick thought about her grandmother but brushed it off quickly. Her mom crept into her head too.

She hadn't been back to visit her since that very first time about a month back.

"Let me be your first for everything," Alex said, as he laid her back down on the bed.

"You already are," Simmy whispered, spreading her legs wide.

Simmy felt all grown up driving Alex's Range Rover. He'd taught her how to drive over the weeks she'd been spending all of her time with him. She had two missions that day: use the fake cards to get the stuff Alex wanted to sell and, most importantly, buy everything she needed for herself for their trip to Jamaica.

Simmy bopped her head to "Hotline Bling," her favorite Drake song, as she pulled into the mall parking lot. Life was good, and she had not one complaint. She grabbed her new denim Chanel bag and dug through it. She separated the credit cards by name and put the identification she had with each name with the right cards. She was all set.

Simmy exited the car and headed toward Nordstrom. She was singing in her head.

"Simone!"

Simmy whirled around, her face folded into a confused frown. "What the fuck are they doing here?" Simmy mumbled under her breath. She thought Veronica was going overboard with the stalking behavior now. Simmy plastered on a fake smile. "Veronica. Dina. Shelby. Sheridan. What a coincidence," Simmy sang, unable to hide that the glee in her voice was phony.

Within seconds all four women were in front of her and invading her personal space in an uncomfortable way. Simmy quickly figured out that this was no chance meeting.

"What's going on? Everything all right?" Simmy asked, the cheeriness completely gone from her voice.

"You driving Alex's car now?" Veronica asked, stepping closer to Simmy.

Simmy's heartbeat sped up. "No, um, not really. He said . . . I mean, he just let me. It's just for this one quick trip." She finally got the words out, a nervous smile spreading on her mouth. "You know he wouldn't let me drive it if I wasn't working." Simmy cleaned it up.

"So you just going to stand in my face and lie now?" Veronica spat. The other three girls moved around Simmy until they practically had her encircled. Simmy looked from Veronica to Dina, to Sheridan, to Shelby.

"What's really going on?" Simmy asked. "Y'all following me now?"

"You tell me what's really going on. You turning into a lying bitch now?" Veronica mocked.

Simmy sucked her teeth. "Look, I don't have to lie. I don't know what your problem is, Veronica. Alex told me he doesn't want you anyway. What y'all had was in the past and, really, you need to get over it. You shouldn't let a man have you out here looking crazy following people and stuff. You're kind of old for this stalking shit, don't you think? I'm the one in high school last time I checked," Simmy said sassily.

"Uh-uh. Hell fucking no. Slap that bitch with her smart-ass mouth," Sheridan spat.

Simmy's eyebrows shot up into arches. She had always been scared of her. Sheridan wasn't like the other girls, all dainty and wearing pumps; instead, Sheridan rocked men's construction Timberland boots, cornbraids all going back, and the best high-end men's jeans and T-shirts she could buy with her counterfeit credit cards.

Simmy clutched her bag and tried to get the clasp open as all of the girls moved closer to her. "So we in high school now?" Simmy asked, her voice crackling with fear. She emitted a nervous laugh as her trembling hands caused her to struggle to get into her bag. She was trying to get to her pepper spray. She knew good and well there was no way she could take on all four of the ladies at the same time.

"You're a fucking liar. You told me you had a man. You weren't interested in Alex. All that shit you talked just to get me to teach you the business was all a fucking lie. You don't think I figured your hoe ass out a long time ago? You been fucking my man for a minute now, haven't you, bitch?" Veronica gritted her teeth.

"We don't fuck with snake bitches in the family. I never liked you," Dina said. "From the gate I could tell you were up to no good. A fucking user."

"Yeah, and you're so fucking stupid anyway. You didn't even remember me being there when your cousin got locked up and when you got locked up. Dumb bitch, I was the one who helped you get those Gucci T-shirts that day. You thought all of that was coincidence? You don't think Alex set all of that shit up? You're dumber than you look," Shelby said, looking at Simmy with disgust.

Simmy's head pounded and the vein at her right temple pulsed fiercely against her skin. She didn't know whether to run, scream, or just stand there. She was frozen with fear. Her heart was pounding painfully against her sternum and sweat burned her armpits until they itched.

"So y'all followed me here to vent about not liking me?" Simmy said, not backing down although she had to fight to keep her teeth from chattering together. "That's lame for grown-ass women like y'all." She shifted her gaze from one scowling face to another.

"This little bitch talk too much," Sheridan announced, pulling back her fist like she was going to punch Simmy. "Let me just lay this bitch out with one punch and get it over with."

Simmy jumped so hard she dropped her bag on the ground. She kept her head up, kept her eyes on the girls, and reached down to get it.

"You think you got a prize in Alex? You think that nigga going to care about you for the rest of your life? Yeah, I thought the same thing. I was loyal to that nigga, and I still am. He plays mind games. He ain't tell you that he's always promising to marry me, right? He ain't tell you how he uses his money to keep me on the line, right? He ain't tell you that just last month I told him I quit and to leave me alone and he sat in my house shedding crocodile tears and begging me not to go, right?" Veronica spat. She chuckled evilly. "You're nothing but a dumb, naïve, little-ass girl. A scared little girl at that. You should've stuck with your little Rikers Island boyfriend. You ain't ready for Alexander Kennedy, fact. You wait until your pussy gets old and he's on to the next bitch. You wait until you all in and that nigga gets frustrated and tries to take your fucking head off. You're going to be just like me, out here looking crazy and about to take the next bitch down over that nigga," Veronica said with feeling.

"I'm not a little girl, but maybe the jealousy is because you're insecure, Veronica. I didn't go after him. He pursued me, so why don't you take this up with Alex—" Simmy started, but her words were cut short. "Ah!" She crumpled to the ground holding her cheek after receiving an open-handed slap to her face. Simmy didn't know who had hit her. The slap had happened so fast that she didn't even know who had administered the stinging hit.

Within seconds, all of the girls converged on her and started pulling her long hair, punching her, scratching her, and kicking her. They were saying things like, "Dumb bitch!" "Traitor-ass ho!" "Little hot-in-the-ass ho!" "Fake-ass bitch!" "Lying bitch!"

"Help!" Simmy hollered. She flailed and kicked wildly trying to get the girls off of her. Her attempts were all for nothing. The more she moved, the harder more intense their assault got. All of the blows to her face and head made it hard for Simmy to stay consistent with her kicking and fighting back. Simmy's scalp was on fire as someone fisted her hair and yanked on it. She took a glancing blow to the bridge of her nose that caused an explosion of small squirms of light in her eyesight. Simmy could feel warm blood running out of her nose and into the back of her throat.

"Help me!" Simmy gurgled, choking on the blood filling up her mouth. She felt and heard the delicate material of her silk Gucci shirt rip in the front, and she could tell that her bra was exposed.

"You worthless little bitch. Get your own fucking man," Veronica growled through her teeth as she landed blow after blow in Simmy's face. "I tried to fucking accept you. I tried to believe you were loyal. You're a nothing but a cheap, young, lying-ass ho!"

Simmy felt her shoes come off and her pants rip. Her knees burned from being dragged across the concrete. More crashing and cracking punches, slaps, and kicks landed on her head, chest, back, and legs. She could taste the tiny sting of blood in mouth, and she'd been kicked in the crotch so hard urine had involuntarily escaped her bladder, wetting the inner thighs of her pants.

"Oh my God! Someone call the police! This lady is being attacked!" Simmy heard somebody yell out.

"C'mon. Let's get the fuck out of here," Sheridan barked at the others.

"You're so fucking lucky I don't feel like catching a case today, or I'd finish your ass off," Veronica snarled. "This shit ain't nearly over."

They all turned and ran, leaving Simmy bloodied on the ground. Everything around her seemed to be spinning, and she couldn't locate exactly where the pain was coming from, but her entire body ached. Simmy raised her trembling hand to her face first. She could feel the gashes in her cheeks where they'd gouged out her skin with their nails.

"Miss, are you okay?" A man rushed over to Simmy's side. "Were they trying to rob you?"

Simmy was dizzy as he tried to help her to her feet. She could feel her lips and eyes swelling with each passing minute. She finally got her eyes to focus and noticed that the entire contents of her purse had spilled out on the ground, including all of the fake credit cards she had in her bag. Panic flashed through her chest, and suddenly her bruises and pain didn't matter as much.

"We called the police, miss. Let us help you up inside so you can wait for them in safety," the man was saying.

"No! I'm fine!" Simmy yelled at the good Samaritan. She squirmed away from the man's grasp and dropped down to the ground. She crawled around and hurriedly scooped up the cards.

"I'm just trying to help," the man said, backing off with his hands up.

"I'll help her," a young girl said. She bent down and began helping Simmy pick up her things. "I totally understand," the girl said. She winked at Simmy.

Simmy looked at the girl strangely, but the girl just smiled.

The police arrived about eight minutes after Veronica and her crew of bullies had gone. Simmy had gathered her things, but she was a mess. Her hair was sticking in every direction, both of her lips were swollen, and red, blue, and purple rings were beginning to crop up under both of her eyes. Simmy crossed her arms over her chest because the front of her shirt was completely gone.

"Ma'am, we've called an ambulance for you," one of the responding officers said. "We will transport you to the hospital to get looked at."

"No. That's okay. I'll just call my boyfriend to come get me," Simmy said, barely able to speak coherently through her swollen mouth. She'd also bitten her tongue, making it more difficult to speak.

"Do you know your attackers, ma'am?" the officer asked.

"Old enemies," Simmy lied. "I don't even know their names. Mean girls from high school."

"Any vehicle description? Anything you can give us will help us get the people who attacked you," he said.

"No. I didn't get—"

"I took the license plate number." A lady rushed forward with a piece of paper in her hand. She seemed to come out of nowhere. She provided Veronica's license plate number to the officers. Simmy panicked.

"I just need to use a phone. They smashed mine," Simmy said, barely able to keep still. The officer pulled out his cell phone and handed it to her. She dialed Alex's number.

"Alex! I need you to come and get me!" Simmy screamed into the phone. "Now!"

Alex's eyes almost bulged out of the sockets when he saw Simmy's wild hair and bruised face. He rushed over to her and pulled her into his arms. "What the fuck?" he gasped. Simmy melted against him. Her sobs came fast and heavy. Her entire body quaked. Everything hurt, even producing tears.

"Shh. Shh," Alex comforted her, holding her. "C'mon, let's get out of here."

Alex gave the police officers a fake name and assured them he would take Simmy to the hospital. He led Simmy to his Range Rover and helped her inside. "Let me go tell Zacky we are good. I'll be right back," Alex told her. He rushed over and thanked his man Zacky for the ride. He was back in his car within seconds.

"You think you need to go to the hospital?" he asked Simmy.

She shook her head. She could not stop the tears from flowing.

"What the fuck happened?" he asked.

"Veronica—" Simmy was saying.

"Veronica did this?" Alex boomed. He almost swerved the car off the road.

Simmy shook her head in the affirmative.

"And the other girls," Simmy rasped. "They attacked me, and all of the cards were out there on the ground. If the cops had got there five minutes earlier, it would've been a wrap. And some old lady took Veronica's license plate down from when they drove away. The police have it now." Simmy dabbed at her busted mouth with a napkin.

Alex's jaw rocked feverishly, and he gripped the steering wheel so hard veins popped up on the tops of his hands.

"She knows about us," Simmy murmured. "She said you're still with her. That's why she did this."

"I don't give a fuck what she said. She fucking put everybody at risk doing this shit while you were out here working," Alex said through gritted teeth. He didn't seem to care about anything else.

Simmy closed her eyes and let her tears flow. She didn't know if she even wanted to be with Alex anymore. She didn't know if any of this was worth it anymore.

Alex pulled his car to a screeching stop in front of Veronica's beauty salon uptown. Veronica had told Simmy that the salon was a front to wash some of Alex's dirty money, but Simmy never understood what Veronica meant or what she was complaining for. In Simmy's assessment, Alex had just bought Veronica her own business with no cash input from her.

"Stay here," Alex told Simmy as he bent over and banged the bottom area of the glove compartment until a small compartment opened up.

Simmy shifted in the seat as Alex grabbed a black handgun from the compartment. "Alex, don't."

"I said stay here," he snapped, stuffing the gun into the back of his pants.

Simmy watched him scramble out of the car and storm into the shop. She shook her head. She knew from Alex's attitude that nothing good was going to happen.

Through the glass storefront window, Simmy could see Alex saying something to the receptionist. The woman stood up from behind the small counter. She shook her head. Alex said something to her; then he stormed toward the back of the shop. The girl raced from behind the counter and rushed behind him. Within moments, Simmy saw Alex dragging Veronica toward the door of the shop.

Simmy shook her head no. "Oh, my God," she gasped as she watched Alex drag Veronica by her hair. He was waving his gun and moving his mouth. Simmy figured he was daring anyone in the shop to try to save Veronica.

Alex kicked open the shop door and pulled Veronica, kicking and screaming, out of the door onto the concrete.

"Get up and walk, bitch!" he barked. "You want to be out here jumping somebody and risking my business? Huh, bitch?" Alex snarled, yanking Veronica's hair so hard she had no choice but to pop up onto her feet.

"This is the thanks I get, Alex? This is the fucking thanks I get for always being your bottom bitch?" she hollered.

"Shut the fuck up!" he boomed. He dragged her to the passenger window of his Range Rover where Simmy watched in horror through her swollen eyes.

"Apologize to her," Alex growled, holding his gun to Veronica's temple.

Veronica sobbed so hard her face was covered in tears and snot. She wouldn't say a word.

"I said to fucking apologize," Alex said through gritted teeth, pressing the cold steel of the gun barrel hard against Veronica's head.

Simmy cried and shook her head. This wasn't what she wanted Alex to do. She didn't want to see Veronica get hurt like this, either. Maybe a slap around in private, but not this spectacle. There had to be at least a hundred people standing outside of businesses, stopping on the streets, and perched in windows watching Veronica get humiliated.

"Oh, you not going to apologize?" Alex said. He raised the gun and brought it down with a crack on the side of Veronica's face.

"Agh!" she screamed. Her legs seemed to give out, and blood gushed from her head.

"Apologize to her and now to me!" Alex demanded, yanking Veronica's head up and forcing it hard against the vehicle window.

Simmy jumped from the thud of Veronica's face hitting the window so hard.

"Say it!" Alex screamed, pulling her head back and slamming it into the glass again.

Veronica cried out in agony. "I . . . I . . ." she struggled. Her teeth were bloodied now.

Simmy closed her eyes. She couldn't watch any longer.

"I . . . I . . . what?" Alex mocked. "Look at her and say fucking sorry!"

Simmy jumped and opened her eyes again. She shivered.

"I'm sor . . . sorryyy," Veronica cried out.

"Bitch, the next time you decide to do something that puts my money at risk, I'ma use this motherfucker right here and put you out of your fucking misery," he spat, pointing the gun at Veronica's right eye. With that, he released her hair with and threw her to the ground with a hard shove. She fell over onto her side, sobbing. All of the girls from the shop rushed over to help her.

Alex stormed around the Range Rover and got in with a fury Simmy had never witnessed before.

"She won't be fucking with you or my money ever again. Facts," Alex said angrily. "I don't play when it comes to my fucking money. I don't care who the fuck you are. Eight to eighty, dumb, crippled, or crazy, you will fucking get it if you fuck around with this nigga's money. She played with the wrong nigga. If those cops would've caught those cards, we all would've been fucked."

Simmy closed her eyes and listened to his rant, hoping that she'd hear at least one sentence about the beating she took and her well-being. She never did. All Alex seemed to worry about was that Veronica had almost gotten him busted when she attacked Simmy. Simmy realized that Alex was very self-centered and she had failed to realize it sooner. She decided she needed to be more observant of Alex's actions from that moment on.

Chapter 17

Karma

The summer came in with a fury of heat waves. July in Brooklyn was hot, and so were the streets. Simmy had grown up in the business and, in the four months since they'd parted ways with Veronica, Alex had come to trust Simmy enough now to send her out on her own to make money.

School was the furthest thing from Simmy's mind at this point. She had never even bothered to call or go to her old school to officially drop out. She was happy with her life as it was. Gone was the schoolgirl with her head always buried in a book. It was as if Simmy were a completely different person. She hadn't seen or spoken to anyone in her family outside of Jayla. She could never stop talking to her cousin. She would always be loyal to Jayla. Simmy had been making sure she had money on the books, her apartment was being kept up, and that Jayla's lawyer was doing his job.

She had gone back to visit her mom two times in the last four months. Her mom was getting annoying with all her talk about how Simmy needed to get right and stop working with Alex. Simmy felt very in control of her actions, and she really didn't want or need anyone coming and telling her how to live her life. Especially a woman who had left her out to dry when she was just fourteen years old. Besides, why would she want to walk away from her life right now? She was making money, and a had a great man who gave her everything she wanted.

Alex had her completely turned out. He lavished her with clothes, shoes, jewelry, and anything else her little heart desired. He'd also gotten her a little ride of her own, a red Honda Accord coupe that she had named Candy Baby. With little convincing, Simmy had also agreed to move in with Alex. Kyan was now a distant memory. She barely had underwear left at Jayla's house, although she still went to check in on the place once a week. She'd go to make sure the cleaning lady was doing a good job.

Simmy put her shopping bags down at her sides and fished around her in Céline bag for the keys to the Brooklyn Heights condo she shared with Alex.

"All this shit in here," she grumbled, moving aside stacks of counterfeit credit cards and several different checkbooks. She finally retrieved the key and opened the door. Simmy stepped inside. "Agh." She balked, immediately dropping her bags and throwing her hand up, covering her nose and mouth.

"What the fuck is that smell?" she mumbled, practically gagging from the strong odor. Her eyes watered and her throat felt like she had swallowed a fire-lit sword. She opened her mouth to call out to Alex, but that just caused her to cough and choke even more. It smelled like an entire aisle of cleaning products at a store exploded inside the apartment. The mixture was caustic.

Simmy moved farther into the apartment and stopped dead. Her hand fell away from her mouth and tears immediately sprang to her eyes. It looked like a hurricane had gone through Alex's living room. His glass tables were shattered, and glass sprinkled his hardwood floors in such small shards it looked like icicles had fallen from some place high and broken into a million pieces all over.

The white stuffing of the couch cushions spilled from long gashes cut down the centers. Every piece of artwork had been knocked off the walls and sliced in asterisk patterns in the middles, the frames were splintered, and the seventy-inch TV mounted on the wall had a gaping hole in the center of it.

"Oh, my God," Simmy coughed, her eyes and nose still burning. She turned swiftly and raced toward the bedrooms. The pungent odor almost became too much to bear the closer she got. Simmy pushed open Alex's ajar bedroom door. The smell almost knocked her backward. She stumbled a few steps. The bed was in the same condition as the couches, sliced and diced until all of the stuff hung out. Alex's fifty-inch flat-screen television was destroyed in same manner as the television in the living room. Simmy stumbled toward the walk-in closet she shared with Alex.

"What the fuck?" she gasped. The closet was almost bare on her side. Simmy rushed inside and flicked through the hangers on her side. All of her expensive shirts, dresses, jeans, pant suits, and T-shirts were gone. Alex's things were left practically untouched. Her heart banged so hard it hurt. She whirled around. There was nothing but empty boxes left from the more than ninety pairs of shoes, sneakers, boots, and sandals she owned. Simmy felt dazed and confused. She raced out of the closet and into the bathroom.

"Agh!" she gagged. She had found the source of the choking odor. The bathtub had been filled with all of her clothes, shoes, jewelry, watches, hats, perfumes, and accessories. Someone had poured bleach, ammonia, and any other cleaning product you could think of over all of her belongings. Everything Simmy owned was swimming in the deadly mixture of chemicals. A slow hissing sound was coming from the tub like it was all about to explode. Simmy moved backward slowly on her legs, her eyes filled with tears from the poisonous gasses coming from the bathtub. She blinked rapidly and looked at the mirror hanging over the bathroom sink. There was a message written in Simmy's red MAC lipstick:

Say hi to your new friend, Karma. Watch your back, bitch.

Simmy ran out of the bathroom, out of the bedroom, and out of the apartment. She raced to the lobby and out to her car.

"Oh, my God!" she screamed, suddenly frozen with fear. She felt like she was in a living nightmare. She had to be dreaming. All of this couldn't be happening. Simmy raised her hands to her head and squeezed her scalp. "What the fuck?" she gasped. Her car's back and side windows had all been busted out. The hood had been dented in like someone had dropped a sack of bricks right in the middle of it. The doors and the entire body had been keyed, leaving long, jagged lines and digs in the paint all down the side. KARMA was written on her windshield in the same red lipstick as the mirror in the apartment. Simmy spun around and around, trying to see who had done this. She had just left her car there and gone upstairs not even ten minutes earlier.

She was really regretting not setting the alarm on her car. She had a bad habit of never setting it, and Alex was always having to remind her. Her car was destroyed. It had to be the same person who'd trashed the apartment. Were they watching her? Were they coming for her? Simmy's hands trembled so badly she could barely press the buttons on her cell phone.

"Alex," Simmy gasped. "You need to come home. No, not later; right now!" she screamed.

***

By the time Alex checked them into the Marriott in downtown Brooklyn, Simmy was exhausted. Her head pounded despite the strong Excedrin she had taken. Her throat burned from inhaling the chemicals and screaming. She felt like shit was out of control. Alex's attitude was on one hundred after he'd seen what had been done to his apartment. He knew right away it had to be Veronica; she was the only other person with a key to his place. There had been no signs of forced entry from what they could tell. Simmy had copped an attitude with him, too; she didn't understand why after all that time, Veronica still had a key. Alex hadn't bothered to explain himself, either. There had been nothing left for Simmy to salvage. All of her stuff had been destroyed. Alex had promised to replace it all, but Simmy didn't care about all of that. She knew she could have her stuff replaced. She was more concerned about what else that crazy bitch might have up her sleeve.

"Get some rest. I gotta make a run," Alex said. He'd taken her to get a few things to tide her over.

"No. Please. Don't leave me by myself tonight," Simmy pleaded. "There is just too much going on, Alex. Don't leave."

"I have to make this run, Simone. Shit is way out of control right now. I have to go check a few people. I'll be back. Get some sleep."

Simmy sucked her teeth and flopped back down on the hotel pillow. She jumped when the hotel door slammed after Alex. Simmy lay there thinking about her parents. Even her picture of them had been tossed into the deadly chemical mixture in the apartment. It was the only picture she had of her mom and dad, and now that was gone.

"You need to get right and stop dealing with that man." Her mother's voice kept resonating in her mind. The last

time Simmy went to visit her mother, Alex had accompanied her. Carla seemed to be visibly disinterested in talking to or getting to know him. He kept trying to make small talk with her, but she was responding with one-word answers. When he'd excused himself to go to the bathroom, Carla told Simmy that Alex was bad news. She told her daughter that the man gave her a really bad vibe.

"Oh, Mommy. You're overreacting." Simmy tried to brush her mother's comments off and chuckled.

"No, I am not," her mom responded, a stern expression on her face.

"Mom, I really don't think you're being very nice right now. All he wanted to do was come and meet you, and you're acting like a bitch to him," Simmy said.

Carla's mom slammed her hands on the table so hard, two of the correction officers immediately sprang to their feet and put their hands on their waists. Carla put her hands up to show them she was all right.

She leaned in toward her daughter. "Listen here, little girl. Don't you ever in your life talk to me like that again. If I even think that something like disrespectful is gonna come out your mouth, I promise you I will slap the shit out of you. And don't think I'll hesitate to do it. I don't care if they put me in the hole for thirty days. On my life, you will feel my hands on you if you don't watch the way you speak to me," she said through gritted teeth.

Simmy was taken aback. She had never seen this side of her mother. She sat there silently, waiting to hear what else her mother had to say.

"That motherfucker didn't come to meet me. You need to open your eyes and see things for what they are, Simone. He came here because he wants to know, hear, and see everything that you do. He wants to listen in on our conversation because he thinks he can control you."

Just as she finished her last statement, she saw Alex walking back to the table. She sat back up and put on a fake smile.

"Everything okay, baby?" *Alex asked Simmy. He could tell something had been going on between them before he came back.*

"Yea, everything is good. I was just telling my mom that we need to get going," *Simmy replied to Alex, but she was glaring at her mother.*

"All right. Take care of yourself, Simmy." *Carla stood up.*

"Yeah, you too," *Simmy said. Her words were short and dry.* "Let's go, baby," *she said as she grabbed Alex's arm. She stood up, grabbed her jacket, and walked out of the room without bothering to look back at her mother.*

Lord, please watch over her. *Carla said a silent prayer. She was worried for her daughter's well-being and was powerless to help her.*

Simmy thought about her grandmother and even her aunt, Sheryl. She wondered how everyone was doing. She had to admit, she missed her Mummy Pat. She missed the home-cooked meals and her grandmother's big, warm hugs. She missed waking up on Saturday morning to the smell of ackee and saltfish cooking on the stove while Mummy Pat hummed her old-school songs. Tears ran out of her eyes, over the bridge of her nose, and wet the pillow.

Just then, her cell phone buzzed on the hotel nightstand. Simmy eased up onto her elbow and picked it up. She didn't recognize the number, and she started to hit decline. But she answered. "Hello," she rasped into the phone.

"Simone?" Sheryl replied.

"Yeah? Sheryl?" Simmy sat up. It was crazy that she had just been thinking about her family and her aunt called like that. Simmy's stomach immediately knotted up. She hadn't heard from Sheryl since the fight back in November. She didn't even remember giving her aunt her cell phone number.

"Simone, I think you should come by the house," Sheryl said solemnly.

"What's wrong? Is everything okay?"

"It's Mummy," Sheryl whimpered.

"Mummy? What's wrong with Mummy? What is it?" Simmy's voice rose an octave. She got to her feet and paced.

"She . . . she has cancer, Simone," Sheryl said, followed by a loud burst of wails.

Simmy collapsed to her knees. "No. No. No," she said over and over.

"You need to come make amends, Simone. The doctors said she has stage four and there's not much they can do for her. You need to come before she . . ." Sheryl's voice trailed off. She couldn't bring herself to finish the sentence.

"I'm coming," Simmy said. "I'll be there."

When Simmy arrived at Mummy Pat's house, it took a good five starts and stops before she finally knocked on the door. Sheryl pulled back the door and tried her best to smile. Simmy did too. She could see the stress all over her aunt's face. Her aunt Sheryl seemed like she'd aged years in the months that Simmy hadn't seen her; a new patch of gray hair sat in a tuft in the front of her head, fine lines branched out from the corners of her eyes now, and skin sagged under her chin.

"Simone," Sheryl sang, opening her arms and pulling Simmy into a tight embrace. "You look so good, girl."

"Hey, Aunt Sheryl. You do too," she lied.

"Girl, I don't need to you lie to me. I know I look like shit."

"Where is she?" Simmy asked, not bothering to deny or affirm her aunt's statement about her appearance.

"She's asleep in her room. You know she's sick if you don't find her in the kitchen, right?" Sheryl said, sadness underlying her words.

Simmy swallowed hard. The hairs on her arms and on the back of her neck stood up. She bit down on her bottom lip as she followed Sheryl through the house toward Mummy Pat's bedroom.

The entire vibe of the house was different. There was none of Mummy Pat's usual old-school reggae playing throughout, gone was the aroma of whatever scrumptious West Indian dish Mummy Pat would usually be throwing down in the kitchen, and it seemed everything was in even more disrepair than before Simmy had left.

"Mummy?" Sheryl called out softly. "You awake?"

Mummy Pat moaned.

"Someone here to see you. I think you want to take this visitor."

"I don't have on my wig," Mummy Pat said, that sweet Jamaican accent tugging at Simmy's heartstrings.

"You're always beautiful to me. You don't need no wig," Simmy said, stepping from behind Sheryl.

"Simone?" Mummy Pat asked, her voice weak. "Is that you, Simone?"

Simmy couldn't help the tears that sprang to her eyes. She tried to fight it, but it was no use. Her grandmother was tiny now, with every bone in her face and neck jutting hard against the thinness of her skin. Her head was bald; gone were the beautiful long, dark curls Mummy Pat cherished so much as a younger woman.

Simmy sat down at Mummy Pat's side and lay her head down on her grandmother. "Yes, Mummy Pat. It's me. I missed you so much," Simmy cried.

"Oh, Lord. I prayed you would come home. I'm sorry, Simmy. I'm sorry about everything. I am so sorry, baby."

Simmy could not control the hard sobs that overtook her. "I'm sorry too. I'm sorry I stayed away all of these months. From now on, I'll be here. I'll be right by your side, Mummy Pat. I swear it."

Chapter 18

Another Side

"Where the fuck you been?" Alex growled. He was in Simmy's face before she could fully get back into the hotel room.

She put her hand up to her nose and scrunched up her face. "You stink like liquor," she said with much attitude, ignoring his question.

Alex grabbed her neck and forced her up against the wall. "I'm not going to fucking ask you again," Alex said through his teeth. "Where the fuck you been?"

Simmy let out a mousy squeal, and her eyes went round. She was so shocked by his behavior that a tiny bit of urine leaked from her bladder and wet her panties. "Get off me," she said, struggling under his grip.

"Answer me!" Alex growled, pulling her forward and then slamming her into the wall again. Simmy's teeth clicked, and pain exploded at the back of her head as it banged into the wall. Alex increased the pressure of his grasp on her throat.

"Stop it," Simmy wheezed, barely able to get the words out.

"You fucking left here and didn't call me? Huh? You ain't got no car so how you get around? A nigga came and got you? You fucking another nigga? Huh? What nigga you fucking?" Alex accused, squeezing so hard Simmy could feel blackness creeping into the sides of her vision. She dug her nails into the top of his hand but to no avail. The heavy, sweet, and bitter scent of alcohol shot straight up her nose as he hissed in her face. "I took you out the gutter while your little boyfriend got locked up and couldn't do a damn thing for you. You better fucking remember that. You ain't loyal? Huh? You giving my pussy away? You want some other nigga out there in them streets? Can't nobody do for you what I've done for you. You fucking belong to me, and the next time you disappear, I'll fucking kill you," he slurred. He released her neck and staggered backward.

Simmy's mouth hung open. She raised her hands to her throat, willing her lungs to fill with air. Finally, she got enough air to start wheezing and coughing. She rested her back against the wall and slid down to the floor. This was another side of Alex that she had never seen.

"Simone." Alex softened. He rushed over to her. "Shit. Simone."

Simmy put her knees up to her chest and covered her head with her arms. She resembled a frightened turtle retreating into its shell. She cried as quietly as she could.

Alex got down on the floor and pulled her into his chest. "I didn't mean to. I just . . ." he stuttered. "I can't stand to think that you would leave me. I need you. I love you. I just get so crazy when I don't know where you are," he said, the liquor on his breath and clothes permeating the room.

Simmy was too scared to push him away. She was too scared to run. She was too scared to move.

"It won't happen again. I swear," Alex promised.

Simmy didn't say a word. She never said a word about it again. She wanted to believe that it had never happened. It was something she wanted to forget as soon as she possibly could.

***

After the incident, Alex did everything he could to woo Simmy. Flowers, impromptu dinners at fancy restaurants, a new Cartier watch, a few pairs of Jimmy Choo, Sophia Webster, and Aquazzura shoes. Simmy gladly accepted it all. She was fascinated by the effort he was taking to prove that he was sorry. She had forgiven him. But, she hadn't forgotten.

Simmy and Alex spent three weeks in the Marriott Downtown while they searched for a new condo. Simmy worked day and night with fake credit cards and kiting checks. She had to give Alex the lion's share of the money, but she still made enough to give to her aunt Sheryl to help pay for Mummy Pat's care. Simmy had learned her lesson and didn't go anywhere without making sure Alex knew where she was going and if she was alone. Each time she left the hotel, if she wasn't driving Alex's car to make money, she let him know her every move.

"Damn. It's already dark outside. Didn't realize I was in there so long," Simmy spoke to herself as she climbed into the Range Rover. She settled into the seat and rested her head on the driver's side headrest. She let out a long sigh. For the first time in forever, going out working had been a chore. Simmy had been drawn back to the stressful feeling she'd get going out with Jayla to boost the old-fashioned way. Simmy had just left Nordstrom, and it had seemed one of the clerks had been clocking her hard. One even held Simmy's credit card up to the light. Simmy had almost cursed her out, but she thought better of making a scene and having store security come over.

Simmy started up Alex's car and headed back to Brooklyn. The long ride back was soothing, and she was able to clear her mind of some of the things that were bogging her down. She thought about how complicated her situation with Alex was, about Mummy Pat being so sick, and about how bad she felt about how things went during the last visit with her mom. She had been thinking that maybe her mom was right about some of the things she had spoken to her about. She was regretting not staying in school and graduating.

Simmy listened to Drake's latest album and tried to let the music carry her mind away from her problems. She made it back to Brooklyn in what seemed like record time. She whipped the Range down Flatbush Avenue and slowed down for a red light.

Bang!

"Ah!" Simmy screeched and ducked at the loud noise. Her foot hit the gas, and the Range Rover lurched forward. Simmy swerved the steering wheel and hit a parked car and a pole. Her head slammed into the steering wheel. She was dazed.

Bang! Another loud bang and glass from the back window had seemingly exploded into the car. Simmy went to lift her aching head, and suddenly the driver's side door of the Range Rover swung open.

"No!" Simmy screamed, gripping the steering wheel as she was being forcefully dragged from the vehicle. Her strength was no match for her attackers.

"Help!" she screamed, trying to kick and fight, but a black leather glove quickly covered her mouth.

"Shut the fuck up, bitch," a man's voice said in her ear. "Keep your fucking eyes closed, too, or you won't live to open them shits ever again."

Simmy's heart felt like it would explode. The cold kiss of steel from the gun pressed against her temple was enough to give her a heart attack. She could hear that there was more than one assailant. "Get all that shit. Bag, money, phone, everything," one of them said.

"Tell your bitch-ass man that we everywhere and we ain't gonna stop until that nigga does right by everybody.

The nigga can't bite the hand that feed his punk ass and think it's one hun'ned. You too cute to be getting caught up like this, baby girl. Next time that bullet that hit that back window might just make it into somebody's head. Better get away from that snake nigga Alex, before that somebody is you," the one holding Simmy said in her ear.

He threw her down to the ground, and they all took off running. Simmy cowered against another car and sobbed. Why were things constantly happening to her now? When did her life get so complicated? Simmy couldn't understand why so much bad was happening to her. What had she ever done to deserve any of this?

She scrambled up from the ground and limped over to the car. Her cell phone, money, new clothes, and all of Alex's counterfeit cards and checks were gone. "Fuck my life! And fuck everybody who don't fuck with me!" Simmy growled, slamming her fists into the seats. She didn't know how much more she could take.

Alex paced in front of Simmy, his constant movement annoying her. "Tell me what the nigga said about me again?" Alex asked, stopping for a few seconds.

Simmy rolled her eyes and blew out a windstorm of breath. "I told you, he said that you can't keep biting the hand that feeds you and getting away with it. He said they're everywhere and they're not going to stop until you do right by everybody," Simmy paraphrased and repeated for the fifth time.

Alex rubbed his chin, his eyebrows dipping low on his face. He was in deep thought.

"I want to go to sleep," Simmy grumbled.

"Here. I got these for you. They'll ease your mind," Alex said, pulling a pharmacy pill bottle out of his pocket and extending it toward Simmy.

She crinkled her nose. "What's that?"

"Percs. Harmless shit. It'll help you relax, though," Alex said. This time he opened the bottle and dumped two into his hand and extended them toward her. "Take the fucking pills, Simone." He raised his voice. "I don't have time to sit around here listening to you moan and groan about all the fucking bad luck we're having. This will shut you the fuck up," Alex said, grabbing her hand and forcing the pills into them.

Simmy had seen that look in his eyes before. Her heart throttled up. She knew better than to go against him right now. She threw the pills into her mouth, grabbed a bottle of water from the nightstand, and swallowed them.

Some hours later Alex was shaking Simmy awake. The pills had definitely relaxed her, so much so she could barely lift her head.

"How long have I been sleeping?" Simmy asked as her eyes tried to adjust to the light.

"We don't have time for stupid questions. Simone, get dressed. I need you to come with me," Alex said, rushing his words out.

"I'm tired," Simmy groaned. "It's the middle of the night."

"I know. But, you have to do something for me," he panted. "Now put these on and hurry up," he said, throwing a pair of sweatpants on the bed.

Simmy reluctantly sat up and wiped the sleep from her eyes. Her head swam, and her vision was slightly blurred. It had to be the aftereffects of those pills.

"Hurry the fuck up!" Alex boomed.

Simmy was startled. She slid into the pants and stood up.

"Good, now let's go."

Simmy rode in the back of a black Suburban with Alex while one of his boys drove and another one sat in the front passenger seat. They didn't speak to one another. They didn't play any music, nothing. The mood was completely dark and ominous. Simmy felt a sinking in the pit of her stomach, like what she imagined a person walking down death row on their day of reckoning must feel like.

Simmy tried to figure out where they were going, but the driver cut through so many Brooklyn side and back streets, she got dizzy trying to keep up. Finally, the SUV stopped at a double chain-link fence. The front passenger got out and moved the gates aside to allow the SUV inside.

Simmy heard the crunch of gravel under the tires, and she craned her neck to see out of the windows. There was a three-story, plain red brick warehouse-style building directly in front of them.

"C'mon," Alex demanded, opening her door.

Simmy followed Alex and his boys into the building. Goosebumps immediately cropped up all over her body once she was inside. She could hear voices, but she couldn't see the source.

"You niggas thought it was a good idea to run up? How fucking stupid are y'all?" Simmy heard a dude's voice. "What do you think he gon' do to y'all knowing y'all niggas fronted on his girl?"

"I don't want to die. I can't leave my kids behind like this," Simmy heard another dude cry. From what she could hear, he could barely get his words out between sobs.

Alex, Simmy, and the other guys from the SUV finally walked into the room. Simmy's teeth were chattering together so badly she was getting a headache again. The warehouse was freezing, the kind of freezing that made Simmy feel like she was standing inside of a huge meat locker. She could even see puffs of frosty air as she breathed out. The smell of sawdust and industrial chemicals was also so strong that the combination was making her stomach churn. The two young dudes who were tied up flexed their backs against each other and turned their heads as much as the ropes that bound them together allowed. Both were trembling from the subzero conditions in the room.

"Yo, King Alex," one of the young dudes said pleadingly.

King Alex! Simmy screamed in her head.

"We ain't do it. I swear, man, it wasn't us. You got the wrong dudes," the dude begged.

"Oh, yeah, nigga? That's why I brought my girl out here. She gon' identify y'all punk asses and then it's going to be over," Alex growled.

"He's telling the truth," the other tied-up victim whispered calmly in response through his battered lips.

Simmy didn't know how he was staying so calm being tied up, damn near buck-naked, freezing, and obviously already beaten. It was like the young guy had no emotion behind what was happening or like he had already resigned himself to the fact that he was going to die.

"Simone," Alex called.

Simmy stumbled forward, her body quaking like a leaf in a wild storm.

"These the niggas who shot at you?" Alex asked.

One of Alex's boys walked over and lifted the two young dudes' downturned heads so Simmy could look at their faces.

"I . . . didn't really . . ." Simmy stammered. She couldn't remember their faces. She would only be able to recognize their voices, but she could feel the heat of all of Alex's crew's glares on her. She would have to let Alex exact his own form of justice, or he'd take it out on her for sure.

"I think so," Simmy lied. She didn't know at all if those were the guys responsible.

"Good. Now you stay here and watch what I do to them. It's all for you, baby girl. Nobody fucks with you," Alex growled. "Get those niggas up."

"King Alex, man. Listen, I can explain," one of the young dudes stammered. "You . . . you know how this trappin' shit is, man. A lot of jealousy and niggas just want to be treated fairly."

Alex seemed to grow more and more agitated by the minute. There was something about the begging and pleading that seemed to send him over the top.

"Shut the fuck up!" Alex boomed. "You wanted to make power moves on my girl? You bitch-ass nigga. Now you in here, assed out and begging? Nah, nigga, keep them crocodile tears."

"Yo, King Alex. Mad niggas in your camp wanted you gone. It wasn't just us. The ones you think is closest to you really ain't got your back, man! We can help you root them niggas out. Just give us another chance. That nigga RayShawn is the one trying to make deals to get the powder behind your back," the second young dude cried out, snitching on his crew while his voice quivered like an old lady's.

Simmy couldn't believe what was happening in front of her. That meant all along, like Kyan had said, Alex was heavy in the drug business. Simmy felt stupid for ever believing that he had financed his lavish lifestyle off of just counterfeit credit cards, kiting checks, and money order scams. She shifted on her legs. If she could run away and never come back, at that moment, she would've taken off out of that scary place and kept running until her legs gave out.

"Niggas scheming on me, huh? That's too bad, because I am the fucking boss now, and always. I gave all y'all dirty rat bastards a job, and picked y'all stupid asses up off them streets from being hungry, dirty, and broke. This is the thanks I get? Niggas complaining and moaning like bitches. Niggas tryin'a cut deals behind my back. Niggas running up on my girl and robbing her like she some

basic bitch? Nah, ain't no coming back from none of that,"
Alex growled, flames flashing in his eyes. Alex rushed
over, raised his gun, and ground the end of it at the first
young dude's temple.

Simmy felt nauseated. She squeezed her eyes shut.

"Please, don't kill me," the young dude begged. "I got
kids. I take care of my whole family. My moms already
lost two sons. Please, King Alex, give me another chance."

"Shut the fuck up! Don't say shit about your mother and
your fucking kids! You wasn't thinking about them when
you was out here playing bad boy, nigga!" Alex growled,
grinding his gun into the dude's head even harder.

Simmy opened her eyes and immediately regretted it.
She turned away so no one could see the tears rimming
her eyes. She had been upset about getting robbed, but
she didn't want to see anyone die behind it. Especially
right in front of her face.

"Should've thought twice before fucking with my family," he said through gritted teeth, putting pressure on
the trigger. "See you in hell, nigga."

One powerful blast to the dome dropped the young
dude like a sack of potatoes. Simmy jumped hard and
shrieked. She clutched her stomach at the sight of the
spray of his blood and the sight of gray brain matter that
splattered. The thick, metallic scent of blood mixed with
the grit of gunpowder overwhelmed Simmy's senses. She
didn't want to watch Alex do it to the second young dude.

"I gotta get out of here," Simmy huffed.

"Nah, you gotta watch. You need to know I have another
side to me. You need to know who I really am," Alex
replied.

More shots and the second dude went down. Simmy
could barely stand up with her knees knocking together
so hard. She gripped her stomach and doubled over.
Vomit spewed from her lips, just missing her feet.

"I'm not to be fucked with," Alex said, his chest heaving like a beast in the wild after a fresh kill.

Something inside of Simmy shivered. She knew all too well how violence could be just as deep and intimate as love and even worse how obsession could turn into death. In that moment, Simmy embraced the feeling. It was fear. She had finally admitted to herself that everything about Alex had her in constant fear.

I'm sorry I didn't listen to you sooner. You were right all along. Simmy made a silent apology to her mother.

Chapter 19

Growing Up, Growing Apart

Simmy used Mummy Pat's deteriorating condition as an excuse to stay at Mummy Pat's house and get away from Alex as much as she could. She'd had constant nightmares after watching him torture and kill the dudes he thought robbed her. Alex reluctantly agreed to Simmy staying at Mummy Pat's, so long as Simmy still went out there and worked. She did anything he asked, just so he wouldn't ask her to come home to the new condo he'd purchased for them.

The day Simmy got the call about Jayla's release, she couldn't keep still. She couldn't wait to see Jayla. She'd missed her cousin so much. There was so much to tell and so many things they had to do.

Simmy drummed her nails on the steering wheel as she waited outside of the jail for Jayla. She looked down at her watch for the tenth time and realized only six minutes had passed since the last time she'd checked. It seemed like Simmy had been waiting an eternity before she finally saw Jayla in the distance. Jayla still had that swagger about her, even wearing the same clothes she'd had on just about a year ago. That was what Simmy admired most about Jayla, she was the epitome of "can't keep a good woman down." Simmy sat up straight and checked herself out in the visor mirror. Her heart drummed with excitement as she got out of her new whip to greet her cousin.

"Baby cuz!" Jayla squealed, damn near breaking into a run.

Simmy opened her arms and scooped Jayla into them. They hugged each other tight and spun around a few times.

"Ohh, my Gawd! I missed your ass so much, Simmy," Jayla sang as they held on to each other. Simmy had visited her often at first but, over the last six months, she hadn't been able to get away from Alex long enough to go see her cousin. She still made sure to keep money on Jayla's books, and she always took Jayla's calls so, even though they hadn't seen each other, they had still been keeping in touch.

"I missed you more. You have no idea," Simmy said, squeezing Jayla like she never wanted to let go. "C'mon. Let's get out of this godforsaken-ass dump New Jersey," Simmy said, leading Jayla to the passenger side door.

"Mmm, mmm. I must say, Simmy, you look hella good. From head to toe you have made me proud," Jayla said, giving Simmy a good once-over. "A bitch can certainly appreciate those Jimmy Choo pumps you rocking."

"Thanks," Simmy said, blushing and smiling. "You know fashion even if your ass been missing in action for almost a year, huh?"

"Oh, you already know." Jayla laughed. "You still working the business?" Jayla asked, getting right to it.

"Something like that," Simmy answered. "But, we can talk about all that in time. Turn around and look in the back," Simmy said, quickly changing the subject. Truth was, Simmy hadn't told Jayla what she had been up to since her arrest. Whenever Jayla would start to ask questions, she would change the subject or rush herself off of the phone.

Jayla loosened her seat belt and leaned between the front seats to look into the back. "Girl! What the hell?"

Jayla said, her voice rising at the sight of the entire back seat filled with shopping bags from Neiman Marcus, Gucci, Prada, Fendi, and Chanel.

"That's all you," Simmy said proudly. "You know I wasn't going to let you come home after almost a year without the right kind of welcome home gifts."

"Bitch, you the best!" Jayla squealed, leaning over and kissing Simmy on her cheek.

Simmy laughed. "Don't make me crash or our asses won't even make it home."

When Jayla walked into her apartment, her mouth fell open at the sight of all of the roses and balloons that read: WELCOME HOME. She turned to Simmy with tears in her eyes. "Simmy. I love you so much. Thank you for holding my shit down all that time. There are not many people like you out there. Anybody else would've just let my shit fall by the wayside and said fuck it. I really appreciate it," Jayla proclaimed, hugging Simmy tight.

"This ain't shit, Jay. You did so much for me when I needed you the most. I wanted you to know that I'd always hold you down and I still stick to that," Simmy said with feeling.

Jayla swiped away her tears. "Look, chick. I ain't come out here to be all weepy and shit. I can't wait to sleep in my own bed," Jayla said, rushing toward her bedroom. Simmy was right on her heels.

Jayla flopped down on her bed and stretched her arms and legs as far and wide as they could go. "Ahh. Nothing like the feel of your own shit."

"I know," Simmy said. "That's how I feel about mine."

Jayla sat up. "Wait. You haven't been staying here?"

Simmy's cheeks flushed, and she broke eye contact with Jayla. She shook her head. "I kind of have my own place," Simmy said shyly.

"Your own place? Oh, shit, my cousin done grew up on me!" Jayla began clapping at Simmy in approval.

"Well, yes. Kinda. Not exactly." Simmy struggled to get her words out. "I live with somebody."

"Okay, and who is it? Kyan? Shit, I want to know everything," Jayla pressed.

Simmy sat down next to Jayla on the bed. "No. It's not Kyan," Simmy said, her voice trailing off.

"Wait, don't tell me you and Kyan not together anymore. I thought he was 'so perfect' for you." Jayla tried to mimic Simmy's voice.

"No, we're not together anymore. He got locked up not long after you got arrested. Things were okay at first but then he flipped on me getting all jealous and shit, so I'm done with that." Jayla summed things up for Jayla.

"Well, shit, girl. Then who you living with?" Jayla asked, banging on the bed. "Who, dammit?"

"Okay. Okay. I'll tell you," Simmy said, still hesitating. "It's Alex."

Jayla looked at her quizzically. "Alex who?"

"Alexander Kennedy. Used to live up here in Harlem but moved to Brooklyn."

Jayla stood up, her hands instinctively folding into fists and resting on her hips. "Uptown Alex? Always driving a Range Rover? Tan skin? Nice-ass hair?" Jayla interrogated.

"Yeah," Simmy answered, her left eyebrow going up at Jayla's reaction. "When I met him he said he knew you. He never said how though."

"Motherfucker," Jayla blurted, almost under her breath.

"What? So you do know him?" Simmy asked, her face completely folded into a frown now.

"What he got you out there doing, Simmy?" Jayla was moving on her feet.

"I work a few angles with him," Simmy replied tentatively. "Why are you acting like that? You mad?"

Jayla shook her head. "So he's your come up?"

"Okay, Jay. You're acting really weird and shit. Is there something you want to tell me? I mean, he already said he knew you. That's the only reason I even met him."

"Wait, what you mean by that?"

"Yeah, I got knocked trying to boost some stuff for Cassandra so I could make some money and he happened to be in the store. He said he recognized me from being with you at some club so he paid the fine and I was able to get out," Simmy said.

"Are you fucking serious, Simone? You can't be that naïve. He's probably the one who got you knocked and then paid the fine so you would think he was your savior. That's the type of shit snake niggas like Alex do. And, obviously, it worked," Jayla said honestly.

Simmy's body grew hot. "It sounds like you're being a little paranoid or maybe even jealous, Jay. And, it is your first day home, so let's not do this now. I want you to relax and just be happy to be home. Plus, like I told you on the way here, Mummy Pat is real sick. You need to go see here before . . ."

"You're right. Let's not fight on my first day back in the world," Jayla agreed.

Simmy could tell that the topic wasn't dead but, at least for that moment, they both played like it was.

It only took two weeks for Jayla to press Simmy about working. Simmy knew that the day was coming, but she couldn't do anything without permission from Alex. Jayla couldn't wait to see Alex in person again.

Simmy's nerves were on a wire's edge when she pulled up to the tattoo spot Alex owned. He had told her early in the morning that he'd be hanging out there for most of the day.

"So he owns this?" Jayla asked.

Simmy let out a long breath. She was so tired of Jayla peppering her with questions about Alex it wasn't even funny. "C'mon. I told him we were coming," Simmy said.

"Ohh, shit! If it ain't bad-ass Jayla Massey," Alex sang out when Simmy and Jayla walked into the shop.

Jayla's face darkened, and her nostrils opened up. "Alexander fucking Kennedy," Jayla said, almost whispering.

Simmy was confused by the exchange. Alex seemed overly excited to see Jayla, and Jayla seemed pissed to see Alex. Simmy didn't think it'd be like this when they saw each other again.

"You ain't change a damn bit, girl," Alex said, looking Jayla up and down like she was something scrumptious to eat.

Simmy bit down into her bottom lip. Both Alex and Jayla had seemed to forget she was even there. "I'm going to the bathroom," Simmy announced. Neither of them seemed to care or notice.

"Jayla is going to get down with the business," Alex told Simmy when she returned. "We got history, so I think it will be a good thing," he said, rubbing his chin.

A pang of jealousy flitted through Simmy's chest, but she ignored it. "Great! That's exactly what I wanted, to make sure my cousin is put on."

A pretty Spanish girl walked over, stepped between Simmy and Alex, and whispered in Alex's ear, then giggled. Simmy could see Jayla looking from the girl to Simmy and back to the girl.

Jayla grabbed Simmy's arm and pulled her away. "So you just going to stand there and let the nigga play you like that?" Jayla asked.

"Like what? Please. I go home with him at night. I couldn't care less about all of his groupie chicks flocking and trying to get at him. He don't fuck with them ratchet girls."

"Simmy." Jayla exhaled her name on the end of a long, exasperated breath. "You still acting like some green-ass little girl out here?"

Simmy's face and mood darkened. "Jayla, please don't start that bullying shit you used to do with me. I'm not a little girl anymore. I've grown up. I'm confident with myself and my man. I hope me growing up doesn't lead to you and me growing apart." With that, Simmy stormed off. She didn't need anybody trying to tell her what to do or how to react to her own man.

Chapter 20

Losing It All

Once Jayla was turned on to the credit card game there was no stopping her. It took her no time to learn the ropes. In three short weeks, Jayla became Alex's number one.

"Little cousin, I need to speak to you about something," Jayla said as she and Simmy got finished with a day of shopping in the city.

Simmy looked at her.

"I think we can find our own connect for the blank cards, IDs, credit card numbers, and socials," Jayla announced.

Simmy rolled her eyes. "Look, I know you're smart, Jay, but we can't fuck with Alex. There's a side of him you don't know and, trust me, you don't want to see that side," Simmy said seriously.

"I know him pretty well, Simmy. Well enough to know you and me both need to be away from him."

"Wow," Simmy said, shaking her head. "So you're being ungrateful now?"

"No. I'm trying to be smart," Jayla retorted.

"Being smart is keeping your mouth shut sometimes and just going with the flow," Simmy snapped.

"No. Being smart is not wanting your little cousin with a nigga who's determined to fuck her cousin and ain't stopping at nothing until he does," Jayla blurted.

Simmy's head whipped around so hard and fast a pain shot down her neck. "What? What the fuck are you talking about, Jayla?"

"Your fucking dude, the one you think so highly of. The one I've watched over the past few weeks play you right in your face with bitches sliding him numbers and him sending expensive bottles to bitches' tables with you right there. The one who came to my fucking crib three times already trying to fuck me again," Jayla spat. Right away Simmy could tell by Jayla's raised eyebrows that she knew she'd said too much.

"Again?" Simmy said, barely above a whisper.

"I didn't want to tell you because it was the past. I used to fuck with Alex heavy back in the day. That's how we know each other. But, that's when he was pimping, Simmy," Jayla confessed.

Simmy chuckled. "Damn, your story just gets deeper and deeper, huh? Maybe you should've been a fiction writer. Alex is a lot of things, but one, he ain't never been a fucking pimp Jayla; and two, every man who lives doesn't want to fuck you," Simmy spat.

"Say what you want, you know and I know that I wouldn't just lie to you like this. The nigga tried to convince me to let some niggas run a train on me, and I refused, so we had a big falling out. That's why I stopped fucking with him. And now he's trying to get at me, and I told him not to ever play with me again, ever. I also told him that I would take a bullet to the head for you, Simmy. And, right hand to God, that's the truth. You need to check for Kyan. He's the type of nigga you should settle down with, Simmy, not a nasty-ass dick-slinger like Alex."

"I told you what happened with Kyan already. He got nasty and ungrateful with me when all I was trying to do was make paper so I could help you and him. He sat there accusing me of fucking with Alex when I had nothing going on with him."

"Yeah, and look at you now. Riding that nigga's dick whenever he tells you to. I'm telling you, Simmy. You made a big mistake walking away from Kyan."

"Let me out. I'll take an Uber," Simmy said, tugging at Jayla's rental car door handle.

"C'mon, Simmy. Don't do this. I just don't want to see you lose it all behind this nigga," Jayla pleaded.

"Pull over!" Simmy boomed. "I have nothing fucking else to say to you. You're an ungrateful bitch just like Kyan, and I should've known better! Don't ever give me advice on who I should settle down with when you had a parade of niggas in and out of your crib like you had an ad on Backpage! Fuck outta here, Jayla!"

Jayla's head jerked like Simmy had slapped her in the face. "A'ight, this is what you want to do? You want to let a nigga come between family? Suit yourself, but when shit falls down around you, don't say I didn't warn you," Jayla shot back.

She pulled over. Simmy grabbed all of the bags that were hers and stormed away. As she walked, she could not stop the tears from falling hard and fast. She couldn't believe what was happening.

"Didn't I tell you Jayla was a hater?" Alex said, practically laughing at Simmy.

"Did you go to her house?" Simmy asked again.

"She's a liar. I don't want her. She's jealous and unhappy because she ain't got a man like me," Alex replied. "C'mere."

Simmy reluctantly lay against him. "I just feel like I'm losing it all, Alex. My grandmother is dying. Jayla is mad at me. You've been spending almost every night out, saying you're working," Simmy said.

"You always got me," Alex said, kissing her deeply. Within minutes he had Simmy out of her pants. She gladly followed his lead once her pants were off. She opened her legs wide, and Alex lowered his head. Simmy gasped. She knew she was in for a special treat. He used his fingers to gently part her delicate flower and then he took the tip of his masterful tongue and teased her clit. Alex always knew how to get Simmy's mind off of things. She was no longer thinking about Jayla and her accusations; instead, she was concentrating on moving her body like a video vixen or a sexy siren from a porn movie. Alex liked when she let herself get freaky.

"Lick it. Fuck that feels so good," Simmy panted, moving Alex's head to the spot where she wanted him. "Yeah, right there," she huffed. Alex licked up and down her entire opening. She could feel a mixture of his saliva and her juices leaking down her ass crack. Simmy couldn't care less if she ever spoke to Jayla again. Alex was giving it to her like she wanted it. The more she moaned and cooed, the harder he went at pleasing her. The slurping noises were making her crazy. "Yes, daddy! Do that shit. I'm sorry I ever doubted you," Simmy hissed, grinding her hips toward Alex's tongue in response. She was breathing so hard her head started swimming. Alex was doing what he did best. He pressed his tongue on Simmy's clit again, and that was enough. "Ouuu!" she screamed out, her thighs shuddering. She creamed all over his face within seconds.

"Damn, you know how to do that shit right," she panted out.

"My turn now," Alex said, his voice gruff with lust. He pulled his pants down and pulled Simmy off the bed and onto her knees. He went to enter her mouth and suddenly stopped.

"Hold up," he said, reaching over for his cell phone. Simmy's face folded.

"Really? You're going to . . ." she was saying.

Alex ignored her and answered his phone. As he walked away, Simmy could hear a female voice filtering through. She jumped to her feet and rushed over to him. Jayla's words were playing over and over in her ears: *The one I've watched over the past few weeks play you right in your face with bitches sliding him numbers and him sending expensive bottles to bitches' tables with you right there. The one who came to my fucking crib three times already trying to fuck me again.*"

"Who is that, Alex?" Simmy demanded, grabbing for his phone.

"Yo. What the fuck? Stop playing," Alex grumbled, taken aback by Simmy's sudden bravado.

"No! I want to know what bitch that is who's so important that you stopped in the middle of fucking me to answer your phone!" Simmy boomed. She could hear the girl on the other end calling out to Alex and asking him what was going on over there.

"I'm telling you to chill. I'm not gonna say it again," Alex warned her.

"Fuck that! You've been playing me right in my face. You been out there getting numbers right in my fucking face, and now you standing there talking to the next bitch when you were all up in my pussy just a minute ago!" Simmy screamed. She could feel her face filling with blood and her entire body coursing with hot adrenaline.

"Bitch, I made you; why would I play you?" Alex spat. Without thinking, Simmy slapped him across the face. She shocked herself but not more than she shocked him.

"Bitch," he spat. Then he backhanded her across the face so hard blood and spit shot out of her mouth. The force sent Simmy reeling backward and slamming to the floor. Within seconds he was on top of her.

"Don't you ever roll up on me like that," Alex snarled, and he slapped her again.

Simmy saw stars. Her head started pounding, and her ears rang.

"I run the fucking show around here. You want to listen to your ho-ass cousin? I will put your ass on the street where I found you. You fucking understand?" he barked. He stood up, and before he turned to leave, he kicked Simmy in the stomach.

Simmy lay there coughing and trying to catch her breath. She didn't have the strength to stand so she crawled over to her nightstand and grabbed her phone. She called the only person she knew would come to her aid.

"Hello." She heard aggravation in the voice on the other end of the line.

"Jayla!" Simmy cried out. "I need you to come and get me!"

"Simmy, what's wrong? What happened" Jayla immediately sat up in bed.

"He beat me, Jayla!"

"That motherfucker!" Jayla screamed into the phone.

Simmy felt herself calming down a little bit. "Jayla, I'm sorry about everything. You were right. He's a no-good piece of shit," she said as she took deep breaths in an attempt to compose herself.

"Apology accepted, cousin. Don't even sweat it. I'm on my way."

"What the fuck happened?" Jayla said as she helped Simmy into her car. Simmy was limping, and the bruises all over her face were starting to turn black and blue. Her eyes were puffy from the crying and the slaps she took from Alex.

"Some bitch called him, and he flipped the fuck out when I confronted him about it."

"Damn, Simmy. I'm sorry that he did this to you," Jayla said solemnly. She felt guilty that she hadn't been around to protect her cousin. She regretted introducing her to this world. If she hadn't put her on to boosting, she probably wouldn't be in the situation she was in now.

"It's okay; it's not your fault, Jayla," Simmy reassured her. Her phone ringing and the vibration she felt by her thigh startled her.

"That better not be that nigga Alex," Jayla said angrily.

"No, it's not. It's Aunt Sheryl." Simmy said as she pressed the answer button. "Hi, Aunt Sheryl," Simmy said into the phone.

Jayla turned the radio off and drove in silence, hoping to be able to hear what Sheryl was saying. She was being nosey, but she didn't care. Unfortunately for her, she couldn't hear anything.

"What? No! Please, God! No! This can't be happening!" Simmy screamed. Her cell phone slipped from her hand, and she could still hear Sheryl screaming into the other end of the phone.

"Deep breaths, Simmy! What happened? What is it?" Jayla did her best to calm her down.

"Mummy Pat," Simmy said in between sobs. "She's gone, Jayla! She's gone!" Simmy felt like her world came crashing down on top of her. The physical pain she was feeling from Alex's beat down was nothing compared to the pain she was now feeling in her heart.

Jayla immediately drove to Mummy Pat's house. By the time she and Simmy got to Mummy Pat's house, paramedics had already taken her body out of the house and were loading it onto the ambulance.

"What hospital are you taking her to?" Jayla ran up to one of the paramedics.

"She's going to Kings County Memorial Hospital. I'm sorry for your loss." The paramedic gave his condolences.

"Thank you," Simmy and Jayla replied in unison.

"Simmy, I'm going to follow Mummy to the hospital and get all the information we'll need so we can make arrangements. You run in and stay with Aunt Sheryl. I may not like her, but I can respect that she just lost her mother," Jayla said. Her voice sounded shaky from trying to hold back her tears.

"Okay, Jayla." Simmy looked into Jayla's eyes and could see the tears welling up. The two cousins held each other for a few seconds, Simmy trying to comfort her cousin and Jayla attempting to do the same.

"I love you," Simmy said as they let go of each other.

"Me too," Jayla replied before walking back in her car so she could go to the hospital.

Simmy rushed into her grandmother's bedroom and found Sheryl in the middle of the floor sobbing. Simmy fell down next to her, and they hugged and sobbed together.

"She went in her sleep," Sheryl said as she wiped at her eyes. Simmy could tell she had been crying for a while.

"Jayla is on her way to the hospital to get all the information we'll need."

"Okay," Sheryl replied.

"I can't believe she's gone," Simmy said in a low voice.

"I know, Simmy. Me too. It was her time to go, though. She lived a long life and took care of so many of us. It's time for her to rest," Sheryl said as she took a deep breath and tried to stop herself from bursting out crying again.

"Yeah, she took care of so many of us, and look who was there for her in the end." Simmy looked around at the empty room. "People ain't shit, Aunt Sheryl. After everything she did for everyone in this house, they didn't have the decency to pay their respects to her on her deathbed. Uncle Marcus went and moved out on her when she needed him the most." Simmy felt overwhelmed with emotions. It felt good to vent and let it all out. She never thought her aunt Sheryl would be the person she'd open up to but here they were. Simmy had learned a lot about her aunt since she and Simmy were the only ones who had been looking after Mummy Pat. She knew her aunt Sheryl would understand her.

"Men ain't good for nothing, Aunt Sheryl." Simmy looked to the ground.

"No, Simmy, not all men are bad. There's still some good ones out there." Sheryl took a deep breath. "I have something for you," she told Simmy. "With Mummy being so sick, I kept forgetting to give it to you."

"What is it?" Simmy asked.

Sheryl got up from the floor and went over to the tall, old-fashioned dresser Mummy Pat had in the far corner of her room. She'd always told all of her grandkids the story of how that dresser was the only thing she had left from her childhood in Jamaica. But, as Simmy got older, she'd figured out that there was no way Mummy Pat could've gotten that dresser on a plane from Jamaica. That was what her grandmother would always do, tell them stories that made them feel proud of their heritage and proud of her.

"Simone. What happened to your face?" Sheryl asked once she was standing directly in front of Simmy. She was holding something in her hands.

"It's nothing. I slipped down some stairs," Simmy lied. "What is it that you want to give me?" she changed the subject. She could see the doubt creasing Sheryl's brow, but neither one of them wanted to deal with it at that moment.

"Here," Sheryl said. "Mummy had all of these. She was holding them for you. She wanted to give them to you personally but, since she got so sick, she made me promise to make sure to give them to you myself. She didn't want them to get lost."

Simmy stood up and held out her hands. She looked down at what Sheryl had handed her. She sucked in her breath and looked back up at Sheryl.

"Oh, my God, are you serious? When did they start arriving? I mean, why wasn't I told sooner?" Simmy couldn't find her words. She couldn't believe what she was seeing. Her heart felt like someone had stuck their hand inside her chest and started squeezing it.

Sheryl nodded. "Every single week, one came for you. Like clockwork, without fail. And he had been calling and talking to Mummy Pat once a week, too. Mummy Pat really grew fond of him. She was always raving about her new adopted grandson. When she got too sick to take his calls, he began writing to her. I would read them to Mummy whenever they arrived. We got used to getting two letters a week. One for you and the other for Mummy. He's a good guy, Simmy. And he truly cares about you. A good man is hard to come by and what he's been doing really says a lot," Sheryl said. Then she pointed to Simmy's busted lip and the dark ring under her right eye.

"You deserve so much better. You weren't raised to be with someone who will do you like that," Sheryl said, using her hand to lift Simmy's chin. "I hope you find something in these that will bring you out of whatever it is you're in. I've been praying for you since you left here, and so was Mummy. Even if you don't do it for you, do it for her."

Simmy swallowed hard as she looked down at the stack of letters addressed to her, from Kyan. "I can't believe he was writing to me all of this time. After everything I did." Simmy seemed to lose the strength in her legs. She flopped down on Mummy Pat's bed and tore open the letter on the top of the stack. It was obviously the most recent one. Her hands shook as she unfolded the delicate piece of paper and began reading.

> *Dear Fly Girl a.k.a. Simone,*
> *How are you? I'm maintaining as best I can given my circumstances. I guess this is the last letter I'll be sending to you. I really want you to know that I still love you. That will never change. Real love doesn't just go away because you don't see eye to eye. The good news I was talking about in my last letter is I should be out a lot sooner than expected. They found a loophole in my case, and they're setting everything up so they can give me the date of my release. Now all I have to do is stay out of trouble in here and wait for them to let me*

out. I've been spending all of my time reading, and now I write. I've even been taking a writing class in here. Enough about me, though. I miss you. I been holding out hope that one of these days your pretty face is going to show up here and say, "Let's start over, Kyan." A nigga can pray and wish, right? I hope you're doing well out there. I hope school is still part of that plan you got going on. I read in this book that when you love something you have to let it go, and if it comes back it is really yours, but if it doesn't, it never was. That's like us. We let it go, but I have a feeling it will come back. I always knew and felt that you were mine and we were meant to be.

I'm sorry about everything I said to you the last time you were here. I was just scared that you were gonna get caught up with the nigga Alex and get into the same mess I got into. I know you're a smart girl and I hope you've made the right choices. Being in here, I've decided to make better choices when I get out of here too. I want to start over and leave all that illegal shit in the past. I want to be the best man I can be for you. I love you, and I hope to hear back from you soon. In the meantime, I won't stop writing. You saved me, Simone. Bumping into you that hot summer day in August was the best thing that could've ever happened to me. It gave me the chance to finally be able to talk to you. I will be forever grateful for that summer day that started it all between us.

Love always,
Kyan

Simmy could not stop the tears from falling. She couldn't believe that all of this time Kyan had still been thinking about her and writing to her.

"Like I said, Mummy wanted to be the one to give them to you, but . . ." Sheryl said. She'd been standing there, watching Simmy read the letter.

"It's okay. Better late than never," Simmy said.

"That's what I said. Better late than never."

Simmy whirled around so fast she almost fell over. Her eyes bulged out of her head like a cartoon character's. She lost her breath. She thought she was seeing a ghost standing in her grandmother's doorway.

"What? I thought you would be happy to see me," Kyan said.

Simmy rushed into him. He wrapped her up in his arms so tight she could barely breathe.

"Oh, my God, Kyan. This is all happening so fast. I just got the letters a few minutes ago," Simmy cried.

"And, I just got the word about Ms. Pat and came straight here," he said.

"When did you get home?" Simmy asked, moving back so she could get a good look at him.

"I'll leave you two to catch up," Sheryl said as she exited the room.

"Two days ago," Kyan replied as he locked eyes with Simmy. "I'm back, and I'm ready to claim what's mine," Kyan said, running his thumb over her bruised eye. "That nigga Alex did that to you?" he asked.

"Yes," Simmy responded. She felt embarrassed to admit it to Kyan.

"It's okay, baby. I'm here now," Kyan whispered. With that, he gently placed his mouth over hers and kissed her deeply.

Simmy's mind went blank as she allowed herself to be carried away. She didn't give one last thought to Alex, but she knew he would be looking for her soon. And, when he found out Kyan was home and Simmy had gone back to him, she knew Alex would flip his lid. Simmy was afraid of how Alex would react to everything.

"Kyan, baby, Alex is dangerous," she tried to warn Kyan.

"And so am I. He messed with the wrong one. He's going to pay for what he's done to you. I promise you that."

To Be Continued